OUTLAW LEAGUE

Robert Foust
and
Keith Rogers

Copyright © 2021 Robert Foust and Keith Rogers
All rights reserved
First Edition

PAGE PUBLISHING, INC.
Conneaut Lake, PA

First originally published by Page Publishing 2021

ISBN 978-1-6624-3711-3 (pbk)
ISBN 978-1-6624-3712-0 (digital)

Printed in the United States of America

A man's ability is only limited by his lack of opportunity

—Hank Aaron, National Baseball Hall of Fame
Cooperstown, New York, 1982

This book is dedicated to the memories of Henry R. "Hank" Robinson and J. Bradley Smith and to all fans everywhere who love the game of baseball.

Acknowledgements

We tip our hats with thanks to Jesse Yungner who used his artistic talents and imagination to produce the front and back covers for *Outlaw League* as well as his ingenuity for the dedication page.

We are also grateful to John Schlosser, who through his knowledge and experience working for the US State Department, located the records that verified the timing of revisions to US–Canada extradition treaty language dealing with draft dodgers harbored in Canada and Robert Foust's extradition case.

As always, we are once again appreciative of Nicole Reefer, our book coordinator and the team at Page Publishing who turned our idea about *Outlaw League* into a reality.

Foreword

Buckle up, it's baseball.

And Robert Foust's enduring journey through America's pastime is surely a bumpy one.

His dogged quest for a pro career makes for an often harrowing yet frequently funny baseball memoir. His quest is never for the faint of heart as it weaves his amazing success on the field with equally amazing adventures off it.

Having a promising career waylaid first by a combat stint in Vietnam, courtesy of his local draft board, then a lingering stretch in a Canadian prison for smuggling marijuana, courtesy of his own hubris, are facts that offer a few tantalizing clues of what lies ahead—a true and thus compelling baseball tale like no other that recalls a particularly turbulent time and a talented pitcher trying to find a way forward.

Yet please don't confuse the term *Outlaw League* as being one that's packed with ex-cons and reprobates of assorted ilk, although there is certainly no shortage of strange and colorful characters and head cases in these organized but decidedly minor leagues.

"There was, and still is in my mind, a difference between an outlaw and a criminal," writes Foust. "Criminals don't care about anyone but themselves and will do anything to anyone they feel like—rob, steal, kill or rape.

"Outlaws, on the other hand, follow the Cervantes route. They are chivalrous lovers who protect the have-nots. Robin Hood may be the best example."

Hence, the book's title and Foust's philosophy as he makes his way among kindred spirits, of which I am one, it soon became apparent while reading this engaging work.

After all, we're about the same age to begin with, both mainly California kids and later Las Vegas transplants who shared a love of both baseball and cannabis and ended up playing hardball for as long as we could.

My part-time and undistinguished career ended at age thirty-nine when my pitching arm suffered a spiral fracture that cracked like a broomstick on crisp fall morning while throwing a pickup game at Cimarron High School the week before our adult men's league championship.

I have a lot in common with Foust and cofounded with coauthor Keith Rogers the over-eighteen-year-old Arizona Charlies Orioles team.

The league held a draft of its own and recruited an assortment of former pro pitchers, a solid catcher, and a group of high-caliber position players who could hit the laces off the ball. We even had a bona fide Dominican Republic recruit who could run like a deer and anchor center field.

The team went on to be sponsored by Holy Cow Brewery, located on the Las Vegas Strip and Sahara Avenue. In the early 1990s, we played the championship game at Cashman Field and beat a mix of baseball diehards 10–1 that included a couple of ex-college players and even a former Dodgers pitcher, who probably could have struck out fifteen of us but elected to play first base instead so we would have a competitive ballgame.

Foust would have been right at home here, and our paths could have easily crossed on a baseball diamond, not that I could reach the upper nineties with my fastball or hit a ball out of the park like he could. But I buckled a lot of knees by hitters salivating for my upper-eighties fastball only to sit down on the pine after staring at my plus-plus circle change up.

Likewise, we almost shared the country-damaging Vietnam experience. My father was a marine who served in 'Nam the same year as Foust, and as I soon was also old enough to be drafted as well.

I became a potential military draftee (at number 102) in the last draft before the long overdue move to all-volunteer United States forces in 1973. The list of those who'd be drafted dried out before they got to me but not before they grabbed guys unlucky enough to have numbers in the midnineties. I'm not sure how I would have fared overseas with bullets flying—not well, I'm fairly certain—and suffice to say, it was enough just to read of Foust's near-death experience in a raging river in Vietnam's Central Highlands to get a grip on the madness and fear that infected the doomed American effort. That Foust doesn't dwell on such experiences in this book, perhaps because they are so horrifying and because of his focus on the game is remarkable in itself.

But Vietnam had another unforeseen impact on Foust soon after his return stateside to resume his chosen career in baseball. Teammates and team brass seemed leery of his status as a combat vet and fears that he'll turn into Rambo in the dugout (the gist of an early chapter) unfortunately bring things to light.

"The stigma of Vietnam did so much to returning veterans it isn't funny," says Foust, who was lucky enough to miss the struggles my own father faced in his return from the battlefront at about the same time.

However, Foust's opportunities appeared limited by the same experience in a sport that has deservedly earned the reputation of being conservative by nature.

He captures the country's divisive time clearly and with laudable detail, using the music of Motown and the British Invasion as fitting accent points. Foust remembers the transition in the early seventies when Marvin Gaye's sweet soul songs began "morphing into cries of ghetto pain and the heartbreak of war."

And he doesn't forget 1971 when Hendrix, Joplin, and Morrison all died from drugs within a matter of month. Indeed, his counterculture lifestyle learnings and no-holds-barred opinions help create an alternative universe where the entire history of post-1950 America is up for his discerning comment.

He comes of age in the 1960s at a time when Vin Scully is broadcasting Los Angeles Dodgers games on radio, and baseball is transitioning quickly into more of a television game. The history of the fast-growing country itself seems linked to the history of baseball, and with a war killing so many Americans in a foreign land, the future is uncertain.

As he progresses toward adulthood, there's a night watching Jimi Hendrix in what will be his final concert. In short, Foust is just another red-blooded young man trying to make his way and any willing young woman who is in a similar mood. He's a baseball-loving regular guy.

Of course, as he reminds us in no uncertain terms, there's no crying in baseball, even when you're forced away from the game and end up stuck in a rough British Columbia prison after your shipment of 750 pounds of marijuana goes array.

This comes at a time when a bust for pot was even more of a life-changing event, and this was the biggest bust on record in Canada to date, although what Foust was doing would quite possibly be legal today in half of America.

That's scant solace, and as Foust repeats here in something of a personal mantra, "No good deed goes unpunished, and nothing is going to be okay." That's the sort of cynicism that can only come from a baseball lifer.

He would serve forty-four months on a marijuana-smuggling charge in a dreary place where old-style stocks and caning as punishment still prevailed.

Yet again, he avoids writing about the daily drudgery as he keeps his focus on the game he loves, even becoming a softball whiz while in prison. Though no spring chicken upon his release by baseball standards, he's thirty years old in 1978 and still doing time when the red-hued Canadian Mounties he once fled finally show up to lead him to the American border and set him free.

But even if he's too old for college ball, our narrator hasn't abandoned the dream of a place, any place really, in the bigs. Stints in Vietnam and prison haven't broken him or erased his love of baseball. And he's still brings a fastball in the 90s and has been honing a changeup and even better mechanics.

It's here that *Outlaw League* really takes off, becoming an international adventure when our hero—or perhaps antihero—starts driving across the border to pitch games in Nogales, Mexico.

We continue on to tales of somehow controlling his aptly named Knuckleball Express, not forgetting a school bus that was minus a front window or the one that burned up and damaged a police vehicle.

We also learn why bars shouldn't give free drinks to ballplayers. Foust finds himself living and mostly enjoying a vagabond baseball lifestyle. He will go on to pitch in National Baseball Congress games and hook up with the semipro Orange County As, earning needed money teaching baseball skills to younger players, and even coaching a bit. "Never throw a changeup on 0–2," he cautions from experience. "Throw the damn pitch up and in."

Yet there's no lesson on how to let the first two batters you face get on base, then pick off both before striking out the batter to end the inning, something pulled off by Foust in unlikely fashion. Cool stuff.

And while there's no official Outlaw League Hall of Fame—perhaps there should be—Foust would surely be a first-ballot inductee for winning a few hundred games in these sundry leagues games, many played in classic bandbox wooden stadiums scattered about the West.

He has few regrets, outside of the most obvious ones, and there's nothing one can do to change things anyway. He's having a hell of a good time, dominating on the field and piling up the strikeouts and victories.

All in all, not a bad way to make a living, and he knows in his thirties that he's still just a break or two away from taking his formidable talents to the major leagues.

"I may only be a batting practice pitcher," he says at one point in his remarkable journey, "and I will be ready if they need a fifth starter."

But no major spoilers here as Foust continues on, doggedly facing age without ever losing sight of his dream to be a Major League pitcher. He confronts his own issues with race and revels in the joy of just being on the diamond with his cohorts.

"We are on the baseball field right where we belong, doing what we do," he says in a pastoral memory that seems to sum it all up. He mentors a young pitcher along the way who, under his guidance, eventually makes it to "The Show."

Celebrities are part and parcel of baseball, and Las Vegas of the 1990s finds Foust tossing batting practice to up-and-coming comedian Jerry Seinfeld and winning a bet (unpaid) from the comic's dad to boot.

Major League Baseball players he encounters remain unnamed but are easily identified by fans with a passing knowledge of the game. His adventures as a "Comp King" in Vegas, taking players and coaches to dinner and tossing out baseball betting picks on a local radio show demonstrate the extent of his commitment to the game he loves.

He'd make some changes, of course. He'd rid the game of the rampant nepotism and systemic racism that infects it and better deal with individual character issues that can lead players astray.

The bluntly spoken Foust is also against pitch clocks, having men on base to start extra innings and the "designated hitter" (American League only) can be eliminated as well. On issues of a more national scope, Foust views the country's war on drugs as about as ineffective as the war in Vietnam. Kindred spirits indeed.

Baseball brings fame, fortune, and notoriety to those who only make it to the majors even for the proverbial cup of coffee.

"I'm not crying now, just telling a story based in fact," says Foust. And he doesn't make a fortune but does all right, thank you, dominating sundry if mostly unpaid Outlaw Leagues for more than a dozen years until he's well into his forties.

He becomes a Vegas fixture at a vibrant time (the early nineties) and is often found listening to the vintage rock and soul of Cook E. Jarr in the bustling lounge of the Sahara Hotel.

"I'm not getting rich but I'm having fun and enjoying life."

He harbors few grudges, except for the military draft, which has thankfully been put aside.

"If there's a draft running, you had better be running too," he recalls with surprising good humor that belies his conflicted view of his own country.

"America has gotten really old," he says. "She is aging, and she stinks."

He looks out at a world where conflicts are commonplace and vows to keep things simple and on the straight and narrow. Foust lives today in Las Vegas and likely can still break off a nasty curveball.

Meanwhile, as forewarned, it's time to buckle up tightly. You are in for a wild ride through Robert Foust's world of baseball.

Michael Paskevich

Former Las Vegas Review, Journal Entertainment Critic, the Son of a Vietnam War Marine Veteran, and an Amateur Baseball Player

Preface

The great American game of baseball is the thread that sews together the main elements of this book: life, liberty, and the pursuit of baseball. *Outlaw League* is the story of a boy and his love of the game. It is about an affair that began when this lad was just eight years old and concluded at the age of forty-five when the boy had become a man. It is the story of how baseball guided a young boy through a difficult childhood and into adulthood and helped him survive through daunting times filled with adversity and misfortune.

It is also a story about life—the great American life and how it has changed over the years. Some of it was for the good, some of it bad. But all of it was worth living from the jungles of Vietnam to a prison stretch in Canada to the major leagues of baseball.

Politicians were becoming slimier and more vicious and treacherous by the second. They were pushing their own agendas of greed over the will—and more importantly the good—of the people. Kennedy, Nixon, and really all of them. Much like the frogs on my aunt and uncle's farm, the politicians are the enemy. This book also explores other elements of life and times too. It touches on growing up in America during seven decades of greed, arrogance, racism, and war. It tells the tale of the Civil Rights movement, the drug wars, riots, and the looting of the 1960s.

The book speaks of the rise and fall of the British invasion. It talks about life, love, and death.

Basically, it is about life and the misgivings that often come with that life. There is no doubt that this book will make the reader feel the full gamut of emotions that the writer experienced firsthand.

From the first intrusion into a young boy's life through the death of his grandfather and then his mother's death and on o a remarriage and a stepfamily, as well as conscription into the Army through the military draft.

This story takes an inside look at serving in the Vietnam War and the destruction that was caused by that service, followed by serving in a foreign prison for four years for a marijuana conviction.

The protagonist in this story was alienated and turned into a pariah by his own government for which he had just put his life on the line.

By any measure, this is a difficult story to tell, but it had to be told.

The message from this book focuses on life and how we live it. More so, it is about perseverance and survival and how you can live a better and more meaningful life.

What are the changes that are needed in today's everyday life, the changes that we can make in today's society that will improve it?

Finding that goal is the new mission. Remember Bob Dylan's words of advice: "You don't need a weatherman to know which way the wind is blowing." Oh so true.

CHAPTER ONE

Frogs Are the Enemy

Life, as I remember, began in 1954. That was when I came of age. Not that I wanted to be a grown-up, but I was thrown into a family affair that aged me beyond my years. That affair began with the death of my grandfather. What followed were circumstances that forced me to learn to live independently.

I was six years old and lived in Southern California with my mother, father, aunt, and my mother's dad, my grandfather. I watched my first baseball game with him and my dad when I was six years old.

I was fascinated not just because the game was a live broadcast on our black-and-white television set but more so because it was the classic matchup between the New York Yankees and the ever-pesky Brooklyn Dodgers.

This was the same Brooklyn Dodgers team that had just broken the race barrier by signing Jackie Robinson, the first player of color in major league baseball history. And soon, this Dodgers franchise would set the baseball world on its ear when the team left Brooklyn for Los Angeles, along with the New York Giants, who moved to San Francisco.

Watching this game with my two best friends was a special treat because a lot of people didn't even have television sets in the 1950s, especially in rural areas. The majority of Americans in that era listened to the games on the radio.

This was fascinating to me because I could watch the players live from thousands of miles away, and it was a double special treat because it was not that often that I had a chance to sit with the two men I respected the most in the world: my father and grandfather.

When the Dodgers and the New York Giants picked up stakes, packed up their gear, and moved to the West Coast, the influx of professional stars for baseball fans in Southern and Northern California took professional baseball to a new pinnacle. In reality, baseball had now become a national sport.

The history between baseball and broadcasting is an early and long-themed affair. Radio has been around forever, it seems. The first radio news program was broadcast from Detroit in 1920. It launched a new era in mass communications. By 1956, the radio business had infiltrated sports, but it wouldn't be until a few years later that television would become the main source of entertainment in millions of American homes. And it was baseball that they were watching.

Television broadcasts began in the 1930s with politicians dominating most of the airtime. It wasn't until the 1960s that a television set became mainstream—a must-have item in all American homes despite still being a novelty. The allure of TV was that baseball games—the great American pastime—were now being broadcast in living color.

Manufacturing TV sets were not that efficient. The real problem was that they were just too damn expensive and programming was limited. That's why when baseball married with TV, it was the perfect match for prosperity. The players all became celebrities, and the owners became billionaires.

The 1936 summer games of the Berlin Olympics had just begun, and they showcased the United States' elite African American sprinter, Jesse Owens.

It was in that hostile environment of a packed one-hundred-thousand-seat stadium that Third Reich leader Adolf Hitler had built for the pleasure of the German people. This racial showdown for the eleventh olympiad happened at the time when the White supremacist dictator was stoking the Nazi push for World War II.

The United States' great heavyweight boxing champion Joe Louis had lost to the German Max Schmeling in their first fight on a foul. But then with a resolve that wouldn't quit, Louis won with a first-round knockout the following year in the rematch. Louis did not mess around this time.

Several years later, the first broadcast of a major league baseball game was televised. Sports, however, did not fully gain traction until the summer of 1941 when the Federal Communications Commission legalized commercial television.

The commission allowed commercial advertisements during sporting events. Broadcast money and advertising became engaged to baseball, and they were married in a cozy relationship that produced greed never seen before for their future. The two seemed to never have enough.

A short time after that classic Yankees-Dodgers game, my grandfather passed away. This prompted a trip to Kansas City, Missouri, for the funeral. We took the Super Chief train—the one with the dome to observe the countryside, which was quite spectacular. The Super Chief was known as the train of the stars because of its route from Los Angeles to Chicago, Illinois. Nevertheless, I still longed to have my grandfather back.

My best friend was gone, and that was the bottom line, and if that wasn't enough for a six-year-old child to grasp, when I turned eight, my mother passed away.

My mother, she was my second best friend, really my first. She was the catalyst of my passion for the game of baseball, and she was my biggest fan. She had helped me find my true love, the game of baseball: just the game, not the people who run the game. That's another story.

After my mother died suddenly of a stroke, I continued playing baseball. It sort of became my life, and I guess my legacy. And, yes, I remember it all.

First, there was the stocky, beer-bellied Mexican man, our Little League manager who gave me my first black eye.

I was a ten-year-old kid, playing third base for this thirtysomething Mexican man. He thought he was a big league slugger. One day, while he was hitting fungoes to the infielders, he knocked a screamer at me. It took a bad hop, and *wham*! the ball popped up and nailed me right in the eye. At that moment, I learned that baseballs hurt.

By the time I was eleven, we were in the Little League championship game, and I had to miss it. Why? I was baling hay far away in Belton, Missouri, on my aunt and uncle's farm, my summer job.

I loved life on the farm, but farm life had its drawbacks, like the time when I was seven. My aunt and uncle had this German shepherd, and he was big, and I don't know, maybe he didn't like children or maybe it was the rabies. Anyway, my dad had this brand-new '56 Mercury. It was a blue exterior with an all-white interior. One Sunday morning, I was doing somersaults out of the car when the dog hit me like a Mack truck. Like a bullet, he snatched me by the nape of the neck and started viciously gnawing at my head. Well, my dad picked up a bucket and threw it at the dog. It missed the dog and hit me right in the head.

There is nothing open as we drive around, me bleeding unmercifully on the white interior of my dad's Mercury. We finally found a doctor. He was right out of *Gunsmoke*—yep, old Doctor Milburn. I call him this because his office was on the second floor of this old wooden building. He stitched me up.

Rabies anyone? Yes, the dog was rabid, and my grandmother shot the dog. I had the pasture treatment all the way home, from Kansas City to Los Angeles, and for two weeks after we returned.

Now with that aside, I got to spend two weeks every summer at my aunt's house, which was really a dairy farm on a 250-acre spread, which also yielded a fine crop of corn and alfalfa. The corn was the cash crop and the alfalfa fed the cattle.

Farm life was hard work, but I developed a passion for it. I'd get up at the crack of dawn for a full workday. Then in the evenings, I'd take my uncle's .22-caliber Remington pump rifle down to the cow pond.

Frogs were my enemy in those days. They would hide in the reeds until I walked by. Then they'd leap into the pond. They couldn't stay down forever, and when they'd come up for air, I'd be waiting. I actually became a pretty good shot although it was hard on the frog population; fortunately, it was only for a couple of weeks a year.

At this time, I did not know what the future held for me, but it turns out it was the rifleman's skills that I developed shooting frogs in the pond that was a damned good skill to have because it wouldn't be long before I would be humping the boonies in Vietnam. The enemy frogs had now become the enemy of North Vietnamese soldiers.

Missouri was not the Mojave Desert or even close to the temperature of the sizzling sand outside my dad's home in Southern California. This Missouri climate was not dry heat; rather, it was humid, heavy sweat-soaked heat even though the thermometer that hung in the shade of the barn showed that it was only ninety-two degrees Fahrenheit. But it felt hotter, much hotter than that, it was as hot as a hundred-mile-per-hour fastball from Philadelphia Phillies ace Robin Roberts.

About ten or eleven o'clock at night, we would get a much-welcomed thunderstorm. The brief but steady downpour cooled off the farmhouse, and the constant rhythm and the damp feeling of the raindrops helped me to fall asleep.

My aunt and uncle didn't have a television set. Hell, they didn't even have running water or indoor plumbing. But that didn't matter. They had electricity, and they had a radio, and every night, I'd listen to the Kansas City A's baseball game. In the Midwest, you could get multiple games on the radio. To be sure, you could get the White Sox, Cubs, or the great St. Louis Cardinals with Red Schoendienst. It was quite a mix.

Back at home in Orange County, California, life in the city was great for this hard-throwing tall skinny blond-haired future big leaguer. By the time I was twelve, I had made the switch from Little League to the Los Angeles parks and recreation league, where my game improved because I could wear steel cleats for better footing on the mound. The league offered flag football and basketball as well as baseball—the same team for all three sports.

While I was a good athlete in all three sports, I excelled at baseball. We won the city championship. I struck out the first twelve hitters in a row and then moved to shortstop. That was a pretty satisfying day for a kid with not much else going for him in life. We were poor and motherless, and my father worked nights. It was not an easy life, to say the least.

I had a newspaper route when I was ten, and I also collected the bill. The bill collection? That was often the tricky part of the operation, the collection. You see, people like to get the paper, but they just didn't like paying for it.

My next job was doing the "run." The "run" consisted of getting into the back of my neighbor's '56 Chevy pickup and driving around for two hours to fill the paper racks. He was the distributor for the *Los Angeles Times*.

This was a pretty lucrative-paying job at thirty-five dollars a week plus all the dimes I could snag. You see, newspapers only cost a dime in those days, and the racks didn't have sophisticated coin catchers. Some of the dimes would get caught right below the coin drop.

These fugitive dimes were ripe "pickin'" for my long skinny fingers. I worked nights six evenings a week, and most nights, I would get eighty to a hundred dimes a night. Things weren't that bad, I guess, with the "run" to help supplement the family's income.

I started a lawn service to augment the run. With my first few weeks of income, I purchased a transistor radio, the newest fad, complete with headphones. They were the bomb.

I was mowing the lawn for our neighbor, one of my two customers, and listening to the Dodgers game on the new headphones. Vin Scully and Jerry Doggett, the incumbent announcers for the Dodgers radio broadcast, were announcing the game. With the headphones firmly on my head, their voices came in loud and clear above the roar of the noisy gasoline-powered Sears and Roebuck lawn mower.

My idol Sandy Koufax, the Dodgers big left-handed ace, was on the mound. The game was in Pittsburgh. And Sandy? Well, Sandy was just dandy as he fired a no-hitter. Yes! And it was a perfect game climaxed by him, striking out the side in the ninth inning. *That was going to be me someday*, I said to myself.

Vin Scully was the best sports announcer I had, or for that matter, have ever heard. I learned so much about the game of baseball from him. It was amazing how much knowledge you can gain from the radio, especially if you have a good announcer. When Jerry died in the early 1960s, Vin continued the broadcast solo. That was Vin Scully to the max.

The last stop on the "run" just happened to be at the McDonald's hamburger stand on the corner of Rosemead Avenue and Paramount Boulevard. It was the nation's second or third shop and the largest and most modern McDonald's yet.

The burgers were so good and just fifteen cents; fries, cokes, and, of course, the shakes were the same. So with the pocketful of dimes that I had pilfered from the paper racks, I would have dinner. I ate there six days a week. Does that sound healthy? Well, that was another question, but at least I ate every day.

At this time in our lives, my father and I had an alcoholic living with us. He was an old friend of my dad who worked with him at Ford Motor Company. We didn't want to, but ultimately, we had to put him in a rehabilitation facility. He suffered from terrific hallucinations and was just plain scary. After his wife died, he just seemed to fall completely apart. Although he was a mess, I kind of liked him, yet I was afraid of him too.

The year is 1960 now, and it's the World Series. It is the "Bucs" the Pittsburgh Pirates versus the Yankees. It seems like the "Yanks" are in every World Series since the days of Ruth and Gehring and DiMaggio. But the Bucs prevailed in this series on Bill Mazeroski's seventh game ninth-inning home run.

And we got to watch all seven games. You see, the World Series was played during the daytime. We even had television sets in our classroom to watch the games. It was a big deal.

It was just after the World Series concluded, I was just finishing the seventh grade. I had been attending parochial school, you know, Catholic school. My mother was an Irish Catholic. My father was quite the opposite. He was an atheist. So when my mother died, my dad found no reason to be paying tuition and buying uniforms for school. Well, my dad told me, "Now that your mother is gone, you are going to see what the Catholic religion is all about." It didn't take long.

The Mother Superior called me into her office to inform me that I would not be attending school with them next fall. I had been kicked out, expelled, declared persona non grata! What a hoot!

Homework? Hell yes, I had homework. I did mine every night after two cheeseburgers, fries, and a shake. Education is important, and I realized that at an early age. Reading? I read a book in about two days mostly World War II stuff.

And the newspaper? I read it every day. Tommy Davis, the great Dodger outfielder, now there is a real ballplayer.

Writing and arithmetic were equally important too.

No, it was not my work ethic or the content of my work that got me kicked out. It was my dad.

Or maybe she might have found out about the priest who tried to molest me.

Father Boudreaux was his name. He was a Frenchman.

After my mother passed away, this French priest would come to my house. I was the perfect victim for his villainous and evil plan of preying on young boys. The man was a pedophile. He thought I was the perfect catch. Wrong!

One day, he came to my house in his Renault Dauphine and ordered me to make his rounds with him as he visited the sick and elderly. I had to wait in the car.

After about the third stop, he gets in the car and tries to kiss me on the mouth. I was onto him, and I was too quick for his misguided advances. To put it bluntly, I was just plain leery of him. *Pow*! Right in the nose I hit him, with a sturdy right hand, and his head crashed against the driver's side window, causing it to crack. I got out of the car and walked home. I never said a word about it, and he never bothered me again. One for the little guy, I guess.

CHAPTER TWO

John Birch Society

It wasn't long after that situation was remedied, the school situation, that my father remarried. It wasn't his steady girlfriend that he remarried, the girlfriend who loved me. She had no children and treated me like gold.

Contrary to my preference, he married his pre-Army childhood sweetheart from Springfield, Missouri. He bought her a plane ticket to Orange County, California, and they got married, with me as the best man, at twelve years old. I was growing up way too fast.

Now I had just turned thirteen, and I wasn't fully engaged in politics at this young age. But we were now living in the politically charged conservative landscape of the newly formed John Birch Society. I was often reminded that there were "no niggers and no commies" in the land of the Birch Society. My immediate family, which now was just my father, was not racially charged, but in this new formed society of Birchers with its vision of a pure-White landscape was starting to gain momentum in the political world.

When the hippie population exploded in California in the mid-1960s, it caused quite an uproar.

Orange County's main attraction was the ever-popular Disneyland, a mainstay since it opened in 1955 and the dream that Walt Disney saw come true before he died eleven years later.

After counterfeit tickets let a larger-than-anticipated crowd in the gates on opening day, July 17, 1955, Walt in all his wisdom began a crackdown on security that eventually reached the point that it rivaled security at the White House.

My mother and aunt took me to Disneyland on opening day. It was a big disappointment because the crowd was huge, and none of the rides worked, at least not many.

By contrast, Knott's Berry Farm in Buena Park, a mere five miles away and known as America's "first" theme park, had a reputation since the 1920s as "the friendliest place in the West." As such, there was little or no security, no fences, and free admission until 1968 when Walter Knott started charging an admission fee of a "quarter" to get in.

Because Knott's Berry Farm was open year-round, it was like a magnet to the hippies who saw it as a free campground, open to all. It was a different time, to say the least.

After my father remarried, I suddenly had an instant family, consisting of two sisters and a brother my age. One of the girls was older and the other younger than me and only a month separated my stepbrother and me. I was the oldest by just a few days.

Having been on my own for several years since the death of my mother and grandfather, all of a sudden, presto, I had two sisters and a brother. Without a doubt, this was a major adjustment because my privacy had been hijacked and was absolutely gone, shattered, at the tender age of twelve.

A new mother meant unwanted supervision in the form of another authority figure to deal with. My track record with authority figures in the first decade of my life was something to behold. Simply put, authority figures didn't mesh with me, so this began the love-hate relationship with my stepmother that continued over the next three decades, exacerbating my attempts to cope with them.

One thing that I learned at twelve years old is that I must stand up for myself. I was definitely my own person, a trait that would help me survive in a cloudy and uncertain future. I continued to play sports on a daily basis, my one savior in life.

For the most part, I competed in pickup games at the local park with the other neighborhood kids. There was no shortage of players as there were plenty of boys my age in the neighborhood. By the time high school rolled around, I was a strapping six-footer and still growing.

I won nine games and didn't have a loss as a tenth-grade pitcher on the sophomore baseball team. I played outfield when I wasn't pitching. Our team won sixteen games with no losses that year.

In summer ball, I was twelve and one as a pitcher, and I won my only start on the all-star squad. It was the first time in my life I had been recognized as an all-star at anything. The sense of accomplishment was quite satisfying. The future looked bright.

I found out pretty early in life that pitching was an art form, and good mechanics were the key to success.

I'm not going to lie, I didn't have all the pitches in my repertoire that I would develop later on in life, like a great changeup and a devastating knee-buckling slider.

No, a good old-fashioned fastball that was faster than most was all that I had. They didn't have radar guns in my high school days, but my fastball on a stopwatch was around one hundred miles per hour and a twelve-to-six o'clock curveball that could buckle your knees. But it was the mechanics that made me successful. Don't walk batters. Make them hit the ball, if they could.

Bowling was another sport that I excelled at. I had won a handsome amount of money bowling in tournaments and had elevated my game to that of a scratch bowler.

And I was starting to discover the opposite sex. Both would surface as problems in the high school baseball world.

By my senior year, I had a dilemma or two. I was ready to bowl in the local scratch league where money was involved. I also had several girlfriends but no serious lovestruck relationships. It seems that about every week or two, I fell for a new one.

By far, my biggest goal was that I was a legitimate "draft pick" for the upcoming major league baseball draft in the summer of 1966. The baseball draft was just two years old, having commenced in 1964.

The bonuses are huge—up to a hundred thousand dollars just to sign a contract if you are lucky or good enough to be selected in the first round. In my mind and dreams, I was a first-rounder.

My senior year high school baseball team was looking good. We were runners up for last year's state championship, and now we had all the players from the undefeated sophomore team, talent galore.

The baseball preseason opened, and the first thing the coach did was to ask me about my bowling. I told him the truth, and that turned out to be a mistake, a big mistake.

He immediately reported me to the California Interscholastic Federation (CIF) for a status ruling. I am definitely learning to lie from now on. My first lesson in politics.

The CIF, which was the body that governs high school sports in California, ruled that I was a professional athlete because of my acceptance of money from bowling.

I was furious but to no avail. So I lost my amateur status and, with that, my senior year of eligibility and my shot at the baseball draft. Just like that, it was gone. My dad was oblivious to the situation and wouldn't hire a lawyer for me. Put simply, I was fucked.

I didn't play other school sports mostly at the behest of the baseball coach. He told me when I was a junior that I had the rawest baseball talent he had ever seen. What he meant was, I had the best fastball he had ever seen.

The team won the state championship without me. Could it get any worse?

Never fear, another draft is here! Yes, it is 1967, and the United States Army is drafting and heavily if you consider fifty thousand men per month heavy. I did.

The deadly conflict in Vietnam was about to spiral out of control through escalation by the United States, its corrupt president, Lyndon B. Johnson, and his cronies in the military-industrial complex. To gain confidence from the American people, Johnson eyed the colonization of Vietnam and used the guise of stopping the so-called "domino effect" of communism in Southeast Asia as his excuse.

Uncle Sam was calling up thousands and thousands of young American men a month; the best of the best of the best every single month. What a mistake!

In January 1967, at six o'clock in the morning, my stepbrother and I boarded a bus in Downtown Fullerton. The bus was full of eighteen-year-old men of different ethnicities and different walks of life and different likes and dislikes. Now they were all going to be jumbled into one big mass of "olive drab" green.

The diesel-powered behemoth lumbered up the freeway, Interstate 5, to Los Angeles. We were going to an induction center for our "physicals," the second step in what amounted to conscription, or in other words, "forced servitude."

I did not know that there were that many gay men or "queers" as they were referred to then. They were popping up like weeds on a spring day.

The first mistake I made was when I signed those damn papers, the ones that end your life forever, for all practical purposes—the papers that contract your services to the United States Army, at slave wages, for the next two years and make you a pawn in the game of war.

Still, we, my stepbrother and I, didn't really believe at this time that we would actually get called for the draft. After all, Johnson was losing the war, and he was trying to get out of Vietnam. He wasn't trying that hard to get out. That is what we didn't realize.

College student deferments were one avenue toward staving off the draft with the optimism that Republican presidential hopeful Richard Nixon succeeded in ending the deadly conflict, as well as the draft.

That was his stated goal, to get out of Vietnam, but in reality, he wanted the undeclared war to drag on long enough to see a "victory"; however, that was defined by his advisers and military industrial complex cronies who saw the war as a business regardless of the human cost.

A person really had to understand political jargon and how it differs from the obvious, the everyday truths of life. Would it get worse? You bet it would! Now with the draft barking at my heels, the great silent majority that Nixon, or his buffoon of a vice president Spiro Agnew, had boasted about was shrinking in contrast to the comparative size of anti-war protests and demonstrations that were steadily growing across the nation.

I thought winning a ground war in Southeast Asia was wishful thinking on Nixon's part. Mostly because that is what he really was, a wishful thinker, and that's just what his plan was, wishful thinking.

This was the summer of girls, beer, fun, and a job at a major auto manufacture's assembly plant.

I wasn't really old enough to drink, by law. But I thought, *If I'm old enough to pull the trigger or have the trigger pulled on me, then I'm old enough to drink a beer.*

I worked the night shift at the Ford assembly plant on the maintenance crew. I also attended classes at the local junior college during the daytime. I was not playing baseball except for pickup games on the weekends.

There is one interesting occurrence in 1966. It was the addition of a new major league baseball franchise, the California Angels, and they play right here in Anaheim.

The attendance was terrible, and usually by the third inning they, the Angels, just quit charging for admission, so we would go to the Angels games for free. The attendance would sometimes be as low as three hundred people.

The Angels did have one star. He was a big Black outfielder, and he could hit. He was leading the league in batting at the time. If he hit a ground ball to the shortstop, he could beat it out with no sweat.

If, however, a fly ball was hit in his direction in left field, he had no chance of catching it. On another note, his brother was a running back for the New York Giants of the National Football League.

The selective service was in its finest hour for the conscription of young men. The system was busy cutting more call-up orders as the call for replacement soldiers became the lead story on the news, in print and television. That was all that we heard or read about.

At my home in Anaheim, things were pretty darned okay. I had met a girl—not just any girl, but the sweetheart of my dreams, and I couldn't believe it, she liked me too.

She was tall and very pretty with the mindset and the attitude of a fifteen-year-old going on thirty. In all my adolescence, I was never short on hormones to do what young males do at the ripe age of nineteen. I mean, I had some discipline, though, and I was not oversexed. And that was a good thing because there was a slight problem: the girl's mother.

She was a pistol. She took her daughter to the gynecologist every single month. Birth control pills were just coming out on the market, but we had no access to them, so we just lived with it, and the oral sex was more than good.

As time rolls on and the draft is nearing, we were drifting apart. Me? I blame the damned draft and the fact that she was pregnant when I returned home from Vietnam, for the reason that she and I finally drifted completely apart, for good. And I'm not going to think about her when she's gone.

Maybe it was the specter of the draft and the possibility that I would have to go to Vietnam, and that meant separation and probably war, which meant the possibility of death. Frankly, she was a little too young to have to deal with it, and so was I for that matter. This was unfortunate, but it was inescapable.

That fateful day finally came, on a cold rainy November day in 1967. I think it was a Thursday that the dreaded letter arrived in the mail. You know, the one that starts out, "Greetings! You have been selected…"

I ditched work and picked my girlfriend up from high school. She was in her junior year. It was not a good day, but we made it through; after all, there was Thanksgiving and Christmas to look forward to, and then it was off to the Army and time for me to play soldier for a while. I was stressed out between my girlfriend and the specter of Vietnam. I needed a break.

This break, a respite from the stress of everyday life came to me through one of my other hobbies, test-driving muscle cars, and this was the height of the muscle car era.

Little did we know what a unique time in history this was for these powerful machines. Muscle cars are what they were called. I had always wanted to be a premier test driver. Who knows? I might have been just that during this period, from 1964 to1967, when all that mattered was how many cubic inches and how much horsepower a guy or girl had under the hood, coupled with a four-speed transmission, four-on-the-floor with a Hurst shifter.

Oh, what a powerful feeling it was to grip that big white gearshift knob in your hand. It was naturally high-time all right. I used to go to the dealerships regularly to test drive the hottest and fastest cars of my generation and maybe of all time.

My first choice was the Ford dealers because they had the Shelby line of small-block rally cars. These were the souped-up Mustang GT 350s. I have road-tested a few. They were pretty fast, but there was something really sexy about the big-block engines.

Of course, there was the Ford AC Shelby "Cobra." By the time 1966 rolled around, it had a 427-cubic-inch motor with crazy horsepower packed into a three-thousand-pound shell. This baby could go from zero to a hundred and back to a dead stop in ten seconds. It had a window sticker price of sixty-five hundred dollars out the door. A bonus baby could afford one.

They had a special dealership for this beast, and I just happened to be there one Sunday where I was trying out my best spiel on a salesman. I was there for a test drive of the classic of all classic cars. The answer was, "Nice try, kid. Come back when you have the cash," the salesman told me. "No test drives."

As I was exiting the showroom, one of the "Beach Boys" rolled in. After the release of their hit album *Pet Sounds*, there was no doubt in my mind that with all their royalties, he had the cash to purchase one of the hottest cars of all time.

I had the look and the spiel that no salesman could resist. My next target was the Chevrolet dealers. Street racing, beer, and tacos were what the Chevy dealers were about. They had some tough hardware. It was like a smorgasbord of fast cheap cars.

My favorite was the Corvette with its 427-cubic-inch engine and the 425 horsepower and priced at a very reasonable thirty-two hundred dollars. Its window sticker price was about half of the price of a Shelby Ford Cobra and ten times easier to test drive.

I was a test-driving machine. I left more than a few salesmen with wet pants. The rest of the cars were paltry compared to the Corvette although the Plymouth with its 426-cubic-inch street hemispherical head engine and packing its own 425 horsepower, it was a pretty slick machine in itself, complete with a factory-installed Hurst shifter.

My life was fairly normal as a teenager with a new family at that time. There were vacations every summer to Missouri. My previously mentioned stepmother was also from Missouri, down south of Kanas City in Springfield. Naturally, we had to go there for a visit, but I preferred the farm.

Now in the real world, we had elections, and John Kennedy has defeated the incumbent vice president, Dick Nixon. Kennedy was the wealthy brash son of an East Coast entrepreneur. He was also a Catholic and a warmonger.

Then there was the call issued from our new President John F. Kennedy for a fifty-mile march challenge. He wanted all American youth to get in shape, so the challenge was to endure a fifty-mile march. We made it about twenty miles, a lot for our young bodies, especially the feet. I learned from this, always wear two pairs of socks when on an extended foot march. We made it to the Newport Beach pier from Buena Park and then called my dad to come to get us.

That proved to be a pattern for us, calling my dad to come to get us after a failed venture. Once, a group of kids from the neighborhood went camping in the Idyllwild Wilderness. We were going to live off the land except for the fact we had no food, water, or money. About two days was all we lasted. I hiked to a little store, begged a quarter from a customer, and made the call. Dad came and got us.

There was a little tension in the family, however. It was mostly due to my older stepsister who was really my half sister. As it turns out, I was the only one who knew this fact other than my dad and stepmother. I never said a word, and it drove my stepmother crazy.

Chapter Three

GI Draft Blues

Times were changing and quickly, and I didn't have an inkling of what was in store for me just a few months ahead. One thing was certain: it was going to be a whole new life-changing experience, and the change was going to be for the worse.

From this life that I liked and loved to a life I couldn't stand. No job, no test drives, and no girlfriend. What could be better? No, it is just the "GI draft blues."

I had been working at Ford for a while, and I own a pretty nice car of my own. It is a '66 Ford Fairlane, and it is a convertible. Flashy yet conservative. More importantly, I had grown up a little bit, matured.

Still, there was nothing quite like the feeling you get when planting your foot on the gas pedal of a Corvette Stingray, pushing it to the floor, and running her through the gears, out on the Pacific Coast Highway. When that nose comes up and the "G" force pushes you back in the seat and all the gauges are right there in front of you, the feeling was exhilarating. I could only imagine what it was like for an astronaut on the launch pad at liftoff.

By the time the calendar year had flipped to September 1967, the great summer was grinding to a halt. I went back to school during the days and then to Ford Motor Company at night.

There was no time for my girlfriend or at least not enough. We were slowly drifting apart although we still had weekends. She was in her junior year of high school, and she was going to be a shoo-in for homecoming queen.

The draft was closing in, and I could feel it lurking in the shadows behind the fun I was having. It didn't feel good. It was like the hot breath of a dragon, of some beast or monster, breathing down the back of my neck. It was uncomfortable, to say the least.

My stepbrother was in the same boat, but at least he was excelling in school, unlike me. I thought that he would get a student deferment for sure.

My girlfriend was one distraction for me, but ultimately, the draft was the real problem. I came down with a bad case of the GI draft blues. I was engulfed in the no-one-cares-about-me-but-me mentality. And my dad? Well, he was just totally uninterested. And my girlfriend? She was just a date at this point in my life. I mean, what's a boy to do?

And what in the hell were we doing as a country? This is the real question to be asked. This country, the United States of America, has never attacked another country unless the homeland was itself was attacked first, self-defense, the bombing of "Pearl Harbor," for instance.

This so-called "war," officially known as a "conflict," came with a new mandate and mantra: stop the "domino" effect in Southeast Asia and "kill a commie for Christ."

How do you rationalize the self-defense theory when you blatantly invade another country—a solvent country that does not want or need you there?

Colonization was the word that kept popping up.

What exactly is colonization? I mean, what's that theory all about anyway?

What was really strange was that the same United States government that professed to defend weaker countries—and help them not conquer them—was advocating this nonsense and carrying out the exact opposite of their mandate. This was just a tad hypocritical I would say.

I was really trying hard to cope with the state of confusion. I was really conflicted, but the question *What can I do about it?* kept popping up.

So with a mindset trending toward helplessness, I dropped out of college only six weeks into my first semester. It was time for some reflection on where I've been, where I was at right then, and where I was headed. I was not a great thinker, but I thought that I owed it to myself to have some fun before I died.

Country Joe McDonald had made a hit out of a song about getting drafted for the war in Vietnam. With the unforgettable and oh-so-true lyrics,

> Uncle Sam needs your help again;
> He's got himself in a jam way down yonder in Vietnam.
> So put down your books and pick up a gun;
> We're gonna have a whole lot of fun.
> Whoopee! We're all gonna die.

Country Joe Mc Donald sang this diddy about the time I was destined for Vietnam.

It was really funny to be listening to all these songs about Vietnam and death and all. And in just a few short weeks, that will be me that they are singing about. Crazy.

Music has changed over the years since I was a youngster. Bill Haley lured my ear for rock and roll with his "Rock Around the Clock." Then it was the "king"—Elvis Presley—who hooked me and reeled me in. I can remember when the "king" was drafted and the so-called "conflict" in Vietnam was about to swell into an undeclared guerrilla war.

It would soon consume fifty thousand young American men a month, and I was about to be thrown into the fray. I'll bet I don't get treated as good as Elvis did.

The "Vietnam conflict" was destined to blow up in a horrific, patriotic jumble of disappointment as more and more families heard the news of dead soldiers.

Then reality sank in. They were not only soldiers—they were family members: brothers, sons, grandsons, and nephews. The empty bootprints covered a lot of ground on the home front. The families searched for answers as to why this was still happening in 1969. But alas, there were no answers. No good ones anyway.

Motown Records, the recording label of Detroit's "Motor City," had been cranking out vinyl records for the past nine years. Berry Gordy Jr.'s stars of Motown with their soul-filled sounds, mostly songs of love and joy gone wrong, blared over the airwaves for all to hear and enjoy.

But then the songs changed with the messages becoming about civil rights and the anti-war movement, replacing the broken love songs.

Mostly to Gordy's chagrin, you see, he was just about making money and controlling his stable of entertainers. Control was the most important aspect.

Even Gordy could not control many of the singers who saw the war for what it was: a land grab, the stealing of another country's national resources, products like tea and rubber, and of course, the country's oil. The Gulf of Tonkin is rich and ripe for drilling, but at what price? Five thousand, ten thousand dead American soldiers a day?

There was another conflict simmering on the home front: the movement for equal rights and equal opportunity on all fronts from housing to college, education, and sports.

A perfect storm for violence at home and overseas loomed over America.

It wasn't long before the anti-war and civil rights movement converged on Detroit like a firestorm from hell. Looting and riots replaced the music and muscle cars. Motown was smoking, literally.

Detroit had been riding high with the muscle car industry and the city's sweet soul sounds that had morphed into ghetto pain and the heartbreak of war.

What a mix of music about the downhill direction that the country was rolling toward. Marvin Gaye used his sweet passionate voice to paint the issues in shades of blue with his hits "Inner

City Blues" and "What's Going On"—two powerful songs respectively about the plight of not only the Blacks but also all the poor in America's slums, barrios, and ghettos.

There were far too many African American men dying in the war, and they were being socially punished with a brutality that was hard to fathom. Was this, in fact, the beginnings of systemic discrimination?

Detroit became a crucible for the civil rights and anti-war demonstrators confronting police officers in riot gear. The city was in chaos with all the looting and the burning of buildings and cars.

The Motor City had lost its mystique, and the ghettos were growing from the embers. As the Motown artists saw their prosperity turn to devastation, their visions were turned from top-10-hit musical creations to anti-war and civil rights songs that filled AM and FM airwaves alike.

I was a fan of all types of music. Yes, I liked country too and even a little western. I wasn't much of a two-step dancer, but the sound of lonesome highways and buttermilk skies kept my mind at ease.

The real story that burst on the scene was the British Invasion that swept across the nation like a pandemic of gyrating rock-and-roll mopheads.

Yes, sir. The British Invasion was in full swing. The *White* album was about to hit the Atlantic coast like a hurricane, thanks to the "long-haired" Beatles and the dark and mysterious Rolling Stones with their own "Sympathy for the Devil." Then there were the Monkees and a whole slew of zoo-themed named groups who blended in with the craze.

These tours of magical musicians traveled across the heartland with their infectious tunes playing nonstop on transistor radios from coast to coast.

The robust and romantic rock sounds turned teenage hotties into zombies. This fresh new sound played in homes, cars, and on both the Atlantic and Pacific coast beaches. It was a great time to be alive.

I went to the recruiters just to see what they had to offer. I visited both the Air Force and Navy recruiting offices. The message was the same in both instances. They can't guarantee me anything. I guess I am just going to wait for the draft and take my chances.

Now the one thing I was sure of: I'm smart enough to know a bad deal when I see one, and this was it. If these guys in crisp uniforms think they could swindle me, then they had another thing to learn, and that was, this street-savvy kid was not a sucker. Besides, I just didn't think a career in the military was right for me.

I did complete junior Reserve Officer Training (ROTC) in the eighth grade. I was a platoon leader, but it just didn't do anything for me. Of course, I was offered no advice from my father other than his wisdom about my independence.

"You are going to have to make your own choice," he told me. And so I did.

The days were going by pretty fast right now, and I realized this would probably be my last Christmas as a civilian. In fact, it was. I was going to be inducted into the military right after the New Year. The year was 1968, and I was not thrilled. My life is no longer mine. *This is not right!*

Politics? Not many schoolboys, or at least very few, were interested in that stuff. That's because politics had a boring, humdrum presence. That was about to change.

It was a crisp November morning, and I was in my sophomore year in high school. It was right in between the second and third periods when the news hit, and hit it did. The president of the United States, John F. Kennedy, had been assassinated. It happened in Dallas, Texas.

How could this happen, and who did it? More importantly, what's next? As it turned out, this was not a world conspiracy or an international assassination. Nope. It was just good old-fashioned jealousy, a mere indiscretion that aristocrats are so famous for.

Vice President Lyndon Baines Johnson took the reins of the presidency. The world would never be the same afterward.

The war in Vietnam was on the brink of escalating out of control because the man steering the charade was not only greedy and had many unscrupulous cronies in the military industrial complex—the war machine.

No, he was also galloping down the trail of colonizing a foreign land and at the great expense of American soldiers, sailors, Marines, and airmen.

One thing that did change and change dramatically was the media. Never before had there been coverage like that of the very popular young and now-deceased statesman John Kennedy.

The media was relentless. It was a twenty-four-hour-a-day barrage. There was seemingly nonstop news carried by the major networks. To make things even more bizarre, the man who "allegedly" shot the president was himself shot and killed in the basement of the Dallas police station.

Just two days after the assassination of the young president, a well-known Dallas bar owner shot the alleged assassin to death and on live television to boot.

Kennedy's funeral was no different. It was broadcast on black-and-white and in living color, and it was worldwide coverage.

It started at the church where services were held and on through the streets of Washington, DC, down to Pennsylvania Avenue and to its final resting spot: a hill near the United States Marine Corps War Memorial, the one that features the planting of Old Glory at Iwo Jima atop of Mount Suribachi. An eternal flame was lit and shone its brilliance across the Potomac River to the Washington Mall. There were a lot of tears shed that day.

As the nation continued to mourn, the new president, Johnson, appointed a commission to investigate the heinous act. But the commission was a sham.

The Warren Commission was headed by the former chief justice of the Supreme Court, Earl Warren. Warren himself had just been the subject of an attempted impeachment hearing brought on by the John Birch Society of Orange County.

This was an inside job, the murder of Kennedy. That is what my instincts tell me, and all you have to do is figure out who had the most to gain from this cowardly act. Like most crimes, it is pretty easy to find the truth if you are really looking.

This event awakened my political senses. It was kind of like, who's doing what to whom? It didn't really matter because I could not vote. I was just seventeen. I can't legally smoke cigarettes, chew tobacco, or drink alcohol, but on the other hand, I am somehow supposed to be able to point a firearm at another human being and pull the trigger. Sounds like something that some aristocrat dreamed up. And the beat goes on, as Cher would sing.

CHAPTER FOUR

Queers and Hot Rods

By the time the calendar flipped to January 1970, I had been home from Vietnam for only a couple of weeks. I was in Anaheim once again, back home in the safety of the United States. That was the best part.

There was a slight problem, though. I came home to a different country than when I had departed. It was different socially than when I had left. Or maybe it was me? Have I changed? Could that be possible?

The change came after serving a grueling ten-month combat tour as one of "LBJ's" mercenaries in South Vietnam. I was having a difficult time adjusting back to civilian life. It was not the war memories or bad dreams. No. It was about the hypocrites who were running this country. Our country.

Going from combat patrols in the jungles of Vietnam to the streets of Los Angeles almost overnight developed into quite a shock. It was not just in the terrain but the nature of the beast I had to conquer. Returning to a civilian lifestyle in the hopeful pursuit of a major league baseball career.

The first year that I was in the Army wasn't too bad, except that I missed my girlfriend terribly. All I could think about was how to get back home to her and repair our relationship.

I did everything possible to stay out of Vietnam, including "volunteering" for "jump school," also known as parachute training.

That's where you are taught to jump out of an airplane—one that's just humming along perfectly—then land on the ground in one piece and start killing. That made sense to me, a crazy sense about the nature of what loomed ahead.

After graduating second in my parachute class at Fort Benning, Georgia, I was kept as a holdover for cadre duty. The captain, our company commander, was from Southern California. He had served in Vietnam. He had seen the devastation and the effect that the war had on young men. He tried to keep me out of the conflict, but that was not to be.

I spent the summer pulling charge-of-quarters duty and moving troops around to and from training and meals.

I was also the mail clerk, tasked with sorting and delivering six months' worth of backedup mail. Some of those guys whose mail I forwarded might even be dead by now. Who knows? A lot of that mail got forwarded to the Republic of Vietnam. I also strapped on a .45-caliber pistol and did the payroll once a month.

What was my real duty? I played centerfield on the forty-eighth jump company softball team. I could hit a softball four hundred feet easily, and my arm just blew people away.

"You should be in the major leagues," one soldier quipped to me after a sorry game for his team.

Then there was the war college. Really, there was a war college where it was akin to getting PhDs in night ambushes or how to bury your feces in the jungle. Foreign military officers also attended these classes and studied mostly warfare tactics.

Finally, there was the ranger training school. I attended classes regularly. I did not qualify for the ranger tab because of my rank. In those days, you had to be at least a buck sergeant, E-5, or above. Unfortunately, I was just a private first class, an E-3. The tab didn't matter. Survival in the jungles did, however. I learned a lot.

With a change of fate and through the "good old boy" network, I was transferred to North Carolina as a clerk. Yep, an airborne computer programmer. I was willing to bet there was not a high demand for that MOS (military occupational specialty) in the combat zone.

So that meant that I probably would not be going to Vietnam, at least anytime soon.

I found out after the last leg of my charter flight from Okinawa to Cam Ranh Bay, South Vietnam, that I was right about computer programmers in Vietnam. But infantrymen were in high demand.

I was suddenly thrust into the infantry, and unknowingly, with that, I began a venture on a gut-wrenching downward spiral in my life. It was all over but the crying, and there wouldn't be any of that.

How does a clean-cut, outstanding soldier with a computer programmer MOS wind up walking point for the Fourth Infantry Division's reconnaissance platoon? It was simple, elementary really.

My new company commander at Fort Bragg hated me. He was a bona fide redneck from Georgia. He believed in the adage of Southern folklore that there was nothing but "queers" and "hot rods" that come from California.

"I don't see any tailpipes on you," this dick weed said in introducing himself. How prejudice was that?

Then there was the drug smuggling foray, and finally, the great payroll robbery of '68.

I was assigned to the machine payroll branch of the administration company. We punched up the payroll for the Eighty-Second Airborne Division on IBM machines. I handled the jump pay. One month, a batch of program cards came in for a new battalion. So I punched it up. Lo and behold, it was a fake.

Some guys in the payroll branch had devised a scheme to set up a false payroll. Once the checks were issued, they would cash them. It was about $250,000 worth of what amounted to double pay for these wise guys.

So that got me a trip to Vietnam, and I thought that was better than the jail time they got at Fort Leavenworth. Looking back, I suppose.

When I tried to settle in at home, my mind was still whirling with the horrors of war, stuff that nobody here could conceive. They had no idea what I was trying to wrap my mind around. So I didn't try explaining it. Why? They wouldn't get it anyway.

That's when the real problems began. I had to figure out what to do with my life and adjust my combat mindset to fit this little niche of septic society where flower children and the rainbow people skip hand in hand happily along the peace trail.

I supposed that was all well and good. I mean, I like peace as much as anyone. The flower people have their place in life, but it is a little different when you have seen what I had seen and have done what I had done—and all this just to stay alive.

Looking back at my pathetic bank account, I had a total in savings of about fifteen hundred dollars for my war effort—the typical golden handshake for draftees who resist re-upping after risking their freakin' lives every day at slave wages. It ain't much, as the old saying goes.

I was eligible for the old GI Bill benefits to go back to college full-time. But the classroom didn't sit well with me.

I actually tried sitting—and staying awake—while listening to some monotone professor preaching about the philosophy of ancient war history.

Hell, I had to learn how to fall asleep sitting up with one eye open to say alive at nights in the steamy Central Highlands of South Vietnam for twice as long as it took this geek to get his teaching certificate.

It is no wonder why I would snooze in that ceramic seat in the comfort of air-conditioning. *I was so tired.*

Coming home to this cold reception at this time in history, I was in a proverbial fish-out-of-water syndrome. The feeling was like I was back on recon in the concrete streets and highways of Los Angeles in pursuit of opportunities while trying to shoot a new azimuth in life. But there was no setting on my social compass for the animosity I would be faced with.

I had a friend whom I would get high with at Fort Bragg. He had been to Vietnam and was an infantryman with the 101st Airborne. He taught me a lot about "Nam" before I went. He had the same problem that I have now when he came home. He could not stay awake. The doctors told him he had parasites in his bloodstream from drinking river water while he was in South Vietnam. Maybe that was my problem too? What about the iodine tablets? They taste bad, and they don't work.

At this point in time, I was virtually lost, but I couldn't let on. That would make me a loser. I couldn't have that in my life right now. Then my father piped up and suggested baseball. And this was from the mouth of the man who wouldn't hire a lawyer for me to fight the CIF for my amateur status when I actually had a shot at professional baseball.

The autoworkers union had a baseball team that played on Sundays, and they needed players. I went out for a tryout. The team was a bad one with an 0–6 record. I pitched the first week I went out, and I did pretty well, throwing a complete game. I hit a home run, and we won. The next week was pretty much a repeat of the first week. Then the team folded.

I was not to be deterred. In fact, it was quite the opposite. So I went to the California Angels headquarters and asked for a tryout. I talked to the general manager and told him my hard-luck story. The one about the loss of my senior year of eligibility for winning money bowling and then getting drafted and sent to Vietnam.

I really thought he cared. That is how naive I was. So he sent me to Montebello to pitch for the "Scout" team. Maybe I was going to get a break, hopefully for the better for a change. It was time for the hard-luck to go away.

I got home from the war in November 1969. My girlfriend was pregnant, and I weighed all of 150 pounds soaking wet. I had lost sixty-five pounds off my six-foot-four-inch frame in ten months, mostly thanks to dysentery, jungle heat, and the last combat patrol. That's the one where we survived two weeks in monsoon rains, 24-7 without rations.

On top of that, I had not slept in about ten months. Hell, I still had the remnants of jungle rot all over my arms. It was not a pretty sight.

Nonetheless, I went back to work at the Ford assembly plant. I had lost my night-shift job as a janitor, and now I was working days on the assembly line.

I had a "boss" who was a young college graduate. He liked to "ride" people. Well, he decided to ride me one Friday while I was assembling the grilles on Ford Thunderbirds. For that indiscretion, he got his whole head wrapped in duct tape. The other workers cheered. I was kind of a cult hero to the other workers but not to my old man. He was pissed, but he got over it. This was the second time I had been in a fight at the Ford plant. The first time occurred in 1967 when a plumber decided to punch my stepbrother simply because he had long hair and "John Lennon-style" glasses. Jim was not a fighter, but I was, and I took it right to him. That guy didn't mess with us again.

This was a nowhere job, and it probably won't even be here next year when the environmental regulators shut this assembly plant down for being a polluter. *And no, I'm not moving to Mexico for my job*, I thought.

When I returned home from Vietnam, I brought a little bag of goodies with me. The bottom third of my duffel bag was filled with marijuana, Cambodian red. It was my first smuggling gig, and I had learned this trade while serving in the Army.

So I met this Black guy who has been at Ford forever, and he knew everybody in the plant. He was my man. Every Friday, I brought a kilo of marijuana broken into one-ounce bags. He would sell them all at lunch. I was making about $480 dollars a week in payroll and another $800 a week selling pot. Do you see why I'm still here?

Back to baseball and my "tryout" with the Angels. I drove out to Montebello for my first tryout. I showed up wearing a baseball jersey. It was an old Angels game jersey that I purchased at a thrift store. I thought it was kind of cool.

On this so-called "Scout" team, there were only two only other White players. One was the son of a Hall of Fame catcher, and he was playing left field. His dad once hit fifty homers for the Detroit Tigers. They had offered him a five-hundred-dollar pay cut for his effort.

The other player was a former first-round pick of the San Francisco Giants. He, like me, also had been drafted and sent to

Vietnam. When he returned home from serving his country, he was released by the San Francisco Giants organization.

That was pretty cold, I thought. They said he had changed a lot, but I didn't see it. But then I didn't know him before. Maybe he was like me, and he smoked a lot of marijuana.

The manager is a short Mexican fellow. I would say he is about thirty-five, and he tells me, "We don't need no pitching right now. Can you play the outfield?"

Yes, I can, and I do. In three weeks, I hit two homers and bat .356 with a couple of outfield assists. Pretty respectable, but still, I have pitched zero innings.

So it is my fourth week, and the manager releases me. "You're too slow afoot," he tells me to be a major league outfielder.

"Yeah, I tell him, but I can throw in the midnineties much harder than all those Mexican pitchers that you've got, and I have better control." I'm gone, no big deal. *Do I smell a little racism here?*

I had either quit my job at Ford or the plant had just closed. For whichever reason, I had joined the ranks of the unemployed. I was an aimless bum, and that wasn't good. I had money, so that was not the problem. Instead, the problem was, that I was just not right.

James returned home. I wasn't worried about him, but I was glad he was back. We got along at first, but ever so slowly, we started to drift apart, until it reached the point where we didn't even talk. That silence would continue for forty years.

Would a reasonable man who endured the draft find it honorable to die for his country in Vietnam? Would he have felt downright shanghaied if he was there? Was there one bit of honor or respect shown to those men if they were "lucky" enough to return intact?

I went back to the basics of the marijuana trade. My business was growing. I had always wanted to be a citrus farmer—oranges or lemons, maybe even some avocados. It was a good, wholesome life. And if I could grow a few thousand marijuana plants as a "cash crop," then so what? This had been my second goal, baseball was my first, and now it is my second—ranching was now my first goal.

Jimi Hendrix was playing at the Forum in Los Angeles. I bought six tickets and took my friends and my stepbrother Jim. We got high on mescaline for the concert, and it was spectacular, a great show. When it was over around midnight, we headed home. I was going to bed. Jim, on the other hand, had a Volkswagen bus and had been rebuilding the engine.

I went to bed. When I woke up in the morning, he had installed the engine and had it running. This feat was simply amazing.

Chapter Five

Rambo in the Dugout

I picked up a partner in crime. He was an old friend, and he had served a tour in Vietnam also. He was a former door gunner on a "Huey." We did pretty well for a while, but all good things must end.

Now in every partnership, there have to be rules, and the first rule of this partnership was no chemicals or hard drugs—pot and hash only. We made an exception for mescaline and LSD (lysergic acid diethylamide) although we never sold that much LSD or mescaline.

I was down in Laguna Beach one evening, selling some kilos when there was a big commotion. The cops? Is it a raid? No, it was Timothy Leary, the LSD guru himself alive and in person. As it turns out, it was Tim Leary who sued the government over the marijuana tax laws. He won, and it also constituted the changing of the spelling to *marijuana*.

Finally, he got the laws taxing marijuana at fifty dollars an ounce overturned. This was some thirty years after Anslinger enacted the law. I sold my wares, and then I was on my way. I was never really into Leary's turn on, tune in, and dropout message. It was not my type of message. I was thankful for his work on marijuana laws.

LSD had been legal for a while, but that soon came to an end. I had read *The Electric Kool-Aid Acid Test*, a book by Tom Wolfe, about the journeys of novelist Ken Kesey and his band of Merry Pranksters with the likes of Hugh Romney Jr., also known as Wavy Gravy.

It is really funny, though, how things come to pass. I have been named or more descriptively unnamed in an article running in the *Rolling Stone* magazine about the "Hippie Mafia" operating out of Laguna Beach. Not one fact is right or true for that matter.

My partner and I got a line on a pound of mescaline, and it was cheap, but we had to drive to San Francisco to get it. San Francisco is known as the "chemical" city because that is where all the LSD comes from.

We drove up to San Francisco. When we got there, it was so foggy that we couldn't see a thing. We were sitting at a stoplight on top of a hill when this guy crossed the street right in front of us. He was only about five feet tall, and he was wearing a long overcoat with the collar pulled up around his head, and he looked at us.

It was kind of a menacing stare, sort of like "What are you doing here?" His eyes are wide open and bulging out of his head they look like flying saucers, and he's breathing hard. The condensation from his breath made it look like steam from a dragon. San Francisco's a weird place.

We score the mescaline and hall ass for home. Back in Orange County, we buy horse caps and cap up the mescaline, and by the time we were done capping, we are as high as a kite.

I am an entrepreneur, so I am always looking for a good way to make money, and band management comes my way. I have some friends who've been playing music professionally since high school. I rent the hall, VFW halls, mostly seeing as how I am a veteran.

I am kind of a one-man company as I paid the band, do the advertisement, and hold dances on the weekends, and then comes the cleanup. I hate the cleanup, but all in all, this had been a successful venture and a good way to launder money.

I remember one Saturday we had a big dance party in Bellflower. We had wine bags filled with wine and spiked with mescaline.

Well, the police showed up and asked, "Who is in charge?"

"I am," I said.

"Well, we don't mind the loud music," the officer began, "or the drunkenness, but we can't have people dancing in the damned street."

"Yes, Officer," I replied, "and I will stop it immediately," and I did.

Time is moving along. The year is 1971, and my father has retired or was forced out at Ford. The times are changing, and I'm not sure for the better. Dad bought a travel trailer, and he and my stepmother are away most of the year, so it is the *Home Alone* story for me.

My partner and I decided to go to Mexico, Ensenada, to buy floor tiles and cotton shirts. Money laundering was the real reason for the trip and, who knows, maybe a connection.

Mostly, we were buying our marijuana in San Diego. It was safer than trying to run the Mexican border. The border at Tijuana is totally corrupt, and you better have the fix in if you try to run it.

Lately, we have gotten into the bulk sales of marijuana, and it is quite profitable, but we could make even more money by transporting the product to other states. We are not at that level yet, but we are getting there.

Rock stars were falling like raindrops from an ominous dark cloud. Jim Morrison, Janis Joplin, and Jimi Hendrix had all died, not in that order but in the past year.

Hendrix died right after we saw him in Inglewood. Wow, I was at Jimi's last concert, but that's all right, there will be ten more to replace them next week.

In another surprise happening, Satchel Paige, the great Negro baseball league pitcher, was inducted into the National Baseball Hall of Fame, a good and well-deserved honor. I think he was the oldest rookie to ever pitch in the big leagues. I believe that he was in his midforties at least when he signed, after a stellar career with the Kansas City Monarchs of the old "Negro League."

I think this was a great feat because it identified Satchel for what he accomplished—his body of work on the field and not the color of his skin.

I miss baseball, but I can't find a place to play, and the college coaches? Well, they've got more excuses not to take me than I have fingers. The real reason they don't want me is simple. Who wants

"Rambo" in their dugout? It is a plain and real clear fact and oh so clear to me.

It is June of 1971 now, and something pretty interesting has just occurred—the "Pentagon Papers" were published by the *New York Times* newspaper. I guess some disgruntled officer at the Pentagon has released some damaging files on the White House. It would be a while, but soon, this would be the end of that beady-eyed war criminal, Dick Nixon, who now sits in the White House—good riddance.

Tricky Dick Nixon is withdrawing troops from Vietnam at an alarming rate. Why? Is it because we have won the war? No, that's not it. Is it because we have lost the war? No, that's not it either. It is of course money. If the military-industrial complex, who is running this country, wants to continue to colonize, they are going to have to find another way to do it.

Colonization is wrong, and colonizing takes troops, conscripted soldiers to do the dirty work, but there is a better way to do it. Simply, they should use a professional army or, better yet, mercenaries, they would even be better. It seems to work for other despots.

But that's not it either. No, the real reason is the anti-war movement, and they're demonstrations and protests over the draft. And now the civil rights movement has joined forces with the anti-war crowd or vice versa, and the riots, the looting, and burning have reached magnanimous proportions—that is a true and plain fact. The demonstrations were what did Nixon's presidency in. It was because of the draft that's the real reason—Watergate was just a small part of it. But to use draftees your average kid off the street to fight your dirty little guerrilla war? Big mistake. Whoever started this fiasco known officially as the "Vietnam conflict" should be shot. Oh! He was Jack Kennedy.

Well, it is a "Hard rain that's gonna fall," sings Dylan, and it is falling on me. The date is March of 1972, and I got busted at the Los Angeles International Airport. Yep, 150 kilos of grade "A" Mexican pot. I was headed to Seattle then on northward to Vancouver, British Columbia, what was I thinking? Well, to tell you the truth, I was thinking of money.

We were getting almost three hundred dollars (US) a kilo, and that's pretty good when you consider we get the kilos for seventy-five dollars apiece. It is, to put it mildly, a gold mine, and the Canadian border is a piece of cake to cross, not at all like the Mexican–American border.

The only problem is the currency exchange. It takes me about a day or more to convert the Canadian dollars to US dollars and a lot of bank trips.

We are on about our fourth trip to Vancouver, and the idiot traveling with me has one kilogram of marijuana in his carry-on luggage.

Sky marshals have just recently come into service because of a rash of hijackings. The most notable hijacking at the time was D. B. Cooper out of Seattle.

The sky marshal busts my traveling companion and then ultimately me. We have made a couple of trips up to the north country, and it has been good up until tonight. The people we do business with are a biker club. They've got people from one end of Canada to the other, as Canada goes.

The other guy we deal with is a bar owner in Downtown Vancouver. The business is good, and it is never a problem—it has been a good run.

Well, this is the end now of my partnership in the drug business. This did not mean I was quitting. It meant I was just gonna change my way of doing business. So I have to go to court and face the charges of international drug smuggling. I am convicted and get a two-to-ten-year suspended sentence pending a ninety-day psychiatric stay at the California men's prison at Chino. What can I say? It sucked.

There was one thing that stood out, though. They make you take a job screening test to find out what job you're suited for. Mine came back as "inconclusive," that's because baseball players and citrus farmers weren't on the test.

Plus, the fact they don't take into consideration that you are now a convicted felon, and life is basically just shit now. That's just a small equation. At any rate, I get through the ninety days.

When I get out, I have nothing. Time to get to work. I make some money and find a ranch in the California high desert around San Jacinto. The ranch is two hundred acres, and my backyard is the Idyllwild national reserve. I'm in heaven.

The ranch itself is a beautiful layout. It was built by Mary Campbell, the lady author who wrote *Ramona*. *Ramona* was a novel about an Indian princess who married a White man or something like that. Romeo and Juliet come to mind.

I've got a couple of partners, two horses, two dogs, and a cat, tomcat to be exact. We are living just above the Soboba Indian Reservation. They are a tribe of half breeds, half Mexican, half Indian, and they're nasty and even nastier when they had been drinking. We have to drive through the reservation to get to our place, but they didn't bother us, so far anyway, but I am sure it is coming.

They had a softball game one Sunday afternoon, and by the fifth inning, they had five people transported to the local hospital with bat contusions and stab wounds.

One day, I caught one of the little braves on my property, and he was shooting at my dogs with a .22 rifle. I broke the rifle in half and sent him on his way.

That night, we got a big surprise when two carloads of Indians rolled up to my front door. "Do you hippies want to 'fuck or fight'?" one of the drunken heathens bellowed out.

I don't know, but one thing for sure, I hate being called a "hippie."

As you can imagine, I have some pretty unorthodox friends. One of them is a former Marine gunny sergeant. The sergeant, who after serving twenty years in the Marine Corps, became a mercenary.

After the Korean War, he had seen action in Venezuela. Then came the real clincher when he joined the Biafra rebel army. He was a major in the Army of Biafra during the Nigerian Civil War.

Now he owns an extermination business in the area, hence the nickname "The Termite Man." He once told me how they robbed the bank in the capital of Lagos as they were leaving the country. He was a character.

As it so just happens, I'm lucky enough to have him be at my house this evening. There are two carloads of Soboban Indians driving up the dirt road that leads right to our door, and they bellow out their challenge again, "Do you hippies want to fuck or fight?" That seemed to be their message.

I presume this was a retaliatory action for the incident the day before when I ran the young buck off my property for shooting at my dogs.

We have some firepower too. The old sarge pulled out a Thompson submachine gun. "Let's have some fun," he cried out.

"Fight!" we answered just before we opened up.

Those old cars never moved so fast. I was blasting with my .12 gauge while sarge ran a bead along the side of both cars. I don't think that they were expecting that.

The next morning, the tribal chief and the tribe's medicine man / spiritual leader were at the door. They apologized for last night, and we agreed to live in harmony. We finished by smoking a big fat joint of Colombian. We didn't have a peace pipe to smoke and they didn't bring one.

Back to the tomcat. He was something else at twelve years old and a healthy nineteen pounds of pure muscle. Once I reached down to pet his neck and was shocked to find out, he didn't have one.

The Sobobans knew of him too. He was said to have been seen copulating with a skunk on the reservation. There were many other incidents involving Tom the Cat, including his hatred of women.

We had some ladies over one summer weekend who were anxious for a dip in the natural hot springs. They also wanted to explore the mountains. And with the horses, this was kind of like paradise.

When the ladies arrived, they had left the sunroof on their car open. Tom must have liked the smell and/or felt a bit like his privacy was being intruded on, so he hopped in the sunroof, landed like cats always do on his feet on the front seat, and started peeing up a storm. That car now reeked of cat urine that would last forever, you could never escape it.

That once-hot car was now burned toast.

There were other capers too. Tom was an older cat. He ate some poisoned meat on the reservation, and then the wind blew a door shut on his tail, and he was never the same after that.

I went away on some business, and while I was gone, a wildfire erupted as they were known to do with westerly Santa Ana winds blowing out to the coast.

I was racing the fire on state Highway 60 in my Porsche. When I reached home, well, most of the property, with exception of the house, was just ashes, charred wood, and sooty concrete.

And what happened to Tom? Who knows. I hope he made it out. Both of the horses perished; the dogs survived; all the buildings were destroyed, except for the house.

I guess we need a new hacienda.

Chapter Six

Outlaws versus Criminals

The year 1973 came after a bad year in 1972, one that had spiraled down to the nub, the bottom rung.

I had been well on my way up the social ladder toward buying a citrus ranch when the idiot who was traveling with me decided he had to carry that one kilo on board the aircraft.

Worse yet, I was a fugitive.

I was given probation for the marijuana bust at the Los Angeles Airport, but the probation officer who had my case, I swear, this guy was like Jack Webb of Sergeant Joe Friday fame. I mean, he was a crusty old Chesterfield-smoking bureaucrat. That was who this clown reminded me of because that was who he was.

My first probation meeting was a disaster as this Jack Webb guy went to court and got a urine test order for me.

I had to pee in a jar for him. I don't think I ever saw a *Dragnet* episode where that happened before. Of course, I hadn't watched much TV, and when I did, it was always just baseball.

So I told the probation officer, "That's fine. I will just go pee, and I will be right back."

I always wondered afterward how long he waited for that jar of urine.

There was, and still is in my mind, a difference between an outlaw and a criminal. Criminals don't care about anyone but themselves and will do anything to anyone they feel like—rob, steal, kill, or rape. Those are the things that criminals do.

Outlaws, on the other hand, follow the Cervantes route. They are chivalrous lovers who protect the have-nots. Robin Hood may have been the best example.

So I have some problems right now, and it is time for me to get cracking. First, I needed a place to live. I found a rental house just off the 91 Freeway with easy access. I would get up at six every morning, and some days, I would make three or four trips between San Diego and Orange County. I'm making money off the hundreds of kilos I'd take with me each trip.

My identification issue was next on the list. How do you get a false identification? First, you must go to a rural Department of Motor Vehicles office. Then you tell the receptionist that you had an unrecorded birth somewhere in Montana or Wyoming right after World War II.

That poor kid. "We'll fix that," she must have thought.

And then you smile for the camera and you have a driver's license and a valid one at that legal identification.

I had four of them. James Rockford, also known by his real name, James Garner, of the *Rockford Files* television series, had nothing on me.

Now I need even more money. I purchased fifteen kilos and then headed up north to Bend, Oregon, in my 1967 Volkswagen bug. When I arrived at Bend, I went to my friend's house to hang out for a couple of days.

It was really quite nice in Bend. There were groves of different types of soft fruit. This probably would be a nice place to live. I didn't sell one kilo, however, and I had been there for a week.

This lack of business wasn't that the pot was bad or that people didn't indulge. Like too many things in this world, whether it was baseball or the military-industrial complex or just plain dealing marijuana, it always seemed to be about the money.

That was the problem—no one had any. So I was dejected and frustrated, and I was heading south for home.

Then something flashed through my mind.

Hell, I might as well stop in at Lake Tahoe.
And so I did.

It was snowing lightly when I descended around the turn and stared down in awe of the cobalt-blue waters of this giant lake.

On the Nevada shoreline side, I stopped at one of the casinos to get a bite to eat, and guess what? I won a thousand dollars playing blackjack.

The quarters' lady cashed me out. I gave her a nice healthy tip and was back in the VW on the road again.

By the time I reached Encinitas, California, I was so tired I had to find a hotel room.

Before I settled down, I walked to the store to get a beer. I left my jean jacket with four one-hundred-dollar bills in the front pocket on the bed and thought nothing of it.

When I awoke the next morning, I discovered that the four hundred-dollar bills were missing.

Now they didn't walk away, so someone must have stolen them. I canvassed the hotel grounds and found a man and a woman. They told me who they suspected of stealing the money, adding the "Dirty rotten thief is also the hotel bully."

"Is that so?" I said. Now I was not an overly violent person, but this act pissed me off to no end.

Big Five sporting goods stores were having a sale on guns. There were some shotguns, eighteen-inch-barrel .12-gauge pump shotguns just like the riot guns that the cops used.

So I found the nearest Big Five and bought a shotgun and a box of ammo, double-ought buckshot.

The "night visitor" was about to reckon with this lowlife. To say the least, I was pissed off.

It was about ten o'clock at night when I kicked his door in. He was totally shocked by my entrance.

He had been fast asleep in the bed that backed up into a corner. I ratcheted the pump on the shotgun, sending out a loud *clack*! and thereby placing a round in the chamber.

"Let's talk," I said in the most sincere tone I could muster.

It took about fifteen minutes, and I had my money back, or at least most of it.

"Thank you," I said sarcastically. "Oh! And by the way, you are moving," I told him. "And I mean tomorrow." I went back to the hotel a week later, and he was gone.

Now I need a hideout fitting for an outlaw. In February, I'm driving out on state Highway 72 going through Valley Center.

It is beautiful out there with the Bates Brothers Farm—it is a spectacular sight to see. *What, with the gray nut trees and pumpkins all orangish and the sheep ready to be sheared in the field, this is the kind of spread I hope to have someday,* I said to myself.

I continue to drive up to the Pala Indian Reservation and continued through it. When I exit the reservation, I spy an old abandoned property. It must be at least six acres.

Well, I do my best detective work and find out the property is in trust for some Czechoslovakian family. They are scientists who are very old and now live in the San Francisco Bay Area.

I found the trustee, and it was a bank in San Diego. I go to the bank, and after two hours, I leave the bank. I have been installed as the caretaker with an option to buy the property, an option that will soon become a reality. But first, I have to get the money.

Canada is my first choice, and it is time for a road trip. We get a rental car, a '72 Ford station wagon. I score twenty kilos of pot and head out for Missoula, Montana. We, my two cohorts and I, have an old Army buddy who is a ski instructor, and he is glad to see us. He sells all our pot in a couple of days, and then it was on to Vancouver. We make the crossing into Canada at Trail and continue on the CanAm Highway to Vancouver. We picked up a couple of girls hitchhiking on the way.

Once we arrive in Vancouver, I go to work, rounding up the bikers whom I dealt with before. I find them after a couple of days, and it is going to be business as usual. We head for the ranch, but I'll be back.

Back at the ranch, it is hotter than hell. I've got a little over six acres with an option for forty-two more acres ripe with avocados and persimmons. Who eats persimmons? Anyhow, it is a great spread, and the house is just as spectacular and fully furnished with tons of antiques. Simply put, this was like finding the proverbial gold mine in the desert.

The house was constructed in 1932 and is built from adobe brick. Surprisingly comfortable, it is warm in the winter and cool in the summer. I mean, it can reach temperatures in the 115-degree range out here in the high desert. The house itself has two wings and a sweet courtyard in the middle, perfect for a croquet court. Then there were some garages, a barn, and an old laboratory.

The two-story building, which is the laboratory, is in good shape, and I'm thinking a recording studio is its next use. Anyway, it is quite satisfying where I'm at right now. I can access Vancouver, and I have buyers from several American cities plus Canada. Overall, I'm in pretty good shape, better than CBS who just sold the Yankees to George Steinbrenner for a paltry three million dollars more than they paid for them.

So I've been pretty busy, but the world has also been busy. Richard Nixon, who is up to his eyeballs in the Watergate scandal himself, has declared a new war—the war on drugs. This guy wants to spray the marijuana fields in Mexico with paraquat so that when you smoke the pot, you will die. Brilliant idea for such a loser of a person.

Lyndon Johnson, the former president, has died, and I wonder if Ladybird is at again? I wonder what it is like to live a life that is so shallow that you have to sleep with one eye open because you can't trust your spouse. Doesn't it make you wonder?

March 29, 1973, was when the last American combat soldiers departed Vietnam. I say, "No!" There were MIAs and prisoners of war still being held there, plus Nixon was still bombing Cambodia. The secret war was not over and was still going full bore. For so many, it would never be over.

The summer moves along, and it is a hot one. The smell of the lemon grove across the street is so sweet it is a sensual delight.

The peacocks are strutting around with their tail feathers displayed, and we have a quail family that lives in the front yard. Yep, it is pretty spectacular.

I had a visitor from Canada this past week. I wasn't sure if he was going to survive the heat. It was 115 degrees. I'm a heat monger, and he made it through barely. He bought 125 kilos, though. This is too easy.

The year moves along uneventfully. I make a couple of trips to Vancouver. On one of the forays up north, I meet this tugboat skipper who operates an oceangoing tug. He brings barges from Thailand. He is about sixty years old, and he smokes marijuana. He has just started to smuggle Thai sticks, a great connection to have, though I'm leery about smuggling back into the United States.

He has a great house in Horseshoe Bay, and I'm invited to come over one night for cabbage rolls. What I got was a spectacular brunette about five feet ten inches tall and built like a goddess. I go home with her naturally. She has a penthouse suite in some high rise in Downtown Vancouver or her beau does. At any rate, it was a really great night for me.

It is now the fall of 1973, and the vice president Spiro Agnew has resigned. Income tax evasion was the reason—good riddance.

He will be replaced by Gerald Ford. Nixon is next, thus leaving us with an unelected president and vice president!

The year closes out, and I'm left to ponder what the future holds. One thing for sure, this has been a good year, much better than the last year.

Time kept on turning into the future. The year was 1974, and I had reached the ripe age of twenty-six. At this point in my life, I felt like it was prime time for me, and I should be pitching someplace in professional baseball.

Don't get me wrong. I loved my life with the ranch, cars, and traveling, in addition to the strange women that I had met. *But! And that is a big but*, I thought, *smuggling is a dangerous profession with a sentence of up to life in prison if you are caught. I mean, you can be the best smuggler in the world, but it only takes getting caught once.*

Those were not good odds, and I felt that most successful smuggling operations are done by the government through diplomatic passports. One thing for sure, I was going to do less transporting after this year.

The "cause"—the legalization of marijuana—was a worthwhile, fair, and legitimate one. There was nothing criminal about it. But was it worth serving a life term in prison?

I was doing quite well in my other ventures. Nevertheless, I miss baseball to death and the money they are paying now is a lot different from the old days' games before television.

I had to go on a February run to Vancouver in the ice and snow. Despite the frigid conditions, it was an uneventful and profitable trip, the kind I prefer.

February 1974 started with a bang. The much-publicized kidnapping of newspaper heiress Patty Hearst. The nineteen-year-old Hearst newspaper heiress was snatched from her Berkeley, California, apartment on February 4, 1974, by urban guerrillas from the Symbionese Liberation Army (SLA).

The SLA had popped up on the US intelligence community's radar months earlier, but the group's motives and targets were unclear.

The SLA was a left-wing, multiracial revolutionary band of militants who defied capitalism and followed founder Donald DeFreeze's philosophy that dissimilar people can live in harmony. From my vantage point, they were just a bunch of ragtag losers bent on ruling society through threats and violence.

A couple of months later, Hearst, in her new supposedly "brainwashed" role as the SLA's "Tania," posed in her rebel getup. She was armed and holding a military-style assault rifle during a bank robbery. Was the rifle even loaded?

I was sitting in an apartment in Tustin in May 1974 watching television when a news flash scrolled across the screen, followed by a live broadcast.

Los Angeles police officers had surrounded some SLA members who were holed up in a house in South Central Los Angeles. A shootout erupted, and police were pinned down by automatic weapons fire. Police had tossed tear gas canisters onto the house. Although the SLA countered by deploying gas masks, the hot tear gas canisters caught the house on fire. This led to the death by self-inflicted gunshot wound to the leader, DeFreeze, also known as "Field Marshal Cinque."

This was his moniker coined from the leader of a slave ship rebellion.

Patricia "Tania" Hearst remained on the lam with two of her captors until September 18, 1975, when authorities closed in and arrested her at a San Francisco apartment. At this point, she was arrested for her role in the previously mentioned armed bank robbery.

She was eventually convicted and sentenced to serve a seven-year sentence in prison. Instead, she served only twenty-two months until her release on March 20, 1979, from a "Club Fed" facility at Camp Parks in Dublin, California.

Reporters from around the world descended on this East Bay Area town for the finale of what had been a televised, fairy-tale, drama-queen crime spree. President Jimmy Carter had commuted her sentence, but he didn't pardon her. Why? She then married her bodyguard and later received a full pardon from President Bill Clinton.

This charade was another example of how folks with money and connections, a worldwide audience, and an ear to presidents can knock the jail time down.

The whole time the Patty Hearst–SLA story was unfolding, here I was just a few months away from getting my own seven-year stretch in prison for drug smuggling.

Right now, though, it was time to go. I had some friends who just got married. This is the start of my downfall. I went askew. I was using amateurs to smuggle.

I was in every sense of the title a "professional smuggler." Discipline was, or should be, a big part of this business. I was about to become an undisciplined smuggler—the worst kind.

Never mix pleasure with business was one rule to follow. Another was, don't do favors and disrupt your success.

Breaking either one of those rules was like hitting a trip wire on a booby trap in Vietnam. Rule number three was, always be ready to shield the explosion.

The married couple had a travel trailer that I had stocked with kilos of grade A Mexican pot, a hundred kilos to be exact.

They were in Vancouver near the border while I traveled to Seattle. I rented a car and drove to meet them and deal the kilos.

The rental car lady in Seattle was a "hot one," whom I always looked forward to seeing. I had taken her out a couple of times. She was a really nice girl, but for this trip, I would have to take a rain check.

However, I did take time at the SeaTac Airport to watch the baseball game. It was on the hundreds of television sets scattered around the airport. It was the Angels and Rangers, and yes, Nolan was pitching. And yes, he threw a no-no, and I watched every pitch of that game. Now back to work!

I arrived in Vancouver and retrieved the kilos and delivered them to my people. They have them sold in two days. For some reason, unbeknownst to me, I take the married couple with me and leave their trailer in Vancouver, to be reclaimed next trip.

So we drive up to Horseshoe Bay and catch the Nanaimo ferry to Vancouver Island then drive south to Victoria. We stay there for a day, and it is spectacular with the roses all in spring bloom.

We hop on the Seattle ferry and head for home. Just our luck, it is graduation time or spring break. The ferry is packed with drunken eighteen-year-olds. When we get to the port in Seattle, it is a mess with drunken teenagers everywhere, so the customs people wave us right through, and with that gesture, they let thirty-five thousand dollars into the country. This was my easiest trip yet. The first rule of smuggling has been broken, never mix pleasure with business. I will pay the price for this one.

My worst trip? Well, there were a few. Like the time I airfreighted 125 kilos in footlockers to the airfreight terminal in Seattle. Once in Seattle, I then had to retrieve them. So I got a U-Haul van and drove to the airfreight terminal. There, I picked the stash up. I then drove to the airport, where I parked the van in the airport parking complex and got a taxi to the rental car place. I drove the rental car to the airport garage and parked the rental car with the trunk backed up to the rear doors of the van. I opened the trunk and started chucking kilos. Lo and behold, I didn't have enough space in the trunk for all the kilos.

What am I going to do now? This is a full-sized Chevrolet Monte Carlo. Under the seats is my next move. I took the van back and turned it in. Then I got a cab back to the airport, and I am ready to roll the Monte Carlo north to Vancouver. Just one problem, I have diarrhea, just my luck. I wonder, is it really worth it?

Back to the present. Once we are back in Seattle, we get a hotel room, and I buy a truck, a 1972 Ford F-250. It is equipped with four-wheel drive and has just about every option on it, including a winch and a spare fuel tank—quite frankly, it is the bomb of trucks.

On we go to California, except for a stop at the beer gardens in Tacoma, where they have free beer. We get pretty inebriated and drive on. We are now back at the ranch. Life is good.

April is now here, and it is baseball season, and Hank Aaron has broken the home run record set by the "Babe," Babe Ruth. Ruth did it in fewer games and arguably under tougher circumstances. The fact that he, Ruth, played in fewer games is questionable, but the circumstances were quite a bit more challenging. After all, the travel was by train, and the accommodations were quite different. Then there is the game itself, and by that, I mean the baseballs.

Have you ever played catch with a 1920s era baseball or even held a ball that old? The old balls? They were looser stitched, and quite frankly, they were a bit softer than today's baseballs. They were quite different from the tightly wrapped baseballs of the future. In other words, you had to hit them really hard to make them fly.

As they said in the old west, "Back to the ranch." My guy from Montreal popped into the ranch unexpectedly and bought two hundred kilos. It was a welcome boon. I am going to have to get out of the business sooner or later—maybe, just maybe, this is going to be my last year.

My guys from Vancouver are down south now, so no use going to Vancouver. They are vacationing and buying turquoise jewelry, the latest fad. Turquoise jewelry is also my "cover" for going to Vancouver. I deal in turquoise jewelry. I drive over to Arizona every once in a while and buy from the Navajo or Hopi Indians on the reservation—it is a good front.

So anyway, I have the boys over, and we party it up, and I sell them some jewelry and a hundred kilos. "Now go home."

I have to get my friend's trailer and make some money.

Chapter Seven

No Good Deed

The phone was ringing one muggy early June morning. I didn't want to answer it, given the sleepless night that made me sweat until my bed was soaking wet. Finally, the ringing had stopped, and just as I was about to doze off for one more nightmarish dream, the damn phone started ringing again.

"Hello," I said in a gruff tone while thinking, *This better not be some jerk trying to sell me aluminum siding or earthquake insurance.*

The telephone call was from a guy I know in Spokane, Washington, and he wants some pot.

"Are you going to be anywhere near Spokane anytime soon? If you are, can you bring me some pot?"

Well, I hadn't planned on deviating from my routine, but the world's fair was underway in Spokane, and that sounds like a good cover story. I saddle up my new Ford truck and head out. It's June now.

The road north to Spokane is no easy drive. Mostly, a two-lane state highway with lots of potholes and no lights. Maybe this wasn't such a good idea.

We got to Spokane and find the guy's farm. He works as a carpet layer, and he works long hours. He is off to work.

My buddy and I decide to go rafting on the Snake River. I have bought all kinds of camping and fishing equipment and a big yellow raft. Might as well get it dirty.

So off we go to raft the day away. We get back to the farm at about four o'clock, and he is not home yet. We fiddle around until he arrives. I have some killer Thai sticks for him, and we smoke a little. I don't know what happened, but he just freaked out. He starts on this rant about he knows there is pot in my truck and we are all getting busted and he is going to be deported and on and on. He was definitely a paranoid schizophrenic.

Now it is true that he is Dutch, a citizen from the Netherlands here on a green card. If we did get busted, he might get deported, but that's a far reach.

It was about ten o'clock at night. He says to us we have to leave.

But he would keep the Thai sticks.

Well, that's a fine "how do you do."

We have no choice but to leave. This fits perfectly with my theory: "No good deed goes unpunished, and nothing is going to be okay."

We head north on Route 395. I think that we will probably get a hotel room, get some sleep, and go get 'em tomorrow. Well, the road is dark. I mean, really dark and no lights, except for my vehicle, and like I said earlier, it is a two-lane highway.

I am tired as hell. There is nothing on this highway that resembles a business or a hotel, just the Cascade mountains on the left and the Kettle River on the right. I mean, this is "God's" country all right.

Shit! We are at the Canadian border. I mean, right there in front of us, we are at the border crossing. What to do now? It is just past midnight. Maybe we will get lucky. Stay cool. We have already gone past the American border station. We could turn around, but no, that looks suspicious. Might as well drive on.

"Hello," the border guard says.

"Hi," I respond.

"Where are you going?" he asks me.

"We are going to Trail. We have just been to the world's fair, in Spokane, and are going back to Seattle via Canada."

Well, at this point, I expect him to say, "Okay, go on through and have a safe trip." Wrong! He wants us to exit the truck. This can't be good, considering I have 750 pounds of marijuana in the back of my truck. So he searches the cab and finds a marijuana seed.

"I just bought the truck. Maybe the seed was from the previous owner," I say.

So now he has a buddy come and help him, and he wants to search the back of the truck. Well, the marijuana is built into a bed in the back of the truck, and it is pretty cleverly concealed. Maybe he won't find it. He asks us to help unload the truck, but I decline, stating, "You are not going to help us repack it. So you empty it, and we will put it back."

To make things even worse, a Mountie car arrived upon the scene, so now this search will be scrutinized by the Royal Canadian Mounted Police.

The border guards are in the back of the truck. We are just standing there, and one of the Mounties is right behind me and little to my left.

I whisper to my friend that they are going to find the stash and that I'm going to take this Mountie out and run back into the United States.

They found the goods. Meanwhile, I took out the Mountie and hauled ass. I'm the only one who escaped back to the friendly confines of the United States.

This is a mess and a big fat one too. What to do now is the question of the day. One big fat mistake compounded by two more—lovely. Let's see what the smugglers' "handbook" has to say about this one. Just what I thought, nothing.

So I am now waist-deep and treading along the Kettle River, and it has got a hell of a current with a lot of debris in it too. So I'm not getting too far out and the logs, giant logs are flowing in the river. I twisted my knee to make things even worse. Fuck!

I make my way about a mile downstream. The reason I stayed so long in the water was to throw the dogs off if they used them. I cross the highway and climb up into the mountain wilderness that is the Cascade National Forest. The Cascades are a series of mountains that run from where I stand now all the way over to Seattle.

At this time in late June, the bears had been out of hibernation, long enough to search for food to satisfy their voracious appetites after the winter's famine. Bears were the only real threat in this wilderness. For the most part, black bears patrolled the woods, but a few grizzlies as well roamed the northern border.

My knee was swollen and throbbing badly. I had about ten Thai sticks and a pack of orange Zig-Zag rolling papers. But damn it, I had no matches. I also had $750 in cash.

I made my way about fifty miles or so south. I knew that with my survival skills from the Army, I could last quite a while out here.

Nevertheless, I felt the need to try to help the married couple. It had been a few days since I had eaten, but water was abundant, and that was a good thing.

Food was still at the top of my want list. My body was craving nourishment, regardless if it was for only a box of saltine crackers, a bag of potato chips, or perhaps a main course like a Big Mac hamburger. Heck, I would have devoured a peanut-butter-and-jelly sandwich in a microsecond.

I could hear the deputies patrolling on the highway with their loudspeakers blaring, trying to coax me out.

My plan, entirely different from their plan, was to make it to Spokane, catch a plane, get to Los Angeles, and get a lawyer for my friends in Canadian custody.

Now it was time to execute the plan.

On the third day at large, I literally stumbled from exhaustion into a gas station that had a pay phone booth. I called for a cab. The dispatcher sent a driver who was a friendly gent.

"Where you going?" the driver asked.

"Spokane," I answered.

"How did you get out here?"

"My car broke down on the road a ways back, and I have got to be in Spokane."

"Okay," he replied. "Let's go. The fare is fifty dollars."

So far so good.

We started to drive southward toward Spokane. He was rambling on about the county fair and the annual rodeo that was taking place in the small local town. There was no traffic because that was where the local folks were.

All I could think about was what a fuck up this was all because I tried to do a favor for someone.

At the minimum, this was going to cost me a couple of hundred grand. I remembered that old saying, and although it sounded redundant, it was so true.

"No good deed goes unpunished, and nothing is going to be okay."

We were cruising along, and the cab driver kept looking in the rearview mirror and checking his speedometer.

The police were right behind us. Not only that, just as we rounded a curve in the road, there were six squad cars blocking the road with twelve deputies. All of them had shotguns pointed in my direction. At that moment, I realized the jig was up.

There was nothing I had experienced like this summer's vacation. I was about to spend in the Spokane County jail.

I made my first court appearance soon thereafter, and the charges were read, and I faced extradition to Canada for drug smuggling. I could not believe this shit was happening to me, but it was. My knee was a mess, and I received no medical attention for it other than the hot compresses that I put on it four or five times a day.

When the trial began, the Canadians were not messing around. This was the biggest marijuana bust in Canadian history. The case had been featured on the national television broadcast for three evenings. The marijuana smuggling escapade had made it onto the British Broadcasting Company network and on prime time too. It was the lead story on the evening news.

I was brought into federal court in Spokane with shackles and handcuffs. I had been appointed a public defender. He was a big fat ninny who didn't give a rat's ass about me.

The case continued for a couple of days. I had been doing a little research on my own and had found the ticket out of Dodge, I thought.

When we went to the courthouse on the third day, the US marshals who were escorting me were particularly rude assholes. When we walked into the courtroom, I asked for permission to address the court.

This particular judge had been really cool as if he found my saga amusing. I had lucked out. He granted my request.

"If it pleases the court," I began, "I would like to act as my own counsel and represent myself."

The judge asked me if I understood the proceedings.

"I do, Your Honor," I responded.

"Very well then. Your request is granted. Will there be anything else?" he asked with a wry grin on his face.

At this moment, I sensed that he knew exactly what I was going to do next.

"Yes, Your Honor. I would like to make an oral motion to dismiss the case against me. I am basing my motion on the treaty by which the Canadian government is trying to extradite me," I explained.

"It seems as though the Canadian government has breached the agreement. The treaty, therefore, is now or should be declared null and void," I continued.

A treaty had been forged in 1917 during World War I between the United States and Canada to extradite any fugitive accused of a crime punishable by death, including draft evasion.

Canada had actively and openly harbored draft dodgers during the Vietnam War.

"That, Your Honor, is the grounds for my motion for dismissal."

"Hmmm," he muttered as he pondered my request.

After only a few seconds and with that same mocking grin, he announced to the court that he would take my motion under consideration.

"The court is adjourned," he declared with a quick knock from his gavel.

The Canadian attorneys were flabbergasted. They thought they might even lose this proceeding.

This time, the marshals were nice to me on the way back to the county jail.

The next day, we were back in court. The judge had made a decision, and it was in my favor. He was convinced by my argument that it was unfair to extradite a Vietnam War veteran to Canada without putting equal weight to draft evaders who had federal warrants out for violating the selective service laws.

Well, that's the cat's meow, I thought.

I had just beaten all these high-priced government lawyers even though my public defender was the worst. Still, the verdict was not in yet, and I could wind up in Canada. Just because one judge saw it my way, that didn't mean the appellate court judges would see it my way.

Did my maneuvering just get me more time in the Spokane county jail? That was not at all what I wanted. Be careful what you ask for.

The Canadians immediately told the judge that they were going to appeal, and they did.

Then something happened behind closed doors that changed not only my case but the extradition agreement between the two countries, the one that had been forged on December 3, 1971, decades after the original pact of 1917.

Known as the Canada International Extradition Treaty, the parties suddenly amended it by "an exchange of notes" that had been signed in Washington, DC, on June 28 and July 9, 1974.

It is unclear who "signed" the notes that led to the change, but my gut feeling was that it was none other than Secretary of State Henry Kissinger.

The result of the "changes" to international policy and related hubbub was apparently triggered by my case because of the timing. As such, I became a catalyst for a reckoning of international law.

In order to be fair to me, the judge would have had to call for the extradition of tens of thousands of draft dodgers from Canada to face felony draft evasion charges: something that Nixon and Kissinger wanted to avoid on the home front, where they were already on shaky ground because of the anti-war movement and the Watergate affair.

In a matter of just a couple of days, the Canadian attorneys had a signed extradition order, bearing Henry Kissinger's signature. Then on the fourth day, after the court appearance, I was on my way back to Canada to stand trial for drug smuggling and assault on a federal police officer. Lovely.

The saga continued when the marshals came for me. I figured that I could appeal, but to what avail?

I mean, the courts were fixed, and I did not have the money. Anyway, I needed to get back to Canada and my buddy. He had received a seven-year sentence, but his wife got off the hook. She retrieved their car and trailer from White Rock, which is where I had a little place.

So I had been extradited under one of my aliases. This could prove to be useful, but really, what difference did it make? I was probably going to get life in prison. I should be thinking about trying to escape.

So this journey continued in a shiny new Ford Crown Victoria with two fully armed United States marshals for the escort.

We pulled out of Spokane about eight o'clock in the morning for the two-hour drive to the border. We headed north on US Highway 395. The scenery looked a lot different in the daytime. The ride to the border was uneventful, and we pulled up to the same crossing where this all had begun some three months ago. The human exchange was made.

The Mounties then took me into custody and transported me to the Trail City jail.

I was treated like a celebrity much to my surprise. After all, I had put this small town on the map.

One of the captains of the police department came in to talk with me. It was a pretty interesting conversation beginning with if I will sign over the pink slip to my truck and agree to forfeit the $750 I had in my possession, the court will drop the assault on a federally protected person charge, and I will be sentenced to the minimum of seven years in the Canadian penitentiary for drug smuggling.

And by the way, here's fifty dollars, you might need it when you get to the British Columbia Penitentiary. This guy was pretty sharp, and that was a good deal considering. I took the deal.

We were in court for trial the next day. The courthouse was a rustic old two-story building with no air-conditioning, and the courtroom is on the second floor.

As I waited for the proceedings to start, I noticed an open window.

Hmm. Was this my chance? No! My knee is still gimpy, and with my luck, I would break an ankle or something else. Just sit tight, I thought.

The judge was now on the bench. This was destined to be the fastest big case that had ever been heard in this courthouse. It took less than an hour, and I became a convicted international drug smuggler.

The next day, two Mounties came to get me for the trip to Vancouver and the infamous British Columbia Penitentiary. I mean, I was going directly to prison. "Do not pass go. Do not collect two hundred dollars."

They took me to the airport, and we flew to Vancouver on a twin-engine turboprop airplane. The flight was smooth. I was in the British Columbia Penitentiary by five o'clock that evening.

Holy shit! How did I get here? This place is a dungeon.

I pondered my predicament as stood in the center of this seemingly medieval detainment structure and eyed my surroundings. I couldn't believe it. I had seen some bad times more than most in Vietnam but nothing like this.

The prison was built in the 1890s. It had not been renovated in a hundred years. The place was five stories high with four wings. I sensed that this was going to be a gut-wrenching experience.

Naturally and befitting my bad luck, my cell was on the fifth floor and posed as a treacherous test with all those stairs for my still-bothersome wrenched knee.

I was not in my cell for two minutes when some guy came up from behind me. I heard him say, "You are a child molester."

He could have at least said, "Hi" or "Hello" or something a little more cordial.

I still had my back turned to him when I retorted.

"No. I am a drug smuggler and a Vietnam combat veteran. If you are still in my doorway when I turn around, you are going over the rail."

Hell, I figured I might as well establish myself.

When I turned around, he was gone.

There were stockades in the basement of this formidable and inescapable building, bolstered atop its foundation by two-foot-square-thick limestone blocks. The Canadians had kept these reminders of corporal punishment still being used until just a couple of years ago.

There was nothing like a good "caning"—a beating with a bamboo cane—or maybe just a day or two in the stockades, dangling your head and arms out the wooden holds like some Revolutionary War prisoner until they went numb from lack of circulation.

What century was this anyhow? The Dark Ages maybe?

I went through the new-guy drill, getting outfitted with clothes, a toothbrush, and of course, the rules of the prison.

At this point in my life, I had one rule: there are no rules.

It was really pretty simple: "Keep your nose clean and do your time."

At this time, my partner had been processed for a transfer to a satellite prison. He was being moved to Matsqui prison in Abbotsford. He has been told that he will serve twenty-eight months of the seven-year sentence and then be deported.

I got the same deal, and I'm still here under an alias. Meanwhile, my knee had completely healed.

I went for a screening and was told that I will also be going to Matsqui. Things were looking up.

Chapter Eight

The Mayor

When the day of my transfer to Matsqui arrived, I climbed aboard the prison bus for the ride to Abbotsford. I was not going to miss the British Columbia Penitentiary with its beautiful view from the fifth floor of the Fraser River idling its way down to the Pacific Ocean or, my favorite sight, the Labatt's brewery right down the street. Now that was torture.

Nope. I ain't gonna miss you at all, I thought.

I couldn't believe my eyes when the bus rolled into Matsqui. The prison was built smack on the American border. If I had to escape, this was the place from which to do it.

The introduction process began with the "Welcome to Matsqui" orientation. It was all bullshit.

There was an older Chinese gentleman working in the induction center. He was an inmate like the rest of us. He was serving fourteen years for heroin trafficking. He was apparently connected because he lived up front, away from the main housing unit.

What was Matsqui prison all about? In reality, it was a social experiment destined to go bad because the theory behind it was flawed.

Put simply, there were too many incarcerated people who should not have been there. Conspiracy theory types and drug users and dealers made up 60 to 70 percent of the inmate population.

And just like in the United States, efforts to correct the flaw fell on deaf ears with Canadian politicians who had the power to change it.

Pierre Trudeau was the prime minister. He was married to Sinclair's daughter. Sinclair built the CanAm Highway and was a very rich and powerful man.

But his daughter? She was another story. She was a giant drug freak (LSD), and there were rumors about her husband, the prime minister, himself.

Matsqui sat on about twenty acres of flat open land. It had a central housing unit with four wings. It stood three stories tall and reminded me of the brick and mortar barracks we had in the Army.

The cells were eight-by-six feet with tile floors, a desk, a chair, a bed, and a window that opened and closed. Of course, there were concrete obstructions fashioned into the window wells to discourage unwanted departures.

What more could an inmate want? There was a chapel and an infirmary, a kitchen and mess hall, and finally, a gymnasium. They had industrial buildings with some shops for job training. We did not make license plates, though.

So what was I going to do for a job?

Remember in the California state prison system the test said that I wasn't qualified for any job? I wonder if the Canadian test was going to be any better.

Basically, I was just existing in no-man's-land. Then one day, while walking in the yard, I was recruited for the softball team.

Now we're getting somewhere.

"Hey, Yank. Can you play ball?" one of the veteran prisoners asked. "How about trying out for the team?"

"Okay, I'll play," I replied.

We had several tournaments and won them all.

This enthralled the inmates who rooted for us against the outside teams that lacked fans. I was now a sports star, at least at Matsqui. I parlayed this into a job on the recreation crew.

We had an inmate government. It was sort of like the administration from a small town. After all, that was really what this was: a small town. We had a population of three hundred men. They had an income of at least a dollar a day apiece. That meant we could pool three hundred dollars a day. But what really was the inmate committee? A joke. It was more like a high school student body.

In the meantime, my buddy had been industrious and had procured the janitorial contract for the prison. I was in. We whiled away the morning hours stripping and waxing the floors. We would do one job a day and sometimes the front offices.

In the afternoon, we would go to the exercise yard and run. The yard was expansive with a full-sized soccer field, tennis courts, and a one-quarter-mile track for running or walking. Of course, the best part was the softball field.

The track was probably the most important asset because inmates could walk off a lot of pent-up anger or frustration or whatever. What more could we have asked for?

A golf course, that's what! A nine-hole, par-two golf course. We constructed it in about three months just in time for the 1975 season. I was absolutely lousy at golf.

The temperatures had cooled and left a crisp fall feeling in September 1974. Things at the prison were livable. It looked like I was going to get out with just twenty-eight months served. What else has been going on in the world?

We got the newspaper, the *Vancouver Sun* every day. Somebody on the tier had a subscription.

I was third in line to read the paper. The horoscope was so important, along with sports—baseball—and the news. The point is, we could keep up with the affairs of the world.

What was the big story, even in Canada, in 1974? Watergate!

"Tricky Dick" is headed out of the door as the president of the United States. Apparently, he had more holes in him than a whiffle ball.

The "Pentagon Papers" were published by the *New York Times*. Apparently, a Marine officer from the Pentagon named Ellsberg had leaked some incriminating documents on Nixon. I don't think that was the real reason Nixon was going down the tubes. The real reason was opposition to the draft. Demonstrations were growing, swelling to a number in the hundreds of thousands, a whole lot of people.

The United States was probably going to have an unelected president for the first time in its history. It was House Speaker Gerry Ford, a Michigan Republican. The vice president was the same way. What about Nixon? He did not spend a single day serving time in jail for his crimes.

Race relations were probably as bad as they had been in years. The Black Panthers were becoming America's third political party. The Panthers had a multifaceted operation in order. They, the "Panthers," had it all: media people, lawyers, politicians, drug-dealing foot soldiers, who were trained during the Vietnam War. Hell, they wanted to get drafted so they could get the training. Then they wouldn't fight.

I remembered those days in Vietnam. "This is whitey's war," the Panthers proclaimed. "America is the Black man's battleground." And so it is and would continue to be.

We made it through the first year of incarceration although we had some rough days, especially Thanksgiving and Christmas. It was kind of tough. It didn't bother me as much because I have no family to speak of—no wife to pine for. I just longed for my freedom that had somehow gone missing.

The year 1975 started off with a bang. I received three days in the hole for opining my opinion of the Canadian justice system.

The hole was a joke. It was just an empty cell where you were locked up for whatever time you had to serve. It was also the protective custody (PC) unit—a necessary evil in prisons because you inevitably have "rats." We had all heard the term before, the two-legged type and then there were the rapists.

The American contingent was sparse, but there were a few of us from the US. For the most part, we were drug smugglers, but the bunch included a few bank robbers.

One was a little older and also a Korean War veteran. I befriended him, sort of. I was not a stranger to the underworld, so I was naturally leery of everyone, and the alias I was using posed a small problem.

He lived on tier One West. I lived on One South in the "Ghetto" tier, which was appropriately named. This was where all the foreigners and Black inmates lived. There were only three or four Blacks in the whole place.

So the bank robber—the Korean War vet—was tight with the man reputed to be the head of organized crime in Vancouver. The mob guy was doing a life sentence for a small number of crimes, including murder. He also lived on One West.

The crime boss eventually moved to One South right next to me. He smoked marijuana, and that was pretty cool. I decided to maintain my distance, though.

Meanwhile, the bank thief made parole. They had just kept him for his minimum sentence and threw him back across the border. That was his fate. It was on the night before he was set to be released that someone slipped into his room and slit his throat, and he bled out. Some said he got too close to the Boss and knew too much.

I'll keep my distance, thanks.

My buddy and I started a new base of operation for our janitorial service: the laundry room. Actually, it was more like a building where prisoners exchange bedding each week, as well as some hygienic supplies and clothes, which it seems we were always out of.

There were sewing machines, so why not tailor some custom duds? Me? I wore shorts in the summer and sweatpants in the winter.

I was just glad we were running the show instead of the transvestites.

The canteen was also located in the laundry facility, which doubled as the "company store."

You could buy almost anything, except freedom.

The dress code was pretty lax. After four o'clock, you could wear anything you wanted, mostly blue jeans, but there were some outrageous homosexuals who would wear anything. They were in prison mostly for fraud and drugs.

Fraud from a man who thinks he is a woman?

The barbershop was also located in the company store. A new barber reported to work this week as the last one expired: the Korean War veteran.

So the year moved on, and time was passing quickly although the winters were a drag.

In the spring, softball started up again. I had also discovered the game of tennis. I was playing every day with the "Chinaman." We had become friendly since the day I saved his bacon from the fire, which could have been a big embarrassment.

The Chinaman was in his early fifties, and he owned or controlled most of Chinatown. That wasn't saying much except that one must understand that Vancouver's Chinatown was the largest contingent of Chinese people in North America.

Rumors floated around that he used to give racehorses heroin at the track. They would run like hell, then die. That's not what he was inside for, though. He was also the biggest broker of heroin on the West Coast.

He sold for the Hong Kong crowd. Hong Kong was destined to go back to Chinese communist control. The colony was being transferred from the Crown, British control, to the government of the communist Chinese. The situation would boil for a few years before the exodus explosion sent anyone and everyone with anything fleeing Hong Kong. Why Canada? Because it is part of the Crown and people from Hong Kong can immigrate freely.

So you liquidate your holdings in Hong Kong, convert it to number four China white heroin—a pinky nails' worth can kill you. "China white" was much more powerful than the Mexican brown heroin, commonly available on the West Coast.

So the Chinaman was the broker. He sold twelve ounces of China white heroin to an undercover cop. It just so happened that his son was a lawyer in Vancouver who primarily ran the family business. He was a nice kid.

So how did I save the Chinaman's bacon?

Some young Chinese lads had gotten a day pass to go "outside" for a day. While out on their day pass, they stole some stuff at a convenience store. Of course, they got caught and then denied it.

Well, the old guy was falling for it. He was going to get his lawyer son to make a big deal about the whole incident.

I didn't know the Chinaman that well, but I approached him anyway.

"This is none of my business," I start with, "but those kids are guilty as hell," I said. "You are making a mistake by getting involved."

I was right, and we became friends. He once offered me a kilo of China white straight trade for a kilo of cocaine, megabucks for me, except I don't deal heroin. Honor is a big deal among the Chinese, and I upheld his.

Days turned into weeks, and the weeks turned into months. Softball was over although I gave the fans something to cheer about, with both my arm and bat.

The first instance came when a guy tried to tag up at third on a fly ball to centerfield. I was playing center field at the time, and I got myself in position to make the catch, take quick a crowhop, I let a mighty throw rip. I threw him out by three feet with a twelve-inch softball. No one could make that throw. The catcher? My buddy, he knew my arm strength.

Then later in the tournament, we were in the championship game, and we were down by three runs. With two outs and the bases loaded in the last inning, I came up to bat.

I hit a fly ball to left field, and the ball just kept on going and going right over the twin fences right past the guard tower, sailing on into freedom.

Yep. When I set that ball free, it was my spirit soaring over those fences to roam the world. Yes, sir! I sent that ball on its journey at last to the moon and back, and we won the game. I was a big-time hometown hero with a cap tip to the applause of all the wannabes who dreamed of a return to freedom.

I could now concentrate on tennis, my new love. I was all decked out too in my tennis attire: shoes, racket, shorts, tote bag, and a sweat towel around my neck.

I look like a real pro and pretty preppy for a prison guy.

In the world of real baseball the fall classic, the World Series started today. There was something in the air other than the smell of hot dogs with mustard. Something was going on, but I wasn't sure what. But I was going to find out.

It seems there was a big meeting up in the front offices. Everybody was there including the department heads and government bigwigs. But that was not it.

I answered a call at the recreation office from the front gate.

"I have a delivery for your department," the gate guard said.

"I'm the only one here. Can I sign for it?"

"Yes!" he said.

So I hustled up to the main gate. There was a delivery truck with thirteen-color television sets on board, one for each of the day rooms, including the Chinaman's room up front. I hooked his up first. Then I scurried down to the main living dorm. I also enlisted a crew to help; the tier janitors. There was one for each floor.

We swapped out the old sets for the new-improved color ones, and they were all installed for the first pitch of game one of the 1975 World Series.

This classic National League versus American League matchup pitted the Cincinnati Reds—The Big Red Machine—against the Boston Red Sox.

The Red Legs versus the Red Stockings as our great-grandfathers might have remembered when the color of your leggings was your team.

And the entire "student body" would be watching the fall classic in living color.

It seemed that the Chinaman and the Boss got together with an outside cosigner, and *poof*, the televisions suddenly appeared. The student body inmate committee had been trying to get this done for a while.

Considering we had an aforementioned guaranteed income amounting to three hundred dollars a day, we had the financing to purchase the televisions on our own. This sounded like a solid argument to make, but there was one problem.

"What's that?" the inmate committee chairman asked.

The warden wouldn't budge.

"You have no credit and with no cosigner. No dice."

So the Boss and the Chinaman stepped in.

It was about three o'clock in the afternoon when the warden called me to his office.

"I said 'no' to those television sets. You go down to the housing unit and take them out, and then you will put the old ones back in!" he shouted.

My mind slipped to the jungles of Vietnam for a millisecond.

Warden or not, when someone shouts at me in anger, I am not intimidated.

I explained it to him cooly, like this, "First, the old television sets have been removed from the property already. Second, I don't want to be deceased just yet. And third, I don't care if I get sent back to the British Columbia Penitentiary. You are the warden of a pretty successful prison. You make good money, and it is an easy job." I reminded him with a cold stare into his steel-gray eyes. "If you take those television sets out of the day rooms, you will have a 'parking lot' by nightfall, and you will be nothing more than a parking lot attendant."

In less than a millisecond, he heeded my warning.

"Get out of my office."

On a happier note, Reggie Jackson, the notorious baseball slugger, was busted today in Montreal, Canada. The charge: possession of one kilogram of marijuana. He is a free agent and was traveling to meet with the Expos.

"I thought it was legal up here" was his only statement.

I wondered if they will send him to Matsqui. If so, I would be patrolling in the outfield with him next summer. But alas, he signed a rich deal with the New York Yankees the very next week.

So this is one more piece of evidence of the "straw" that stirs the drink.

My buddy told me today that he is transferring to another prison, the one on Vancouver Island. He says he needs a change of scenery. I feel that he needs it too. Moreover, I think he needs to be away from me, and I wish him well.

The reason I think that he needs to be away from me? Well, that's simple: I'm still under an alias, and I don't want that fact to interfere with his parole.

Throughout this whole ordeal, we have had dorm officers.

I don't know what else to call them. They are really creepy, though.

You know, they try to be nice to you pretend to be your friend then screw you. I stay away.

We have counselors too. You know the type, guidance counselors, more aptly put, social workers are what they really are.

My first counselor was a guy who in his spare time played wide receiver and punter for the BC Lions of the Canadian Football League. He mostly punts because he has hands made of stone. Good for boxing but not for football.

My buddy and I would go to the yard every day after lunch. Sometimes we would throw a football around. So my counselor sees us throwing the football out in the yard, and he tells me who he is and if he can come work out with us. What a gig you go to your job and prepare for your other job all on the taxpayer's dime. Sure, why not? I need all the help I can get.

"Whoops," I told you about my arm. I turn his fingers back on a five-yard crossing pattern, and he is pissed. That's the last time he comes out. Oh well.

There is one other brave soul who comes out with us. His name is "Spike." He is not the dog from the *Looney Tunes* comics, but he is a beast. He stands about six feet two and about 220 pounds, and he is really fast.

He's got great hands. This guy could be a pro fullback easily, except for the heroin. It is amazing how many addicts there are in Vancouver. I think, in all honesty, he was the one who slit the bank robber's throat. He got a day pass shortly thereafter, and he overdosed on heroin. Sounds like the Boss.

It was a normal day up at seven in the morning, stand in my doorway for a head count, then go to breakfast or back to sleep.

It is a Saturday, so no work. About eleven o'clock, he comes down on to our tier. All three hundred pounds of him. The notorious "Headhunter," no, really. We have this freak called the Headhunter running around loose in our town. He is a big bald-headed beast of a human and weighs, like I said, about three hundred pounds.

He wasn't always like this, and let me tell the tale. He was a skinny Jewish gay guy, and he met a guy in a bar one night and took him home. One thing led to another. Basically, the guy tried to rob him and wound up dead. Now what to do? I know I'll put the body in my bathtub and cut it up. Well, that didn't go so well, and now the Headhunter is out driving around in his car, totally distraught, and he gets pulled over. They find the head in the trunk of his car, and my man is now doing life for murder. Well, he has been in now for five or six years and has gained two hundred pounds from lifting weights, and among other things, he has been locked up in a mental institution, where he endured countless hours of shock therapy. Fittingly, it didn't seem to faze him. He has this head complete with dripping blood tattooed on his humungous arm.

What's he doing down here? Well, I've only been in a few weeks, and I don't know all this lore about the Headhunter at this time. Damn, he comes right in my cell. I hear him say, "You're from California, and you're going to be my new lover." He states in a loud clear voice. *Really?* I say to myself, half amused. It just so happens I have a tennis racket in my room and I lay it right between his eyes. He goes down. I shut the door.

Now I should explain that the doors are electronically operated and we have a call box that doubles as an AM FM radio. Anyway, the door locks, and I take the stake end that's left from the tennis racket and put it right up under his chin to his throat. "I'm not really into bullshit!" I tell him, "You can die now, or we will have an agreement. Don't fuck with me again." What's it gonna be?

"I was just kidding," he says.

I ring to have my door opened. Now there is a "fishbowl" at the mouth of the tier where the guards are stationed, and they have a view of all four tiers. So they saw the Headhunter come onto our tier, as well as ten or twelve inmates. There are twenty-five cells to a tier, and I'm in One South 23. Anyway, the door opens, and the Headhunter comes staggering out onto the tier, and he has a pretty gnarly-looking gash right between his eyes. Now that's how you get respect. We would go on to become friends, and he even turned me on to a business deal when I got out.

So it is a quiet fall day, and the Expos are on the television. I am watching the game with our tier cleaner "Frenchy." We call him that because he is a "Frog," which simply put means he is a Frenchman from Montreal. He is also a smuggler, but that's not what he's in for.

What he did was the best smuggle ever. Let me spin this story for you. Frenchy went to Lebanon and bought some Lebanese red hashish. He then shaped the hash like soap bars and wrapped the hashish in rose-scented paper and shipped it. Then with that done, he goes back to Lebanon. There was a lot of surplus heavy equipment in the Sinai Desert. It was left over from the "Seven-Day War" between Egypt and Israel. He buys a huge crane, fills it with fifteen hundred pounds of hash, and ships it. Pure genius, if you ask me. I am always impressed by the independent smuggler. I mean, the governments all have diplomatic passports, and those are basically just a free pass. Being an independent smuggler takes smarts, nerves, and brains.

Chapter Nine

The Big Yank

My partner is gone now, so I'm on my own. Probably better that way. He has been in about twenty months now, and in eight months, he will get out with me right behind him, just a few months later.

We have a racquetball court. Just one racquetball court.

I play a lot because I work on the recreation crew. I've been challenged to a grudge match, a money match, and the challenge is from the Boss himself. I mean, I will slay him, but if he wants to put up some cash, what the heck?

Winning at racquetball is one thing, but staying alive after you win is another. The Boss likes to win. So do I. Well, word of the challenge gets around the prison. Nothing is secret in here. Lots of money being bet on the match—most of it on me. So the day of the big match arrives. We play the game, and I win, and I lived to tell about it.

So the winter of 1975 has set in, and it is miserable. I have a new counselor, the last one, the football player, is gone.

The new guy is an American, and he is from Riverside, California, and uh-oh! I'm a fugitive from California's penal system, a two- to ten-year prison sentence. Red flags are going off in my head. My parole hearing is next year, which is only a few weeks away. I am not overly paranoid, but I'm suspicious as hell and do my best to avoid the guy. The winter is horrible. There is no tennis and very little yard time, and it is cold and dark a lot. Up north, the sun comes up late and sets early in the winter. This is where the radio comes in. It is the one line to the free world. It's a privilege to have these devices. Plus, the color TVs have made a big difference in the morale of the inmates. I have myself in a pretty good position for a parole hearing, considering.

The "Big Yank" is what they call me, a nickname if you like, and well, I've had it since the incident with the Headhunter in my cell. It was the "Coyote" who tagged me. The Coyote lives in the Ghetto, and he works on the recreation crew. They say that coyotes are very smart and are the only animal in North America that are increasing in population other than humans.

Canada has too many people, and that's why they put them in prison. I mean, Canada does have the highest incarceration rate per capita than any country in the free world. When you take into consideration, Canada is part of the Crown, and Crown law doesn't prosecute drug addicts. It treats them at least in England. And, of course, drugs can be a death sentence in some places, say Hong Kong for instance. Anyway, the prison is 25 percent drug addicts. And I mean bad addicts. People who would sell their soul for a "fix."

Then there are the fraud convictions. What do you expect from a drug-addicted society? And of course, there are the murderers, rapists, bank robbers, the people that really belong in prison.

Then you wouldn't have everyone screaming about prisoners' rights. But no! Canada is going to rehabilitate these poor unfortunate souls—bullshit! Criminals are not made—outlaws are made, created out of an unjust unequal system. But criminals are born, and with larceny in their hearts, all of them, there is just no way to explain it, and there is no way to alleviate that situation either. So we have prisons and the death penalty. Both necessary evils my view. Then there are rapists, we have a few, and there is a special place in hell for them. But they are mostly kept in the British Columbia prison, or they are in protective custody.

And that is what Matsqui is all about. I've said it before. We are just a small town surrounded by twin twenty-foot fences and guard towers, and don't forget, the barbwire and concertina wire atop the fences. But what is the real difference in prison convictions between the United States and Canada? "Conspiracy" charges. They will get you a boatload of time behind bars in Canada, and they don't have to have any real evidence against you, just hearsay will do it. And that's the difference between Canada's "justice" and American justice. In the United States, you must have factual evidence to convict, not just hearsay. Proof beyond a reasonable doubt. That's how the Canadians got the Boss, and he got life.

So speaking of the Boss, he made the move to One South, the "Ghetto," from One West, and he lives one cell over from me.

He is about forty-five or so, and he is in pretty good shape, considering. As I think I mentioned before, he is doing life for "conspiracy" to commit bank robbery and murder.

The Boss, well, he owns skyscrapers in Downtown Vancouver, and it is rumored that he has a big heroin trade too. I don't know. I'm friendly with him but not too friendly. His brother is a lawyer, and he is coming in for a racquetball exhibition. I arranged it. I won't be playing.

The recreation crew doesn't have much to do in the wintertime. I'm bored. So I talk the inmate committee into buying a 35 mm camera with a few attachments. I'm in the photography business now and just in time for the first open house this winter. The warden's idea was to keep morale up during the winter, and it would turn out to be a monthly event. It also would start the supply train for drugs. I'm surprised no guns made it in.

We would have these open houses on Sundays. Friends, relatives anyone could come in. The event was held in the gymnasium. There was one time one of the Americans, a guy from Louisville, he was a thespian and singer, he got four years for LSD. How do you get caught with acid? Must have sold it to the cops. Anyhow, at one of these open houses, he had a girlfriend visitor. She went into the bathroom, changed into some prison garb I had stashed in there, and continued with him up to his cell. Now that was a real visit.

Another time, I had a visit, not a visit, but one of the counselors at the prison was there. She gives me a big tongue in the mouth kiss and slips something into my pocket. It is an ounce of weed. Now that was unexpected, but it made the days go better. I mean, I think

I smoked every day I was in there—at least a joint before bed. But now I had power, marijuana. Joints are a powerful bargaining tool in prison. Everybody smokes.

One time, I tried to get the "Righteous Brothers" to perform at one open house. I went to high school with one of them. But alas, they turned me down.

The year is now 1976, and time is moving along, and news flash, the '76 summer Olympic Games are going to be held in Montreal. This is a big feather in Canada's hat. One of the recreation officers here at Matsqui is a former Olympic decathlete. He is a Chinese immigrant, but in the 1960s, he was the decathlete for Taiwan and performed in the '60s Mexico Olympic games.

He was a big guy for an Asian, considering most Asian men are smaller, but he was at least six feet tall and weighed about 175 pounds. He was supposedly proficient in martial arts, so he was on the prison response team as well, which was never deployed while I was there.

We played sports together, basketball, ping-pong, racquetball. Some inmates were giving me grief about my interaction with him. He never wins at anything, and I get more information from him than I give out. It was settled.

One time, while I was waiting for my release, this was after my second parole hearing, we were playing basketball in the gym, and he made some bogus move and caused me to turn my ankle. Well, I will tell you the truth, it popped, and I saw the "white light," and it swelled. He came to my room every day and did acupuncture on my ankle. It healed quickly, and I was as good as new. The Chinese national teams don't have doctors, but they all carry acupuncturist. Not one inmate said one word. There is a code among inmates, and I know it well. But you have to deal with these people, the prison cadre, if you want your life to be as good as it can be while you are in here. I mean, hell, I have the civilian head of inmate living over once a week. So I have that unique ability to play both sides of the fence. Maybe it is the fact that I am not a criminal—that is the difference.

I guess now is about as good of a time as any to talk about these two characters. One is an American, and the other is a lovely Canadian lass who is a prison counselor and a social worker.

Where should I start? Ladies first? Usually, but in this case, I'll start with the man. He is a bank robber or, more so, a restaurant robber. His MO (method of operation) was to call the restaurant, always a high-class one, and tell them that he was a bodyguard for a celebrity—Zsa Zsa Gabor was one celebrity he used often.

Anyway, he would make arrangements to "inspect" the facility because his client was coming there to dine, a pretty good idea when you think about it. There were no crowds, no employees to speak of, and they probably hadn't made the bank deposit from the night before.

So he would pull up in a rented limousine and proceed to tie the restaurant employees up and then rob them. As so often happens, in these cases, he gets caught, convicted, and he is serving a ten-year prison sentence.

It just so happens he has some newspaper articles portraying him as Zsa Zsa's bodyguard. I had seen them, and they looked fake to me.

He also professed to be a black belt in karate. Everybody in the whole prison is scared to death of him. My partner was the first to acquaint with him. Me? Well, I am skeptical. I mean, this guy doesn't have any athletic skills, and he doesn't work out, so I'm just leery of anyone who projects themselves to be something that they are not. Simply put, it is a fraud.

I know what I am, and if you are a badass, show me. We play cards with him and smoke a little marijuana with him. He really has a charming personality, but what con doesn't have one? I know that he has larceny in his heart, and I personally have had enough of his fake badass routine.

So one day, we are in the gymnasium. He, me, and my partner just the three of us. I say, "Show me some moves."

"Oh, not now. I'm not stretched out and warmed up," he retorts. The next thing he knows, he's lying flat on his back. I'm on top of him and have him by the throat.

"You don't know karate at all, do you?" I ask.

"No," he replies.

"And you have never been a bodyguard, have you?" I ask.

"No," he replies.

At this point, I let him up off the floor.

"You won't tell anyone, will you?" he asks.

This time, it is my turn to say, "No!"

My partner is flabbergasted, and so it goes.

The restaurant thief transfers to the prison at Victoria, on Vancouver Island—good riddance. But no, it is not over yet.

Now comes the lady, and this is like *Lady and the Tramp*. She is the counselor for One West, and that's where the restaurant robber resides or resided. So she is his counselor. I have become friendly with her. I don't know why. After all, she is not my counselor, and I have no business talking with her.

She's a pretty girl. She has a master's degree in sociology, social work, and she is going to change the world. At twenty-five, she is an idealist. You know, she has all kinds of great plans that will never work. Besides that, her only drawback is she is a bit heavy. I don't know what drives her really, but she gets way too involved with inmates. Inmates who don't care about her and will use her to an end. So was the case between her and the restaurant bandit.

This girl, twenty-five years old, puts her whole life on the line for this bum. I mean, career, reputation, and even criminal liability. How did she do this, and why did she do this, is even a better question.

First of all, she gets him a day pass. She then rents a motor home and takes him to Seattle via the ferry. Once in Seattle, he is gone but, alas, not to be forgotten. She then tells me about the whole scenario, and my advice to her is, "Keep your mouth shut." Maybe it will blow over.

Well, there is little chance of that. The escaped convict returns to Vancouver, where he has a lover in the Matsqui prison. This surprised me a little because I just did not see that. His lover is a ratty little piece of manure, and he escaped too with my next-door neighbor.

Then they travel to Toronto and murder the warden of the Toronto prison. This really happened. you can't make it up.

Now she has a real problem. There is no statute of limitations on murder, and though she didn't participate, she was a conspirator, and conspiracy in Canada is worse than if you did the crime. The escape, well, if you don't get caught for seven years, it goes away.

I guess something's up. We are on lockdown. An escape? Indian uprising? Maybe there is a knife missing from the kitchen. What could it be? I don't know, and furthermore, I don't care. There is a foot of snow on the ground, and I'm just going back to sleep. Most of the time in the winter, I don't even get up for morning count, a punishable offense by the way. The guards don't care. Why?

The supervisor of the guards is a big fellow. I call him the "Duke." He walks a little like John Wayne, the movie star. He is about six feet six. He is just a little taller than me. He is in his sixties, and he is a pretty good egg. He and I get along. I heard him tell some of the other guards one day that everyone knows that the Big Yank hibernates in the winter, and so I did.

And the lockdown? They found a brew some Indians were making. When they drink alcohol, you better circle the wagons because it is going to get rowdy. They have several tribes in Canada, and a good chunk of them are in prison and mostly for violent crimes. Murder comes to mind, the number one offense for Canadian natives, and they are real alcoholics. The "Natives" as they are called are treated as second-class much like the Blacks and minorities in America. They just kill each other and then go to prison. Canada has no Black population for the most part, and the prisons here are predominantly White, at least from my perspective anyhow.

So the weather is getting better and the days are getting longer and the yard is opening up again. That is a good thing because there is too much tension inside during the winter months. I was lucky because I had my photography business. It keeps me occupied. That, plus my job on the recreation crew kept me busy during those cold bleak winter months. And my new love, tennis, is back.

It is March now, and the warden calls me up to his office. I find this kind of strange because the last time we talked in his office, he threw me out. So what's this about? I know that I'm not in trouble for anything. Maybe he is going to tell me that this is all a big mistake and I can go on my way, but I doubt that.

No! It's not my release that's pending. The warden is worried that there is going to be a riot. And why was he worried there was going to be a riot? The Olympics. That is his reasoning. Yep! That's the honest-to-gosh truth. The warden thought that because of the 1976 Summer Olympic Games being held in Montreal, we were going to have a riot at Matsqui. Well, what the hell? That makes perfect sense.

"Why did you want to see me?" I ask.

He says to me, "I thought you might create some sort of event to take the inmates' minds off rioting."

There may or may not be a riot this summer, but it won't be because of the Olympics. No, it will be because of your meddling, and more importantly, it goes with the chemistry of the prison. More lifers that can't be rehabilitated are being shipped in every day. That's where your riot will come from. But that's not what I say to him.

No, instead I ask him if he has five hundred dollars to put in my inmate account.

To my surprise, he didn't even blink. "Yes," he said. "I will deposit the money at the end of the month. What is your plan?" he asks.

"Well," I say, "first, I call the local sporting goods stores and get some prizes donated, and then I set up an Olympic-style venue that will run for two weeks and has several events daily."

"Brilliant," he says.

And I say, "Only if it works," but I got paid in advance and US currency.

So March of 1976 is in the books, and the summer is nearing, and I have to perform. I really am determined that this is going to be a really good event. I take pride in my productions, inmate or not.

I recruit a few helpers, but mostly, I run the event on my own. The first thing I do is get on the phone and start my getting spiel down. By the time the third phone call was made, I'm a verbal machine. The prize stash is mounting. Now there are three natural gifts you can have in life: the gift of looks, the gift of gab, and the gift of the purse. I have two of the three. I work the phones for most of April, and by May, I have plenty of prizes. Now I have to dream up some events.

You have to work with what you have. So I will have events like tennis, the Chinaman is favored, racquetball, golf, softball throw, ping-pong. I think I can make this work, and I do although I don't participate. But I do manage to get a little loot—three hundred thankful inmates and not to mention the warden. I am now the "mayor" of Matsqui, this small town of ours.

Among the donated prizes were some Olympic T-shirts, and they were very popular. And the events? Well, they went well, and to top it off, we had an open house at the end of the events and presented the prizes.

I should mention Canada Day was in the mix too. Canada Day, for those of you who don't know, is like America's Fourth of July, except for the fact that Canada is not free—it is part of the Crown. Just another hypocrisy in Canadian lore.

Now I didn't know it, but the recreation officer, the head guy, had entered us in a new "fast-pitch" softball league. The league was for the greater Abbotsford area and consisted of seven teams. They just let us in the league because they wanted eight teams. We were the equalizer, and it was kind of fitting. I was named the manager of the prison team. Probably punishment for the lost prisoner on a golf outing. Just what I need, another task for the summer. Goodbye tennis for a while.

So I start holding practices in the afternoon on the first day of May. The league starts in one week and runs through the middle of June then the playoffs. We have no chance at the playoffs.

Then in July, the Olympics are held in Montreal, and they run for two weeks. That will take us to August, and that is when I have my second parole hearing coming up—and my last.

So we start the fast-pitch league. We have a pretty good team. The only problem is that we have some road games, and that seriously diminishes our odds of winning the league.

OUTLAW LEAGUE

The home field advantage is huge for us because we can use all our players. We win a couple of games at home, and then we have a road game. The surprise of all surprises occurs. I'm on the travel list. They are giving me a pass to go out and play softball. We go out and win the game. I get three hits. That's the last time I would go out until my deportation.

We wind up a game or two over the five-hundred mark and a good experiment it was and the last. Part of the problem was funding, but the real problem was that we couldn't get our best players cleared to go outside the fences and play the outside games. A sad state of affairs.

Olympic mania is here, and it's pretty raucous. We have color televisions and our own Olympics hosted by none other than me!

Between officiating events and taking pictures of the participants, I am worn out. All in all, it was a really successful event, and no riots either. Everyone is happy, and it is August, and my parole hearing is just weeks away. And credibility? I am beaming with it. It is like I said earlier, this is a small town, and I'm the mayor right now. What could go wrong?

We got a new tenant in the Ghetto today, and his name is "Kelloggs." That's his nickname. I don't know his real name, and I don't care. He is a murderer and not just an ordinary killer. No, he is a mass murderer. He committed what is termed "family annihilation."

I mean, they captured him in the woods, but they said his daughter's stomach was slit open, and her breakfast of cornflakes had been re-eaten by him, hence the name Kelloggs. Pretty nice story, eh.

Now he is living five cells from me. I have an uneasy feeling with him around, and I'm not the only one. The attitude in the Ghetto has become somber.

Then one day, about a week or so later, I come in from work, and lo and behold, we have had a fire. Really! Someone burned Kelloggs's cell out. That's one way to get rid of him, and the fire was ruled as an accidental incident, just sweep it under the carpet.

I have got to admit, I am a little nervous about this parole hearing, and I have some butterflies in my stomach.

Now the trash all goes out of the south tiers rear door on Monday mornings. So if you're the tier janitor, your job is to bring your trash down at ten o'clock on Monday morning.

Well, we have a small problem with the tier janitor from One West. First of all, he is a rapist and should not be in the general population. I think he is bait to get some other inmate to attack him, then the government is rid of him, and the attacker gets more time.

Anyway, he has started bringing his trash over on Sunday night so it can stink us out all night. The Boss is unhappy, but worse yet, so am I. We, okay I, confront the guy and tell him trash call is at ten in the morning and come back then. He then tries to blow right past me, and that, my friends, was a mistake.

The fight didn't last too long. I hit him, and he hit the ground. "Maybe you didn't hear me," I restated. "The trash call is at ten in the morning. Come back then."

All this takes place right in front of the fishbowl, and the guards don't even move.

One of the inmates on our tier is this really wild kid. Pretty good size too. He is doing six years for armed robbery, and he is a weak junkie, and I hate him. He lives right next door to me. How do I get rid of him? It just so happens I have a pair of bolt cutters. Hey, you never know! I have them hidden out in the outside recreation shack. I know now. I'm not going to use them, and they are a problem. I could get another two or three years added on to my sentence, and I don't want to take the risk. So I offer the cutters to my unsavory neighbor, and he takes them. I figured he would. Three days later, we are missing two inmates, and there is a big hole cut in the fence just outside the living dorm and another hole in each of the two main fences. Problem solved. Footnote, they captured him two days later, smacked out on heroin in the slums of downtown Vancouver. he is in the British Columbia Penitentiary for now.

Well, the day is here. It is my parole hearing. Ah, and a fine day it is! I'm feeling pretty good about my situation. Well, by ten o'clock, it is over. I got a one-year bump. How did that happen?

Well, it is simple. I am in the front offices walking toward the parole hearing room when the girl counselor from One West comes running up to me, and she is crying big crocodile tears.

"What is wrong?" I ask her.

She is blubbering pretty good, but I managed to eke out the fact that they, the parole board, knew my real name, and once again, the jig was up.

So I have to think fast, and here's what I came up with. I walk into the parole room, and there are five members on the parole board panel, four men and one woman. They are older people, at least in their sixties, mostly retired police chiefs, and the woman is an ex-alderman, a very staunch-looking group, to say the least.

I take a chair and begin with this piece of dialogue, "At this time, I would respectfully like to withdraw my application for parole." I continue, "I have not been completely honest with you, and for that, I am sorry. Furthermore, I don't think I am completely rehabilitated yet."

They all five looked at each other and cracked up. They were laughing so hard one fell out of his seat.

"Well, son," the old police chief says, "that took a lot of courage, and we will see you next year. Courage, my ass, that was just common sense. Deep down inside, I was livid. Never show your emotions."

So it's been a pretty good year so far, except for my parole fiasco. Another year inside and another bleak and dreary winter to suffer through.

Chapter Ten

Where Is My Pardon?

Baseball playoff games were still on the television when the Canadian winter approached and temperatures dropped. Watching the Montreal Expos almost daily helped us pass the time even though they are now Reggie-less, since he signed with the Yankees.

Seattle has a new professional football team—the Seahawks. We'll start getting their games on TV on Sundays.

The Canadian Football League games are on too, but they are not as good as American football. Frankly, it is a talent problem. The CFL will allow only two foreigners per team. There is a lot of talent in the world, you know, but Canada is a strange place. I mean, they had corporal punishment up to and into the twentieth century.

Women could not go into a bar unescorted in Canada, some archaic law of theirs. Really! It is the 1970s, and women could not enter a pub unescorted. They would hang around outside the pub until some gent came by and escorted them in. The currency is different too. That's why I told the warden five hundred dollars US currency for my Olympic services. In Canadian currency, that would have been 10 to 15 percent less.

On a positive note, my partner was released today from the prison at Victoria. That's a big relief.

We got a new American inmate today. He is doing nine years for smuggling a ton of Thai sticks in a load of teak from Thailand. His distinguishing mark is that his father is a general in the Army.

He commands the presidio in San Francisco. Guess Dad and the boy don't get along that well.

I asked him, but he has no comment. Wow, nine years! He will do three. He winds up not being too talkative. It is strange that we don't hang out more, but that's life.

So it has been a banner year for the Canadian border guards as we just got another American inmate today. He is young, maybe twenty years old, if that. He is a strapping young man.

Seven years, the minimum, was his sentence, and he only had fifty pounds of marijuana. I have heard of doing hard time before, and when you do hard time, you make the others around you do hard time too, and it is not a pleasant situation to be in. Now this is definitely going to be a long year.

So the Expos turn into the Seahawks as baseball switches to football. The winter arrives. It is a cold one.

It is time for Seattle's first ever professional football team to come out and play its first ever game. It is my time to hibernate.

The winter of 1976 is in the books, and it is a New Year. The year is 1977, and I'm doing a little harder time. That might be due to the year bump that I got at my parole hearing.

No matter how resilient you are, prison life takes a toll on you. I don't know what is really. It could be the monotony of every day is the same, but I think it is the everyday same routine that gets you down. Then, of course, there are the surroundings, and I'm not talking about the buildings.

So I have to make it to August before my next parole hearing and then the thirty days to process the paperwork.

So I'm out in, say, probably September. I cannot wait as this is getting old, and the winters, well, they are almost unbearable.

So 1977 is here, and with it, a whole new slew of problems. First of all, the Olympic threat is over, and the warden has announced budget cuts, and we, the recreation department, got hit pretty hard. Second, the inmate elections are being held, and I was elected sports commissioner.

Funny, I don't remember putting my name on any list for the inmate committee. Oh well, the voters have spoken, and speak they did. They elected a totally radical inmate committee, a bunch of lifers, and a big Yank.

Now, as for the state of affairs with the inmate committee, one, there are four guys who are serving life sentences on the committee, and probably, they are not too rational. On the other hand and in the alternative, who knows more about prison life and the dos and do nots of prison life than lifers? There has definitely been an attitude change in the prison from good to the not so good, and it came quickly in just a matter of weeks.

So my boy from Seattle is driving me crazy with his complaining. He has a sister. She is about a year younger than him and a real looker too.

"If I got you a pass when the golf season starts, can you have your sister pick you up from the golf course?"

"Yes!" he says.

"Well, they don't give day passes to foreigners very often. My pass for softball last year was a first."

"Yes," he says. "Can you really get me a pass? Can you do that?"

"I'll try," I say. "Meanwhile, stop the complaining."

Well, golf season comes along, and I get him a pass, and his sister does her part and picks him up, and he is gone. Two things: One, he was only twenty years old and did not deserve the seven years he got for fifty pounds of pot. I mean, that was just wrong. He did a year, that's too much. The second thing is that the head of the recreation is pissed at me. He doesn't speak to me for a month. Oh well.

So it is a slow-moving year. Jimmy Carter has taken the White House from Ford. Ford, whom I believe is the first unelected president, is thrown out of office, and the first Southerner in seventy-five years to sit in the White House takes the reins.

One of Ford's last official acts was to pardon "Tokyo Rose," the infamous voice of the Imperial Japanese army for her propaganda barrage against the allied troops in WWII. It was a strange move in my opinion but not as strange as Carter's presidency is going to be.

One of the first moves that Carter makes is to pardon Patricia Hearst. Then he proceeds to pardon all the draft dodgers from the

Vietnam War. As Carter's presidency goes, it was the Iran hostage situation that did him in.

As we move to the summer months, it is getting hot, and not just the temperature outside, the inmate population temperature is up as well. The inmate committee is at with the warden, and they can't win. They have no tact.

So as summer comes along, the top three members of the inmate committee are shipped back to the British Columbia Penitentiary.

It is funny. Well, not in the humorous term but in the odd sense that all the heads of the inmate committee wind up back on Fraser Boulevard, overlooking the Fraser River at the infamous British Columbia Penitentiary.

This doesn't really affect me, or does it? I'm the new "de facto" head of the inmate committee and not too happy about it either. Does this mean I'm going back to the British Columbia Pen too? I don't think so. My résumé is too good, and I have tact, plus I am making parole really soon.

August is finally here, and it is time for me to go for my second parole hearing. The same panel of five men and one woman. I didn't know it at the time, but the woman, a retired alderman, has a son serving a five-year stretch for drugs, and he is in Matsqui. He is a total a-flaming faggot, or he is just deeply gay. Seems like a conflict of interest to me. This doesn't concern me, though, as I have to make a good showing.

And I do in a forty-five-minute hearing, and now I have been granted parole, and I will be home in a month. I mean, what could go wrong?

It is strange how this coincides with Vietnam just a little bit. The first thirty days you're in the jungles, you are scared to death, then you get over it. Until the final thirty days of your tour comes, and then all of a sudden, you become human again. Well, it is kind of the same here, and now I am a short-timer, and I don't want anything to go wrong.

Well, that's exactly what happened. Something went wrong. No fault of mine, except that I was in the wrong place at the wrong time. It was on a Sunday evening, and I had just returned to my tier, One

South. I had been playing tennis as usual with the Chinaman when it happened.

The staircase from the upper floors empties right at the fishbowl on the ground floor. I'm standing approximately fifteen feet inside the tier opening when this inmate comes stumbling down the stairs. He is bleeding profusely from his rear lower left back area. It is not so bad at first glance, but I notice the blood is blackish, and this usually means a kidney or another organ has been pierced, and that's a bad thing. In other words, he is a "dead man walking."

I turn and head for my house, stopping and telling everyone in the dayroom to get in their cells.

When the guards finally come out of the fishbowl and start to treat the fallen inmate, they call an ambulance, but this guy is lying on the floor, bleeding out. It seems like forever.

The ambulance arrives, and they take him away. The next day, we find out he did not make it. I knew that the minute I saw him come downstairs.

Well, they find the guy who did the dastardly deed, and he says he has an alibi. He says he was down on One South, One South 25 to be exact. That's the cell right next to mine. Oh, and he drops my name too. He says that I saw him, so he couldn't have possibly stabbed the guy. With that said, I'm now a witness in a murder case. Lovely. This all started when one faggot liked another faggot who had a faggot boyfriend.

In other words, it was a lover's quarrel, plain and simple jealousy. I really do not understand homosexuals at all. Men that think they are women and women who think that they are men. It is just plain crazy.

Anyway, my parole is in jeopardy, and what am I going to do now? The investigators come to the prison to interview me. I spend an hour trying to convince them that I saw nothing, that I wasn't even in my house when the suspect said he was there. Despite my best defense, they tell me that I'm going to have to testify. they are putting a hold on my parole. Lovely!

Well, it is now December, and I haven't heard a fucking word. I am pretty short-tempered right now; in fact, I had a physical run-in with a guard the other day. The worst thing about prison is how easy it is to pick up another "beef"—you know, another case or charge like assault and battery on a protected person. That's good for another five years or so.

Well, nothing came of it. December passes, and the New Year is here, and I still have not have heard a fucking word. Hell, I'll wind up doing my whole seven-year stretch at this rate, and then get a hold on me as a material witness, I'll never get back home.

New Year is here, and it becomes January 1978 just like that. The Mounties are at the prison today. It is early February, and they are here to drive me to Vancouver but not to the courthouse. Instead of taking me to the courthouse, they take me to the British Columbia Penitentiary.

"What the hell is this?" I say. "What!" I scream. "Why?"

"Because they don't know what day you are supposed to testify, so you need to be available."

"Oh, I see."

Bullshit, you are making money by switching me around. That's what this is all about. This punishment for the Seattle caper.

"Is this my punishment?"

"Have a nice stay," they say.

So here I am back at the British Columbia Penitentiary, and it is as disgusting—no, more disgusting than before. I know a few of the inmates, I mean, hell, all my inmate committee guys from Matsqui are all here, the hard-core prison lifers. Face it, all these men are destined to die, to die inside these prison walls, and what's more, they know it. Now there is someone you can ration with.

The second day I'm at the British Columbia Penitentiary it starts. It is cold outside, maybe twenty degrees, and the wind is blowing at a forty miles per hour clip, and just for good measure, it is snowing.

This would not be a good time to lose power. But that's exactly what happened, thanks to the prison officials. And to boot, all the windows have been broken out. I don't know how or where it started, but I do know four or five of the inmates who started it. A full-blown prison riot. It is total chaos.

There isn't a prison guard in the place, and the power is off because the warden shut it off. Bastard! So as I have stated, the windows are broken out, doors ripped from cell walls, toilets, and sinks likewise.

To make things worse, the inmates have gotten into the warden's office and have found the list of snitches.

These are the informants who tell on other prisoners for monetary gain or privileges. Six of them are killed.

The national guard has been activated, and they are throwing C-rations over the fence. Thus, the action causes a wild scramble for food.

The best scene, though, is of the four guys from the Matsqui inmate committee. They are on the fifth floor, the top tier of the prison, and they have a bedsheet draped over the rail, and it reads, "Under New Management." The photograph runs on the front page of the *Vancouver Sun* the very next day. Anarchy at its epitome.

After about five days, the riot is quelled, and peace is somewhat restored. I mean, the place is demolished. *These Canadians sure know how to riot.*

On the sixth day, I finally am called to testify, and I am shocked. My trial was just a normal court hearing with one judge who wore a robe. But these guys? I mean, what a getup. They are wearing wigs and red robes, and there are three of them. I feel like I am in a seventeenth-century courtroom. I guess it is a tribunal of sorts, and I am flabbergasted.

It was a really short hearing. I did most of the talking, and I made the judges laugh. I was excused as a witness.

Back to the British Columbia Penitentiary and the next day back to Matsqui after having survived another disaster, and today, I am being discharged.

The next morning, the Mounties come to the prison to escort me to the border. Now the next adventure begins.

Sex in prison is the final category. Is there sex in prison? Heterosexual sex in prison? Why, of course, there is! It just a question of how good it is. Prison bunks, I wouldn't call them beds, are very uncomfortable, and they are small. So I guess you would have kinky sex, standing up or whatever. Me? The infirmary was the best. Full-sized beds, and privacy, it was the bomb.

One morning, I get a call to report to the infirmary. Why? I'm not sick. There is no epidemic in the prison, so why the infirmary?

The female counselor from One West had the keys. How she got them? I don't know. But when I got to the infirmary, she was waiting for me, wearing a hospital gown and nothing else.

It is evident what she had in mind, and I didn't mind either.

A fitting going away party I guess.

Well, what a long strange trip it's been, sang the grateful dead in their hit song "Truckin'." And it is not over yet.

The Mounties took me to the American border where I was processed and released.

I can't believe it. I am a fugitive from the American justice system; after all, I was sentenced to two to ten years in 1972, and that still has to be resolved. And I am fully aware of this.

But the border guards haven't a clue. And they let me go.

The year is now 1978, and I just completed forty-four months of an eighty-four-month sentence. I am a free man for now, but for how long? I love the fight for the right to smoke marijuana. It is a just cause, and I am a warrior, a soldier in the fight. But warriors grow old and get tired. I'm thirty years old now, not a young man anymore in most eyes, but I feel much younger. It is like I have had so much of my life stolen away from me. First, the war and then prison. It is time for me to have some fun now and make money if I can. After all, I have quite a résumé.

So when I leave the border crossing at Bellingham, I'm headed for SeaTac International Airport. One problem, no, the main problem, is that it is two hundred miles from the border to Seattle and SeaTac Airport and I have no car.

Hitchhike? I could do that, but it is February, and it is cold, windy, and raining. I think hitchhiking would be a waste of time. I do have about $750 that I saved in my "inmate welfare fund," plus the $500 I got for "saving" the prison from a destructive riot during the '76 Olympics.

So I walk to the border town where I know the Greyhound bus stops. Sure enough, the Greyhound is running, and it is due right now. So I climb aboard and go to the airport and then catch a flight to Los Angeles. I get completely inebriated on the flight by consuming two liters of red wine, the first alcohol I have had in fifty months. And this, my friends, was a bad idea, the drinking of the wine.

The plane touches down in Los Angeles, and what am I going to do now? I've got about a thousand dollars, no car, no place to stay, and I'm drunk as a skunk.

Well, as luck would have it, I run into an old buddy of mine who is flying out. He tells me to go and see his brother, and I do. He, the brother, lives in Costa Mesa. He is a boat salesman, or for that matter, anything else he could sell. For instance, the kilo of cocaine he sold to an undercover cop. All he got was fifty-two weekends in the county jail. So I stay with him for a while. The days of ranch living are gone for now.

Gradually, I am getting reintroduced to society. I get in touch with one of my old cohorts, and he has some really bad Thai sticks, and he can't sell them. I take ten pounds, and I buy myself a Greyhound bus pass. A one-week bus pass cost fifty-five dollars, see the USA Greyhound way.

First stop, Seattle, where the man that I helped escape turns three pounds then eastward to Tennessee. I turn a couple of more pounds, but the weather is so bad. I gotta go. I mean four feet of snow at your door in the morning, well, that is not exactly my cup of tea.

I go on to Louisville where my acid guy from Matsqui has just gotten home. There is two feet of ice in the alleyways; to put it mildly, it was freezing. The whole Midwest is in the midst of a terrible winter storm.

I am heading west back to Seattle. I have two pounds left. I board the bus heading for Seattle when this fine-looking honey gets on the bus, and it just so happens she sits down right next to me. We start chatting, and it turns out that she is going to Seattle too. One thing leads to another, and we get pretty cozy. It is a long ride to Seattle.

We make it to Missoula, where that's the end of the road for now. Snow advisories are out, and we are stranded, and we are going to be here for thirty-six hours. Well, I have money, so we get a hotel room. We eventually get to Seattle. She gives me a contact number. I lose it. I turn the final two units that I have and head back to Costa Mesa—not a bad week.

Ah, the warm Southern California sun. I was at the beach, getting some rays when I ran into some old high school friends. They have a weekend baseball team. One of them says to me, "You use to be pretty good. Can you still play?"

"Probably. When is the next game?"

They tell me when the next game is, and I say, "I'll be there."

This is the start of a thirteen-year baseball odyssey. I wouldn't call it a career, but it is close. This is the very moment where the "Outlaw League" begins for me.

Now at this same time, one of my friends has a Pony League baseball team that he is managing. His son plays on the team.

"We just had our draft," he told me. "Could you help me coach the team?"

"Well, yes, but, and it is a big but, I'm a 'convicted felon,' and that might be a problem," I said.

It was not a problem at all.

We opened the season with one win and seven losses. We couldn't even play five innings in one game, but it will get better. And it does as our team proceeds to roll out ten games in a row winning streak.

We win the division playoff game and then the league championship game.

Now it is onto the state championships. We are the runner-up in the state tournament for nine- and ten-year-olds. I really admired these young boys. Not once did they quit on us.

So I join my high school buddies' baseball team. They play in a recreational league on Sundays. The games are doubleheaders, two seven-inning games.

The first game is always pitched by this lefty who pitched in the major leagues for the Chicago White Sox for six years, and he is damned good. These guys are just one pitcher away from winning this league. It just so happens that I was that pitcher. The team went undefeated. In one game, the lefty struck out ten in a row. Not to be outdone, I opened the next game by fanning the first twelve. I remember one player asking me, "How hard are you throwing when the seams on the ball are whistling?"

I answer, "Pretty damned hard."

Our center fielder is a tall skinny blond kid who has grown five inches since graduating from high school. He didn't put on any weight, though.

Much like me, he didn't play baseball his senior year of high school. So he is working or has been working a job at a doorknob factory. He has been thinking, and he decided he would rather be a professional baseball player, so he quit his day job.

Well, he couldn't find the mound on this team. Maybe two or three innings all season, but he is a damn good athlete. As a result, he gets an invite from one of the two-year college coaches in the area, and it is a really reputable team.

Fall rolls around, and he and I are pretty close now, especially seeing as how I am funding his baseball career—not only funding it but diet and training plus pithing tips and he doesn't need many of those.

Spring practice starts, and I walk on at the same school as the kid, I mean, GI Bill and all. The coach of the team is the same guy I had in junior high school, the one who pulled me out of a game because I threw too hard and the catcher complained. What could possibly go wrong?

We are on the baseball field, and there is a scrimmage going on. I'm due to pitch next in the scrimmage game, and I am warm and ready to go, and I am just sitting in the dugout.

The guy who is pitching in front of me is a Marine veteran who had just gotten a discharge at Camp Pendleton. "Ball four!" the umpire cried. "That's twelve balls in a row, and the bases are loaded."

The coach looks at me and says, "Are you ready?"

"Yes," I say.

"Okay, you're in. Let's go."

So I take the mound throw, my warm-up pitches, and make the first pitch to the batter. Fastball on the inside part of the plate, he swings, and I jam him. He hits one-hopper right back to me. I field the ball and throw home. That's one out. The catcher then throws the ball to the third baseman. He tags the base two outs! Could it be?

Well, thank God for slow runners because the third baseman rifled a throw across the diamond and got the guy at first. Just your ordinary 1–2–5–3 triple play. What's next? I'm cut, that's what's next. I didn't even ask why.

Well, what now? I go to another junior college, and I catch on not as a pitcher but as the pitching coach. Make that as an all-around coach. I don't mind that I'm older than these guys, and no college coach is going to feature and me as a starting pitcher. No, the college playing days are over. That's just a reality and a fact of war. I'm over the hill age-wise for college baseball.

There is a weekend scout team in the area. Maybe I will try out for that team. The manager is a little Mexican fellow who managed for fourteen years in the Yankee organization, all of them at "A" ball. I have a few friends that are playing on the team, and they tell me that I should come out. I probably should. This is a chance to be seen by scouts. Pure baseball politics to its nth degree. Is there some Systemic discrimination here?

This manager has a lefty who is his number one starter. I will be the number two starter. At least this is a chance for me to outpitch a former pro and be seen by scouts. The lefty was released by the Astros after two seasons at triple "A" Tucson.

Now I may not have mentioned this, but I have one awesome temper. "Donald Duck" has nothing on me. I struck out in a game, and I threw the bat, and that got me a one-game suspension. But not a game I pitched, one of the lefty's games, which I didn't play in, anyway. But that changed when while under suspension, the manager puts me in to pinch run at third base in a tie game. I scored the winning run on a passed ball, the left-hander's only win of the season. I mean, he is horrible. The man can't pitch a lick, and he goes one and eleven. I win all twelve of my starts. He makes the all-star team. I guess there is systemic discrimination present.

College baseball is going pretty well. The team started, 9–0. It is now spring break time for colleges around the nation, and the team is tired. We finally let a game get away, and we took our first loss. So I'm ready to relax for a week when this guy shows up. He is the phantom infield coach. He wants to run my championship team because they lost a game.

"Bullshit!" I say. "And you?"

"Well, you have no say out here."

The players love me. We went on to tie for the league championship. Now we have a one-game playoff, and we win the game at a neutral field.

Onto the state championship. We finish second, and we are ranked number two for the season after opening the season being ranked fifty-second. The coach who beat us for the championship just happened to be the winningest coach in the entire nation at the two-year college level. And just as a point of interest, this was his last game before he retired.

Chapter Eleven

Orange County A's

The LaFonda Stars is now my new baseball team. I've been with them for a couple of months. The owner is an older Mexican gentleman who owns the LaFonda Mexican restaurant in Downtown Santa Ana, and the food is really good—no, great. I have eaten there many times.

He played in the Mexican leagues for thirteen years, the "Norte de Sonora" League. I think he was an outfielder.

The manager of the team, the Stars, is a big bully-type guy. A big bag of wind is what he really was. I'd like to introduce him to the Headhunter. I am not going to last too long here. I already know that.

This team is made up of a tightly knit group of players, mostly from one high school and one college. There is one guy I can relate to on this team. He is a Marine veteran, and he did two tours in Vietnam as a door gunner. We got along.

So I wouldn't be on this team, except for all their pitchers can't pitch. Now I have learned a few things while playing in these leagues. It is almost like the minor leagues, but I have learned about hitters, and there is very little quality pitching around. I've won fourteen starts in a row, and I throw as hard or harder than anyone around, and now I have developed a changeup and a devastating knee-buckling slider.

One of the reasons I sought this team out was the fact that they travel to Mexico to play exhibition games. The owner of the team does charity trips down to his hometown of Nogales.

Now Nogales is a wild and wooly border town, and it is about a four-hour drive from Orange County. The team announces, "We are playing there, Nogales, next weekend. Who can make the trip?"

"I can," I say.

"There are going to be three games. The first one is a nine-inning game on Saturday night at 7:00 and then two seven-inning games on Sunday starting at 11:00 a.m. We need you," meaning me, "for the getaway game. That's pretty smart, save your ace for last."

The border crossing is simple, and the guards love baseball players. So it is late Friday night, and I am coked out. I had a little bit of cocaine, and that is okay. It is pretty good for the long drive late into the night to Nogales from Orange County.

I get a hotel room on the Arizona side of the Nogales border. I will sleep until about two o'clock in the afternoon, then I will get some dinner, and then cross the border into Mexico. So I execute the plan and get a hotel room. It is about two in the morning, and I am tired as hell.

To my astonishment, there is a Mexican girl, about twenty years of age, with a baby sleeping in my room. I go back to the front desk. They tell me no one should be in the room. I go back to the room. She is still there.

Now I am coked out, and some sex would be good. But then I think again, and I decide that I came to play baseball, and that is my goal. That's what I am here for. So I decided to let her sleep. When I get up the next day, she is gone, and good riddance.

Up at around two in the afternoon, I shower, shave, and get some dinner at the Denny's located right on the border. Then it is time to cross into Mexico and head to the ballpark. The border? The guards at the border love baseball and baseball players, as I've stated before, so it is no problem.

I cross the border and arrive at the ballpark around five in the afternoon. It's hot and humid. What a great ballpark. It holds upward of fifty thousand fans, and the stands are wrapped with chicken wire.

That is kind of odd. We're playing tonight against the Mexican National team. Christ, they must have forty players out here. We have fourteen.

I'm scheduled to pitch the second game on Sunday. I'll coach a base tonight. Our starting pitcher has just been released by the Giants. He's pretty good, and he throws fairly hard. He goes eight and is done, humidity.

We bring in a relief pitcher. He's a lefty, a high school senior. He gets hit hard, but he doesn't surrender any runs. Dilemma time. We're out of pitchers.

Now the fat bully manager didn't make the trip, and my buddy, the former Marine, is at the helm, and it is a tie game in partially due to one of the finest catches I have ever witnessed in baseball. The center fielder made it in the bottom of the ninth inning.

Now they turn to me. "Can you throw an inning or two?" I'm asked.

"Hell yeah!" I respond. "Let's go."

I enter the game in the eleventh inning, striking out the side on nine pitches. Same in the twelfth inning.

It is the top of the thirteenth inning, and we get a run. We are in the lead now. It is the bottom of the thirteenth inning. There are two outs and a man on second base. The cleanup hitter is at the plate. He's five for five in this game tonight. Three fastballs later and we win, as I sit him down with a backward K—— caught looking.

Well, so much for the wild and wooly town of Nogales. I mean, it is only eleven o'clock at night, and everything is closed.

The ballpark was wild and wooly, though. Mexico is a crazy place, and like I said earlier, they have chicken wire surrounding the stands. Why? Well, in the fifth inning, we had a smoke bomb near the mound. In the seventh inning with runners in scoring position and two strikes on our hitter, a bottle rocket comes whizzing out of the stands from behind home plate. As the batter turns to look back to see where the bottle rocket came from, the umpire raises his hand and calls, "Strike three! You're out."

I remember walking out of the stadium, and people were offering us tequila, chickens, just about anything you can think of for a reward. Pretty interesting, the Mexican fans really love the game of baseball and are not afraid to show it.

We're back in the hotel room. I shower and roll a big fat Thai joint. I offer to share with my teammates—big mistake. Okay, I'll smoke it myself.

I go out to get some dinner, but everything is closed. Fuck, it's only eleven o clock, and the sidewalk is rolled up. I head back up to the room. I'm locked out, and no one will answer the door. Fuck. I'm sleeping in my car, I guess. As I head to my car to call it a night, I pass the rooms where the Mexican team is staying. Actually, it is several rooms, but this room was the "party" room.

"How hard did the first guy throw?" they ask me.

"I don't know, ninety-three," I say.

"You throw much harder," they tell me.

"That's good to know. Now pass the mescal."

After the worm, I don't remember much. I woke up at about eight thirty in the morning. I slept in my car. Must have had a rough night 'cause there's puke all over floorboard, and uh-oh, hangover! It's already eighty damn degrees out. I walk or stumble or crawl, however you like it, over to the pool and fall in. The pool? It's ice-cold. That woke me up. Now to the yard. We're playing at a different location today. Nothing like last night's forty-thousand-seat attendance stadium. that was the biggest crowd I've ever pitched before, and I loved it.

Today's venue is smaller with a skinned infield, no grass.

The guy starting for us pitched in the Angels organization, and his brother is still with the Angels.

We scored a pair of runs in the third inning, and he gave up a walk and then a two-out, two-run homer in the bottom of the inning. We scored again in the fifth inning and took a one-run lead. In the bottom of the fifth inning with two outs, he issues a base on balls and then throws a big fly. We lose the game, 4–3.

This is all fine and dandy, but I am hungover from hell. It's at least one hundred degrees, and I've got the dry heaves, really bad dry heaves.

"Can you throw?" someone asks me.

"We will find out," I counter.

My Vietnam buddy takes care of me. He gets me warm. I stumble to the mound. The fastball is a slow ball today with lots of sliders. I throw 6 2/3 of no-hit baseball, no strikeouts, nineteen ground balls. We win the game, and everyone hates me. Why? Well, the reasons should be obvious. Hell, I hate me too right now. But the real reason is that the Mexicans brought a bucket of ice water for drinking into the dugout. I have been soaking my towel in it in between innings and throwing up behind the dugout. That's apparently a problem.

Time to face the four-hour drive home, and my car won't start, dead battery. Where can I get a jump? And this hangover, when will it stop. So high yet so low.

Somehow, I made it home. The next week, I show up for the regular game, and I have a stiff neck. I throw one inning, my last for the La Fonda Stars. Find someplace else to pitch, I'm told, short and sweet.

So it's now March of 1979, and I am thirty-two years old, not a young man in the baseball world. But still, five or six years in the big leagues would help me a lot financially, then there's the movie rights, who knows, hell, I might be the oldest rookie to ever pitch in the major leagues.

Satchel Paige was old when he joined the major leagues, he was a Black man, but he had been a professional with the Kansas City Monarchs for twenty years.

I have a great reputation as a pitching coach after a record-setting year at a local community college. One scout offered me a minor league job with the Mets as a pitching coach. I'm not old enough, I tell him. Maybe later.

Life's pretty good, and I'm getting lots of beach time and also plenty of honeys. Gotta stay away from the blow once in a while but not on a daily basis, at least for me. Nothing like getting coked and kinky, though. It's sinful, but what the heck?

I need a place to pitch, and I start scouting the area for teams. There's an "open" amateur baseball tournament going on here locally. They are playing at the field that Connie Mack built for the old Philadelphia Athletics in the early twentieth century. And it was also about that time that the Wrigley family bought the island of Santa Catalina for their professional sports teams, the Cubs and the Bears. Their thought was, it would keep the players away from the women.

So I go out to see a few tournament games, and the Orange County A's are one team that is playing, but they lose to a San Diego team. It's funny because the A's have a former big leaguer pitching for them and a future big leaguer catching. They are arguing nonstop for three innings over pitch selection. You won't last too long arguing with a thirty-two-year-old pitcher in the show. And he didn't. All in all, some of these teams are pretty darned good.

The owner/manager of the A's is a flamboyant man in his sixties, and he is quite the dresser.

He is wearing a yellow jumpsuit with green accessories and yellow casual shoes and an A's baseball cap that sits kind of cockeyed on his head, no uniform for this guy, Charlie Finley all the way. He even looks like Finley. He is a tall thin man with a hawkish face and cold gray eyes. *This is a real character*, I say to myself, as he drives off in his Kelly green Jeep with the A's logo painted on the door. One thing is for sure, he's all in. This is my kind of team. Hell, if I can't make the major leagues, this is the next best thing. Maybe I'll fit in. We'll see.

Amateur league baseball has been around forever.

The most prominent of the leagues is the "NBC" or National Baseball Congress. It has been around since the forties. With teams from the Cape Cod League on the Atlantic Coast to the North Pole. Seriously, the North Pole "Nicks."

The league was designed to be a summer instructional league for college athletes to continue to develop their game. But many teams use whatever players they can to win the championship held each summer at the "Hap Dumont" stadium in Wichita, Kansas.

There are probably one hundred NBC teams nationwide, and the teams are supposed to be made up of college players, but a few old pros sneak in anyway, and these are the elite teams in amateur baseball.

Then there are your "club" teams, made up of players from the same area high school, college, etc., the "Weekend Warrior" faction of baseball because they usually play once a week in a league.

Then there is the Southern California Baseball Association, and it's been around for a while, at least as long as the NBC, that is for sure. The Southern California Baseball Association, I think that's what they called it. My friend, the old coach and Baltimore Orioles scout, had a team in this league. There were the Pasadena Redbirds, the Long Beach Rockets, and so many more, including the La Fonda Stars. It was quite a league. Hell, the Rockets played at Blair field and fielded a major league roster every week.

Then there are the local leagues. Mostly, sandlot players many who never even played high school baseball. For the most part, the NBC teams are well-funded professionally run organizations, and almost all of them are nonprofit organizations.

Then you have the "Scout" teams run by professional baseball scouts and sponsored by the major league franchise.

The Dodgers were the sponsors of the scout team I played for. These teams played among themselves but would play exhibition games too with teams like the Orange County A's.

Then there are the semipro teams. These are teams made up of higher-caliber players, many of whom had professional experience, including ex– or former major league players. These teams usually compete year round with very few weekends off and games played during the week.

The owners of these teams are mostly flamboyant and very serious about proving their own worth in the baseball world, sometimes to their own detriment. What I mean by that is that these owners are bigger than the game. They are bigger than the players. They are the show, and that's is a sad statement.

The Orange County A's is one of these semipro teams. Let me tell you my little story about the Orange County A's and my time with the team.

In the mid-1970s adult or amateur baseball, any way you like it, took a turn. Teams were popping up all over the West Coast, like sunflowers in the sun on a sunny day, and especially in California. There were teams from one end of the state to the other.

The "Outlaw League," does it really exist? Depends on who you ask. Some folks call it amateur baseball or adult league, semipro baseball, "Club" ball. I call it the "Outlaw League."

We will talk more about this phenomenon later.

In the meantime, my friend has another Pony League team. This time, it is eleven- and twelve-year-olds. Could I, would I, help coach? Well, I don't know. I mean, I have the time, but after the last experience with the nine- and ten-year-olds, I mean, it was not the kids—the kids were great. No, it was the parents—simply stated, they are the worst. I have no children, so I shouldn't be allowed to coach, but what they really meant was, we can't beat you, so you can't coach.

Funny, it seems all the parents that berated me now wanted their kids on the team that I am coaching. Well, I don't have much going in baseball at the present time, so I agree. We start the season, but it is not like last time. No, this time, we come out winning. And I mean we didn't stop winning until the season was over. We had won both halves of the league. There was no playoff, and our reward is we don't get to coach the all-star team.

My decision is made, and I have joined the Orange County A's. I didn't know it at the time, but this would be the start of a fifteen-year battle, a real love-hate battle, mostly love between me and the skipper, and he is a hard man to love, and I'm not much different.

The first weekend I'm on board, we have two doubleheaders—one on Saturday and then again on Sunday. Saturday's games are in Riverside. I'm not pitching, but I am coaching third base in both games. I'm pitching Sunday against Waldrons Pirates in San Diego. Wow, we are certainly going to put on some miles this weekend, and how do you get all your players to the game anyway?

Well, the owner tells me to be at the shop no later than eight Saturday morning. I am there and find the answer.

An old white shorty school bus with the A's logo on the side. Twenty players show up, load on the bus, and we go to Riverside. I coach third base, and we win two games. Back to the shop, and we will do it all over again tomorrow.

Sunday morning arrives, and we drive to San Diego, and it is hot, probably ninety, where I make my Orange County A's debut. And it is a dandy, a seven-inning shutout against the team that beat the A's in the recent tournament. And I haven't pitched in a game in six weeks. Sweet revenge.

One thing about me, I'm honest, to the point it sometimes hurts me; after all, I have some baggage.

After the game, I'm in the restroom pissing in the urinal when the owner comes up to the urinal next to me.

"That was a hell of a performance!" he says to me.

"Yeah, I say. I can pretty much beat anybody anywhere, anytime. That's not the problem. The problem is, I'm an ex-convict. I did four years in prison for a thousand pounds of pot. So if you don't want me around your baseball team, I understand. Oh, and I'm a Vietnam combat veteran to boot," another whammy.

"Well, don't fret," he says to me. "I did time for a bank robbery that I didn't really commit, and I had seven PT boats shot out from beneath me in WWII. So welcome to the club."

Chapter Twelve

The Surrender

Now you are probably wondering what about my fugitive situation and what's going on with that. Well, I'll tell you. I got up one morning and decided I had to get that situation straightened out.

So I rolled and then smoked a big fat joint, and then I went down to Santa Ana, the county seat and the home of the courthouse.

I went in waited for all the calendar to clear, and then I made my move. I am going up before the duty judge. He is the judge that hears messed-up cases.

"Your honor," I began, "I am a fugitive, and I wish to surrender myself."

"Oh!" he said.

"I received a two to ten years' prison sentence back in 1972. I have been in prison in Canada, where I served forty-four months. I just got out last week, and I want to clear this matter up."

The district attorney wanted to take me into custody on the spot, one of the downfalls of surrendering this way.

"No, that won't be necessary," the judge told him. "Come back in one week, and I'll give you my final decision."

So I returned on the date the judge set, and to my surprise, the judge just lets me go. There is to be no parole or probation. He gives me time served. What a relief.

"One thing," he warned me as I was leaving the courtroom, "don't ever come before me again on a drug charge."

I had been admonished. The district attorney was fit to be tied, and that was the end of that.

This year was going by pretty fast. The college where I coached last season and set nineteen school records won the first championship in school history, and the head coach was named coach of the year.

They called today, and they want me back.

"Okay," I say.

Well, I'm out there for two days, and the athletic director called me up to his office.

"You're done," he says. "There was no real reason. Just pack up your gear and move on." Short and sweet.

Well, there was a reason—there is always a reason. It is called systemic discrimination. You see, the baseball coach was not very popular, and the AD wanted to bring in a new and younger coach, but with me hanging around, there was no chance of that because we were going to win.

So with me gone and a losing season in the books, the new coach comes in the next year. That's why I dislike the people in the game. It is all backstabbing.

The Orange County A's have joined a league, and it is the Greater Inland Empire League. We play Sundays in Ontario at a couple of different fields. The league is pretty good, and I now have a twenty-four game winning streak.

My pitcher, the young kid I was working with, signed a professional contract with the Mets and pitched at "A" ball his first year out, and now and he is home.

He pitched in excess of three hundred innings this year between college and pro ball. He is beat, and his arm is dead. The Mets scout and not the one who signed him, but another scout calls and wants my guy to pitch this winter on his scout team. The kid is distraught about pitching winter ball in some meaningless games. The kid's in a bind, and he's scared to death.

"I'll handle it," I tell him.

So I get the scout on the phone, and he agrees that I'm better equipped to handle the kid's off-season workouts.

"I will have him ready for spring training," I say. "You can count on it." And I do.

So the winter passes. We take a week off at Christmastime and New Year's. We have a routine of running five miles in the morning. The course is a cross-country route that I have found. Then we eat breakfast, and then we got to the beach, got to keep the tan up, then it's a little baseball activity from three to four in the afternoon. This might be the best thing we do. Keep your baseball muscles stretched and, more importantly, keep the feel of the ball. Plus, you can work on new pitches. Remember this, reinventing yourself is a big help to staying in the big leagues. Then it is dinnertime, plenty of food good, healthy food. The kid has put on about fifteen pounds this winter, and it is all good weight, not fat. Good food, balanced meals, and the beach—ah, the beach.

I have a small house in Costa Mesa just a mile or two from the beach. This is actually the best time of the year for us just lounging at the beach and working out. Oh, and honeys? We've got a slew of them. The year ends as they always do, and now it is 1980.

It's January 2, to be exact, and we are on the baseball field at the college where we do our winter prespring training workouts. There are about twenty professional baseball players who are on the field from nine in the morning to twelve o'clock Monday through Friday; after all, spring training is only weeks away.

We join in, and it will be this way for the next six years or so. Up at six, five-mile run, breakfast, then to the field for baseball drills, then lunch, and down to the beach for some beach volleyball. Good life, eh?

One of the players is an old knuckleball pitcher. He probably smokes two packs of cigarettes a day. That is his business. But smoking cigarettes on a college baseball field could cause a problem seeing as how it is posted, "No Smoking," no tobacco of any kind. So "Knucks" is out in the center field, puffing on a nail.

"I hate to break it to you," I say, "but you can't smoke out here."

We became friends, and I used to catch his bullpens, and his "Dancer?" Well, it was the best one I had ever seen. So my guy is off to spring training, and I wished that I was going too.

But no, I am going to Canada with one of my associates from the underworld. He comes from a strong Italian family. His uncle is a big-time fight promoter, and he manages some pretty famous heavyweights also, and his cousin owns a grocery store in South Central Los Angeles. This was a rough neighborhood, to say the least. I used to sell to him. He was a good customer.

So my friend is in the music business, and he is a producer, and he has had some pretty big opportunities. He has promoted The Ramones. They tore up the auditorium at Irvine University, and that cost thirty grand. Insurance? We don't need any stinking insurance, but he was glad he had it, or he would have had to self-indemnify. The B-52s, he did them too.

So he wants to expand to Canada. We take about a ten-day trip up to Vancouver. I reengage with some of my people from the past.

"Can you get kilos?" they ask.

"Is the world round?" was my response.

So we traveled back home. I'm pretty excited that I have reconnected with my people in Canada. Maybe there is a little business in my future in Canada. And the promoter? When we got back to California, he got a bag of cocaine, and he overdosed on the shit and killed himself. What a dummy!

On a lighter note, I found out, while we were in Canada, another death. Yes! Matsqui was dead. The cause was listed in the paper as a prison riot. The warden didn't heed my warning about to many lifers in that prison. Lo and behold, they burned the place to the ground. Inmates were sleeping in a tent or tents in the yard. It is not that bad now, weather-wise, but just wait until the winter comes in like a lion.

The Orange County A's play baseball on a year-round schedule, taking only Thanksgiving, Christmas, and New Year's off.

This year, the National Baseball Congress has commissioned a league for Southern California. This is to be the inaugural season. We, me and the skipper, meet with the commissioner one night out in Corona. We are set to compete in the league.

There are going to be eight teams, and the commissioner owns one of the teams. Now I don't mind him owning a team, but there is prize money involved, lots of it, for the winner of the tournament to go to Wichita. The commissioner's team is loaded. Well, it just so happens we are loaded too, and I'm on a thirty-game winning streak. The league started, and I won my first two starts. That was no big deal. Play on.

The phone rang at the office one morning. It was the commissioner of the league, and he is calling to tell us, "You have got to kick that guy off your team." He is talking about me.

"No way," the skipper tells him.

"Well then, you can't play in the league."

"Fine," the skipper retorts. "I will just get in another league or play an independent schedule. We are major financiers of the league, so kicking us out kicks out a lot of the funding too."

The phone rings about two hours later. It is the commissioner again. He is calling back to apologize for his morning rant and said, "Let's just continue with the way things were."

"Okay, if you say so."

But that was pretty weird. I wonder to myself if this guy's a "schizo." This guy, the commissioner, is just whacked out, and it is just another example of why I love the game of baseball but hate the people who run it. Maybe someday, I will run into the good guys in baseball. *That is my hope.*

Well, down in spring training, my guy is doing well, and he is going to make the double "A" team at Jackson, Mississippi. That wasn't unexpected though because that was the contract they had sent him.

Meanwhile, we are undefeated in league play, and I've run my winning streak to thirty-eight games.

In the major leagues for 1980, one season is underway, and the Baltimore Orioles have cut their backup catcher. He had been with Orioles for several years, his whole career, in fact. He is from Huntington Beach. Hmmm, I wonder if he is done?

Well, I get on the phone and track him down, and after discussing this with the skipper, of course, and the skipper says, "Damn, son, get a lunch date."

Well, I do. We meet the guy, and he is definitely not done, and he signs on with us. About two weeks later, the 1981 Major League Baseball strike takes place.

The local paper, the *Orange County Register*, runs an article on our catcher. And it is a big article on the sports page, and the title is "At Least He Is Playing," and play he did. I mean to tell you, this guy is a great receiver, but holy hell, he can hit too. I can't believe someone besides us didn't pick him up. We were lucky, I guess.

So we are going to Santa Maria to play the Indians. This is one of the classiest ball clubs you will ever find. The team is fifty years old, and they go to Wichita every year. This should be a good test.

Now the skipper has been up here before and has never won a single game. We are playing five games, one nine-inning game on Friday, two seven-inning doubleheaders Saturday and Sunday, and I am pitching the opener.

One problem, we played pinochle till midnight and drank a half gallon of Scotch, and to put it mildly, I have a screaming hangover.

We get to the "yard" at about five o'clock. The game time is at 7:00 p.m. The game started, and I'm on the mound, and I have no velocity.

Nine innings later, we win 2–1. Their run was an unearned run in the eighth inning. I threw a no-hitter, and the skipper has his first win ever at Santa Maria. We sweep the five-game series.

Now we have made the four-hour trip up to Santa Maria in "Casper," the short white school bus. The skipper is too drunk to drive home, so that falls on my shoulders. No problem.

Back in Orange County. We have a game on Wednesday night in San Bernardino. The game is against the Athletes in Action squad, a Christian-oriented baseball team. I'm at forty-two wins in a row now, and I get the ball for this matchup.

I pitch eight innings, strike out thirteen batters, walk none, and lose 10–9 on nine unearned runs. These guys that we brought out here tonight can't catch or throw. We make nine errors in the game. The streak is stopped at forty-two.

The summer is moving pretty fast, and it is time for the NBC league playoffs. We should win it, but we will see.

We have an older former major leaguer who plays with us from time to time. He is still pretty good, and he pitches the opener, and we win. I'm up, and I'm facing the San Diego Stars, and they're a damn good team, but alas, they have never beaten me.

There are lots of ex-pro ballplayers on this Stars club. I beat them 5–1. The semifinal game is up now, and we are playing the "Goldfield Nuggets" at Redlands College. It is a day game, and it is not going well for us. We are down 8–1 in the seventh inning. Now this is my first year with the skipper, and so far, it has been a good one. But for a man who supposedly had seven PT boats shot out from underneath him, the skipper, well, the skipper is a quitter. We haven't lost that many games since I came on board, and I haven't seen this side of him before although one time before he pulled his team off the field because of an umpire. I mean, that is childish and immature and is not really acceptable, kind of embarrassing, to say the least.

I say to the skipper, "Skip, how about if I coach third for a couple of innings?"

"Okay," he says. "I don't care."

Well, it is getting dark, and there are no lights in this stadium. I take over the coaching duties at third base. And guess what? That is the right guess. I rally the team, and we come back from a pretty good deficit to win the game, 10–9. But the skipper is pissed and pouting. That is not a good sign.

Now we are in the championship game tomorrow, the site to be determined by the commissioner. Oh, and it is his team, the Blue Jays, whom we will be facing. Well, he, the commissioner, calls in the morning, and the game is at some horrible high school field, and it is a five o'clock start.

We show up, and I am starting on the mound. I go one inning, give, and up a home run. This is a hitter's park. I mean, this place is a bandbox. It is tiny and no mound to speak of. I give up a home run on a 0–2 pitch, a bad changeup. Never throw the changeup with a 0–2 count on the hitter—throw the damn ball up and in. No big deal. I can handle this. Wrong! I'm out of the game, and some lefty drug addict is in, and he gives up thirteen runs. We score two. I've always wondered about that game and why the skipper pulled me. Just another one of his hunches.

The A's did qualify for Wichita because we won the league. So the skipper kicks all the veterans off the team, which includes me, the catcher, the big league pitcher, and he takes the team to Wichita, and it is a disaster. He loses two in a row.

So now I have no place to play, and my guy is still out burning up the Texas League. What am I going to do?

Well, the Texas League has wrapped up too. My guy made the all-star team and pitched the game of the season in the league championship, shutting out the Texas Rangers squad 1–0 with sixteen strikeouts. He is now in an extended winter ball "instructional league" in Florida.

A friend who has some kilos calls and asks me if I can sell any of them, or all of them for that matter. Yes, I say, and I take them to Vancouver.

I'm staying with the son and daughter-in-law of the old tugboat captain from Horseshoe Bay. The girl is a firecracker, and she goes off. Cocaine and whiskey are a bad combination, at least for her. The cops come.

Now we are in White Rock, which is right on the border. I have been deported from Canada once already. I book it for the border, leaving my rental car behind. I know the terrain pretty well and make my way to Freedom Park, which is right on the border and cross into the States. There is a Denny's restaurant right there on the border, so I go in and have some coffee.

Well, I decide it is too dangerous to go back to Canada. So I hop the Greyhound to Seattle, tell the rental car place where their car is, and head for Las Vegas. Ah, a nice, peaceful bus ride through Oregon and Northern Nevada to clear my head. I get to Las Vegas and go to my dad's for a few days to relax.

Well, the phone rings, and it is for me. I left my dad's telephone number with the tugboat captain's son as I left. It must be my lucky day. To my surprise, the cops didn't get the stash. It got sold, and they are wiring me the money—totally outrageous.

So I get the money, about four thousand dollars, and I head to the craps table, and I lose about half of it, naturally.

So I then hop a jet and go down to Florida to check on my guy. He is sick as hell with strep throat, and he is flat broke. Time for me to step in. I go find the minor league director, and we have a conversation—okay, I had a conversation, the one-sided kind. The results of which were the player is going home immediately, and he is getting a five-thousand-dollar loan or bonus. "We will see you next spring" was the closing statement.

So I tell my player what transpired, and he says to me, "That's great, but my throat is killing me."

Jack Daniel's to the rescue, a good night's sleep, and the airport the next morning.

Me? Well, I have told one of the outfielders that I would drive to San Diego with him. He was a former first-round draft pick and had lost his bonus money in a high-rise scheme. To make things worse, he just wasn't doing so well in the game. So I have a bag of marijuana, and we head west in his 1968 Volkswagen bug. We make it to San Antonio, where we blow the engine. I'm flying to Vegas. He stays in San Antonio. He grows up to be the general manager of the Oakland A's. So now I guess he is doing pretty well in the game.

I have just returned to Orange County. We get a house. My pitcher is just resting. I go see the skipper as I know that the winter league is just starting.

"God, son, where have you been?"

I'm not sure he could handle the truth, so I just say, "Around. Do you need pitching?"

"Yes," he says, "and we are playing this weekend."

"Okay," I say, "but I am definitely leery."

I have to say, I have seen some pretty strange behavior out of the old guy.

Corky is the skipper's shop guy, manservant, and he is also the team's umpire. That is pretty weird. This guy would do anything for the skipper. I kind of like him too. We go out at night once in a while and have a drink. I have a band playing at a little dive bar. It is harmless fun.

So there is another mechanic who works in the shop, and he is not so friendly. One night, like so many other nights, we are playing pinochle and drinking scotch. My partner is a big Black guy. He was a fullback for the Oakland Raiders, and he has the Super Bowl ring and all. So I have to pee. I go in the back where the restrooms are, and this mechanic follows me into the back and picks a fight with me. A triple left hook later, he is going to the hospital for a hundred stitches, and he is lucky he didn't lose his eye.

The baseball team has gotten stale after the skipper's ill-advised foray to Wichita. One thing, when players at this level lose faith in you, it is hard to reclaim it. And that was exactly what had occurred here. We need a pick-me-up. I have scheduled most of our games. The problem is that we don't have a home field, and I am going to solve that.

After checking around, I come up with a high school field. Buena Park High school, to be exact. It is pretty big for a high school yard four hundred feet to dead center field, and the fences are about twenty feet high chain-link with ivy growing on them, and it is a pretty cool setting, and the dimensions are three-hundred-twenty feet down the lines, and as I have stated, it is four hundred feet to dead center. The playing surface is really good, and for good measure, there is plenty of foul territories, good for pitchers and we can use it for free Saturdays and Sundays. It kind of reminds me of Wrigley Field a little bit with the ivy on the fences and all.

So we are not playing in a league. We are just playing an independent schedule. There are plenty of teams around. One of the reasons we are not playing in a league? The skipper. No one will let him in. With this year closing and me, well, I'm no closer to the big leagues and, more importantly, a job—a job making real money.

My young pitcher is making great strides in baseball. Maybe, just maybe he is going to make the jump from double "A" to the show. Speaking of money, his contract from the Mets has arrived, and it is pathetic although it is for Triple "A." It doesn't offer him much in the way of pay, and what about the five-grand loan we took from the club? Well, he and I argue for a while, and I end the disagreement by saying, "Have I been wrong yet?" I tell him, "Don't sign it. Just send it back," and he does.

About two weeks later, he gets another contract, a split contract with one salary for triple "A" and one for the big leagues with more money and loan forgiveness.

In just five years, he will have gone from doorknob factory employee to college baseball to the major leagues—that is pretty decent, I would say.

Well, he has a good spring but is sent to triple "A" where he will start the season. He is a real phenom, but the Mets have no money in him despite his stellar numbers. You have to remember, baseball is a business. So no matter how good you are doing, there is always a player whom they have invested more money in. So naturally, he gets to go first. One of the problems that arise when you take your girlfriend to your signing instead of your agent.

Right before the strike, we had the owner of the Seattle Mariners over to the shop. We have a switch-hitting outfielder, and they, the Mariners, are interested in him. One of the problems is that for now, baseball is on strike. This guy can't win. He owns Air West, (worst) the airline, and they are on strike too.

So we are telling him about this player, and we mention that he is a switch-hitter. Well, the Mariners's owner says, "We certainly don't need any of those kinds around."

"Um, no, not that kind of switch-hitter. We mean that he bats from both sides of the plate." And I'm thinking, how did this guy become a billionaire?

The baseball club is doing pretty well now, and I'm doing pretty well too. But my pitcher is doing really well. This has been a pretty good year all in all.

It took some time, but I now have the Orange County A's back to where we were before the skipper's insanity boiled up to the surface. I have figured it out. The skipper is crazy.

By the time 1982 rolled in, it was January the 3, to be exact, and we were on the baseball field at the college where we would while away the days until it is time to go to spring training.

OUTLAW LEAGUE

It is the usual list of suspects prospects and players, plus we may have added a few. This could be a good ball team, except we have no catchers. That is me. I catch all the bullpens. My guy first, though, then I usually throw batting practice before hitting fungoes. I'm a regular coach.

Things are moving along, and before you know it, the kid is gone to spring training, and the workouts are over for the most part. The kid has gotten an invitation to Big League Camp. That's outstanding. So I'm just helping run the A's and trying to stay out of trouble. A full-time job for me.

We have a game in Riverside. The skipper arranged it. What a disaster this was! We drove out to Riverside to the park where the game was supposed to be played. It is in a really bad neighborhood. I even say to the skip, "Are you sure we're in the right place?"

"Yes, this is it. I feel good about this one," he states.

Well, that's okay, but I have my suspicions. As we disembark the bus, a group—no, a mob—of Blacks is growing, and they are restless. A few taunts and some bottles are hurled at us, and we are back on the bus. Then a rock comes sailing through the front windshield of the bus.

"Let's go," I say. "No game today."

So we drive back to Santa Ana.

The next day at the office and the phone rings. I answer it. "Is this the baseball team that was in Riverside yesterday?" the voice on the other end of the line asks.

"Yes," I answer.

"Well, your bus ran over my child, and I want five hundred dollars," the voice on the other end says.

"Ma'am," I begin, "and with all due respect, if our bus ran over your child, he would be dead. Stop with the extortion, or I will have you arrested."

That put a stop to that.

The skipper has gotten us a weekend exhibition with the pro team in Ensenada, Mexico. They play in the Pacific Coast League, the Mexican Pacific Coast League, and it is an Easter weekend on top of it. Oh boy, a road trip! Easter weekend, and we're headed to

Mexico. Pretty exciting but not for me. I'm in the doghouse again, so I am not expecting to pitch. No, I will probably just coach a base and drink a lot. I'm only along in case a fight breaks out. We arrive in Ensenada on Saturday at about noon. We are driving in the new motor home "Casper" has been retired. The new motor home isn't new, but it is o us. Wild times are coming. The motor home will eventually be christened the "knuckleball" express. And it was.

We have one nine-inning game on Saturday night, then on Sunday, two seven-inning games. We started the first game, and it goes fairly smoothly. We win although there was one problem during the game, the almost brawl.

Our center fielder homered in his first at bat, so naturally, he gets "drilled" the next time up. Well, this is bullshit, and I let the pitcher know that as I am coaching first base. So the base runner comes to first. He is hurting.

"Rub it off!" I tell him.

"Play ball!" the umpire cries.

Okay. But where is the ball? It is nowhere to be found.

Well, out of the blue, our base runner pulls the ball out from under his armpit and chucks it right at the pitcher.

"We are even!" he shouts.

So after the game, we are out on the town. This ain't Nogales, and this town is jumping. I'm dancing on the stage with the strippers at a strip club. The whole ball club is in the place, and the bouncers can't do a thing about it. One of the outfielders and I then go back to the motor home. It is about two in the morning. There is beer in the motor home, cold beer, and we are drinking beers with some college students.

About four in the morning, the door to the motor home opens, and it is the skipper.

He shouts at us. "What in the hell are you doing?" he asks.

Without missing a beat, I retort, "Skip, you know that the lock on the door is broken." I continued, "And all the equipment is in here, and we are just guarding the equipment and the motor home."

He replies, "Goddamn it, son! I knew I could count on you."

The skipper always called me son, and I am out of the doghouse just like that.

Three or four hours of sleep, I don't think we got that. So it is up at eight o'clock for the team breakfast, and then onto the yard we go.

I'm just vegging in the dugout when the skipper comes up and says to me, "I think that these kids were up drinking all night."

Well, what else are you going to do in Mexico? I am thinking.

And then he continues, "I think you better start the first game." What he really meant was none of these kids can pitch.

So I take the mound, throw my warm-up pitches, and I look into the catcher for the sign. And what did I see? The most bloodshot pair of red eyes I had ever seen peering back at me from behind the catcher's mask. I saw him, the catcher, passed out on the pool slide at three this morning.

This guy, our catcher, is a left-handed hitter, and he can "roll the pole," as they say, and he is an okay receiver, but he can't throw a lick. Have you ever heard the proverb that goes "He couldn't hit a barn door"? In this case, it fits.

I call "timeout." The catcher walks out to the mound.

"Are you as fucked up as you look? I ask him.

"Worse," he says.

Okay, I then tell him, "We are just throwing fastballs in and out. Just move where you want the ball, put the glove up, and I will hit it."

I throw a two-hit shutout. We win the second game too. Time to go home.

So we are all packed up and ready to go. "Mama," the skip's wife, is already gone.

For one thing, she doesn't like riding with the ballplayers. Language is just one obstacle. She's an aristocrat and an heiress, and she abhors swearing, and well, these darn baseball players tend to swear a lot. There is one problem; she has all the money.

Now the skipper knows I am a dealer, and I always have money, and here it comes.

"You got any money, son?"

"Yeah, I say. What's up?"

"Well, we are out of gas, and Mama's gone, and we are stranded."

"No sweat. I've got gas money."

"Well, we have to eat at the border, and that costs too."

"I have about two hundred and fifty dollars. Will that cover it?"

"Yes," he says, and it is onto the Tijuana border, a quick stop at the Bob's Big Boy, and on we go north up the 5 Freeway to Orange County and home.

Chapter Thirteen

Funniest Man Alive

Belushi is dead. John Belushi, maybe the funniest man alive, was found dead in a bungalow in Hollywood. A drug overdose, plain and simple. There was no mystery. No foul play is evident or suspected—just a plain old drug overdose. Still, it is sad because that guy was as funny as they come.

We are playing a game this very night. It's March of 1982, and I am thirty-four years old and not getting any younger.

I have been in Westwood all day, trying to get a passport for my boat salesman buddy. A futile effort is how it would best be described. Anyway, we are playing at Forty-Second and Van Ness. This was basically right in the heart of South Central Los Angeles, Watts. Game time is at 7:00 p.m. I arrived at the ballpark at about 5:30 p.m. Nap? Not in this neighborhood. I'll just listen to the radio. Poor John! He was a real "blues brother."

The team shows up around 6:00 p.m., and it is a typical Orange County A's entry. The white school bus with the A's logo on the side and fifteen lily-white ballplayers on board. It is amazing the games the skipper gets us into.

Sometimes the best and sometimes the worst. His motto is "I will play anybody anywhere, anytime." Like the saying goes, "It was the best of times, and it was the worst of times." This was one of the bad times.

I am pretty sure we are the only White people for ten square miles around. Second of all, this field is a mess, complete with bad lights, gopher holes in the outfield, and a skinned infield.

The mound? What mound? It was as flat as a seven-year-old girl's chest with two pitching rubbers, one at about forty-five feet and then one at the adult regulation of sixty feet six inches.

Tonight, we are playing the Long Beach Red Sox. The manager is a salty old ex-minor leaguer and a World War II guy. I've pitched against them several times and won each outing. He swears he's going to beat us this time. He should. He's got two current Dodgers minor leaguers in the lineup.

This guy always has a lot of Black and Latino players, and they can usually play. He is the one who scheduled this game, and he scheduled it just right. He has this big Dominican who has pitched against us before he has good stuff. I think he is a former big leaguer; at any rate, this guy brings it, flat ground or not.

So in pregame warm-ups, I'm throwing in the outfield, and here it comes.

The skipper comes up to me and says, "Son, I think you better start tonight." His voice was a little gruff this evening.

Oh really? So I'm playing catch and doing my pregame stuff when our second baseman walks up to me and says, "You got a little hop on the fastball tonight, do ya?"

That's a good thing to know because if the ball gets hit tonight, it is going to roll forever, seeing as how there are no fences on this field to stop it.

The game started. I struck out the side, and we get a couple of runs in the first. The second inning is the same, three up three down, and I struck out the side in both innings. As I come off the field at the end of the inning, the skipper says to me, "Sheesh, you must be throwing a hundred miles an hour."

If there's a crummy baseball field around and you need good pitching, I'm your guy. I have pitched on them all.

End of five, we're up, 9–0. I have thirteen strikeouts and two assists on bunt attempts. The skipper in his wisdom pulls me. We win the game, barely by a 10–9 score.

After I came out of the game, an older Black man came over to our dugout. It was open to the rear, just chain-link. He introduces himself as Lou Johnson, and he's a Dodgers scout. I don't know about scouting, but the man could hit. When he played, I remember him as a player, "Sweet Swinging Lou."

He says to me, "How old are you?"

"Thirty-four," I reply.

"And you can still hit 98 on my radar gun? I mean, that's what I gunned you at. If you were ten years younger, I'd sign you right now."

"Thank you," I reply. I guess that's a compliment. I hate it when people talk to me when I'm pitching. We load up the bus, head back to Santa Ana, down a half gallon of scotch, and play pinochle 'til 2:00 a.m.

We are going back to Santa Maria for a weekend series with the Indians. We don't have as good a team as we did last year, and there is absolutely no chemistry on the ball club. We have a bunch of guys with no personality.

The pitching staff is a-shambles. I don't think we will win a game, and lo and behold, I was right. We didn't win one game.

We had this catcher with us who played at Cal State–Fullerton. He is slated to be drafted, but he is also on the national team for the United States, you know, the Olympics. Well, he is a prankster. I hate pranksters. His thing is to get a wad—a big wad—of chewing tobacco going in his mouth, and then he will deposit it in some unsuspecting player's ear. I don't know what makes people act like this, but I know what it is called, "bullying." And I won't and don't put up with it for one instant.

Well, I am sitting next to him in the dugout. He spits not in my ear but on my shoes, then he gets up and moves. In a few minutes, I get up and go to the bat rack. I select a nice wooden Louisville slugger and proceed to shatter the bat right over his head against the dugout wall. That put a stop to his spitting, at least on me.

Well, it has been a pretty embarrassing weekend as we lose all the games by huge scores. Time to go home. We are driving along in the motor home. The skipper is at the helm, and he is pissed. It is a pretty somber ride. What else could go wrong?

We get just south of Los Angeles, and the motor starts cutting out. It is the fuel pump that is failing. We have to make it to Santa Ana.

"Son, is there any scotch on board?"

"Yeah, Skip. We have two gallons."

"Well then, get the cowling off and the air cleaner off and start pouring."

Well, I will tell you what, in an emergency, scotch will work. We belched and farted and backfired the last twenty-five miles, but we made it.

So it is now the summer and time for the NBC tournament, and we win it, but the skip declines the invitation to go to Wichita.

I understand why. It is plain and simple. We don't have the funds and really don't have the team even though we won the tournament, and after last year's fiasco, well, let's just say, no! So we just finish out the summer playing exhibitions.

Winter ball starts, and we are in a league in the Inland Empire. That is San Bernardino and Riverside counties. They are really big on baseball and have some damn good teams. Me? I'm just kicking back, selling a little pot, and being mellow, old age and all.

The kid is home from triple "A," after he got a late-season call-up to the big leagues. He got a major-league call-up and is a cinch to start next year at the major-league level.

The Mets want him to go to Puerto Rico for winter ball. We talk about it and decide that he is still young and needs some recovery time at some point. So we decide that it is okay for him to go and pitch but only until December. The money is too good to pass up.

Now baseball, the major leagues, are not doing that well. The strike really hurt, and the fans have been pretty unforgiving. Baseball has pretty much been the same game for decades. But lately, it has undergone some drastic rule changes, most notably the "designated hitter" rule. But what are they going to do now to reinvent the game? I know, more offense is what we need. Let's make the game longer and more boring, and we will sell more beer. After all, that's what these owners nowadays are—just the sellers of beer and hot dogs and nachos. I go to the ballpark for work. But if I was a fan, I'd go to the ballpark to see the game.

The players were willing to do their fair share. They started juicing. You know, using steroids or performance-enhancing drugs (PEDs). Greenies are a thing of the past. Hell, I heard that one team had a big bowl of prednisone just sitting out in the training room.

One might ask, Is that even legal? We are going to find out. No, they are not legal. So that starts the cat-and-mouse game between the players who try to "mask" their use of these steroids and PEDs and the owners who try to catch them, but not really.

The only problem is that the owners in their own corrupt, greedy fashion do not want to catch the offenders. Baseball is back now, and they are lining their pockets with the fans' hard-earned dollars.

Now I'm a mess with no winter workout partner. What to do? I'm living with my boat salesman buddy in Costa Mesa, doing odd jobs and selling a little marijuana.

We, my boat salesman buddy and I, are in solar energy now. We are involved with the energy-saving products project and solar panels that generate hot water. We can do them commercially for car washes, restaurants, and apartment buildings. This is a pretty big deal, and we now own the energy-saving product's end of the business.

The Southern California gas company is buying hot water, heater blankets, and we are selling them. The executives, the buyers, love fishing and baseball. So I send the kid out fishing with them, and we get the contract to supply hot water blankets to all Southern California through the Southern California gas company. The other part of the business, the energy-saving products, has to do with light bulbs and low-flow showerheads.

So my boat buddy in his wisdom gives thirty thousand dollars' worth of product to the Crystal Cathedral in Garden Grove. They then sold it directly to their parishioners, and then they forgot to pay us. We thought it was a donation they finally tell us.

So the solar panels are the most intriguing deal by far. It was brought to us by some guy from Chicago. He raised four million dollars through a tax shelter. Two hundred and fifty thousand went as a donation to the governor's race. He could approve the tax break that we need to get rich. We would literally own our own utility company selling hot water, and that would be so cool.

Well, it is six months to the election, so the guy who garnered all the investment funds invests some of the money marked for the solar project into the construction of a hotel down in Mexico. What could go wrong, right?

The Mexican builders built a quarter of the hotel, and guess what? The builders are out of money, but another influx of cash will get the hotel finished. Well, that didn't happen, and he lost the money. Fortunately for him, he was killed in a helicopter crash shortly thereafter. His death probably saved us a lot of legal wrangling.

So the boat salesman is a big fisherman, and that makes sense. A few years ago, he bought into a house in Cabo San Lucas. Well, things went south, money-wise, and he didn't pay his fair share; in fact, he didn't pay anything. He had no money and was doing weekends in the Orange County jail.

Then just like that, things changed. The Baja coast got hammered by a hurricane. So we took the company cargo truck, loaded it with every household item you could need, and set off for "Cabo." That's one nasty drive. We made it in twenty-four hours, a two-car caravan, and my pal's partner is in the lead in his pickup truck.

This guy is a specimen. He is about six feet two and weighs about 235 pounds. He is a load and an ex-Navy SEAL to boot. He, the SEAL, is pretty well-known in Cabo San Lucas. He was the guy who set all the buoys that you tie your boat to. You see, they have no docks or piers in Cabo San Lucas. You have to park your boat offshore and use a skiff to come ashore.

We get to Cabo and unload the goods. I have a half ounce of blow that I want to sell. It just so happens that the Rolling Stones are in Cabo, and one of them is getting married at the time.

I gave the cocaine to a friend, and he purportedly went to the wedding. Me? I took the money and drove home alone. Well, two days after I leave and get safely through the Sonoran Desert, the Navy SEAL drowns, and my boat buddy loses the house and everything in it. The drowning wasn't unexpected as the diver had been warned about diving. The doctors said he had too many years of Navy "hard hat" diving, and he was vulnerable to decompression.

So the year is about to turn, and it has been a pretty decent year for me and my pitcher, who is home from Puerto Rico, and it is two weeks off and well-deserved at that.

Chapter Fourteen

Boat People

The year is 1983, January 2, and we are on the baseball field right where we belong, doing what we do. The year 1982 finished with a bang, and we even had a little New Year party. Now we are pretty conservative in our lifestyle, but what the hey?

We got a keg of beer and an ounce of pot. I rolled it all up and a quarter ounce of cocaine and then we just let it all hang out all night long. It was a pretty rousing night. About three o'clock, I heard one of the housemates upstairs in bed, and he was saying, "Please, God, if you let me come down, I'll never do it again." Well, we all know that's a lie, and he was just fine.

You have to have money to run a baseball team. So the skipper tells me about his building prowess. He, the skipper, has gotten himself into a building project in Los Angeles. Well, that's not unusual, but the project will fall through, like they always do. That's one thing about the skipper. He talks a good game, but when it comes time to deliver, well, that's another story.

So he comes back to the shop after a meeting, and he has this young guy with him—another investor—in the project.

So the young guy's an entrepreneur, or anything for money as I call it. The entrepreneur is at a bar in Newport Beach one night, and some guys tell him about a freighter filled with Colombian pot, and they need to get it unloaded.

So he owns a sailing club in Newport Beach, and he knows a lot of "boat" people. He tells the guys who have the freighter that he is the man who can get the freighter unloaded.

He gets a powerboat, and they set a course to meet the freighter. They cast off for the big off-load, a ton of Colombian pot, they find the freighter and unload it. The guys that own the powerboat are pretty persuasive, and they talked the freighter's crew into coming ashore for a party.

Now when they get onshore, there are about fifty federal agents waiting for them. They're busted. We read about it in the *Los Angeles Times* the next day.

The baseball team is playing again. It is the first week in January. We have a doubleheader out in Ontario. So we load the motor home up the "knuckleball express," as it was so aptly tagged.

We head east on the 91 Freeway to State Route 74 and onto Ontario. Well, we are cruising along on the 74 State Highway when it happens.

We are about halfway to Ontario when we smell smoke. The smoke is coming from underneath the cowling that covers the engine. The skipper pulls the motor home over to the side of the road, and we all start bailing.

I was a paratrooper in the army. One night, we were on a jump, and we emptied a C-130 in thirty-two seconds, a division record, and I will tell you, we cleared that motor home faster than thirty-two seconds.

Where's the skip? Oh shit! He is still in the burning motor home. The brave captain going down with the ship? Not today. I go to the driver's window and pull him out. You okay, Skip?

So now a California Highway Patrol vehicle—no, two vehicles pull up—the first cruiser is driven by a lady officer.

The skipper says to her, "Ma'am, I think your car is a little too close to the burning motor home."

She replies that she has been a patrol officer for eight years, and she knows what she is doing, thank you very much.

Well, while she is investigating the fire, all the paint on the front of her car melts. She is pissed—oh, and no baseball today.

Now another friend of mine, a Mexican and a ballplayer, has been named the manager of a team in Mexico. The team is the Puerto Pinasco Tiburones (Sharks), and they play in the Norte de Sonora League. Puerto Pinasco is located right at the top of the Gulf of California or the Sea of Cortez, depending on if you're Mexican or American.

"Would you like to pitch for me down in Mexico?"

"How much? I ask.

"Fifteen hundred dollars, US, a month. Plus room and board."

Why not? I think. I am in.

We travel down to Mexico and arrive safely in Puerto Pinasco. We start workouts the next day, except this manager can't do pregame.

There is another small problem. An ex-Padres big leaguer is down here, and he has been promised the manager's job also. Uh-oh, we have a conflict, and the owner of the team is just an all-out clown.

We make it through the first few days okay. It comes time for me to throw a bullpen, and the catcher has no shoes—he is barefooted. The manager and owner are out too to see me throw. The owner wanted to see what he was buying, I guess. Fifteen hundred dollars is a lot of money down here. You see, the fifteen hundred dollars is about twice what anyone else is making, including the ex-Padre.

It just so happens that there are about ten to fifteen kids sitting on an eight-foot fence to watch me throw.

"Would you like some cleats?" I ask the catcher.

"No," he says. "I'm fine."

Well, he was fine until the moment I threw my first curveball to him. It broke straight down and got him right smack on the big toe of his right foot. The toe is broken. The kids fall off the fence from laughing. One pitch and I've wiped out the bullpen catcher and half of the fan base.

Two days later, the Nogales squad is in for an exhibition game. I am on the mound. The owner wants to see what he is paying for. The first guy up hits a grounder to the shortstop, and he lets it go right through his legs.

The next batter comes up to the plate, and he hits a lazy fly ball to left field, a "can of corn" as they say. This is where we have a Black kid playing, and he was just released by the St. Louis Cardinals. The fly ball is hit right to him. He doesn't even have to move. He drops the ball.

It is the bottom of the first inning, and I have no outs and runners on first and second base. Now the big ex-Padre is playing first base. He once hit five home runs and had nine runs batted in, in a doubleheader in San Diego. He had a little nose problem—cocaine.

Before I ever delivered another pitch to the plate, I picked off both of the runners. Then I struck out the next guy. The first baseman says to me, "I have never seen that done before," referring to the pickoffs.

"Gotta control the base paths," I tell him.

It is a week later, and we are playing in Nogales. The big first baseman, hits a towering home run to center field. The next time he comes up, he gets drilled, and I go to the plate and get him.

We have just finished a road trip. It was about eight days long, and I won two games. When we get back, I am informed that I was released before we went on the road trip. Funny, no one said a word to me. Maybe I was allowed to go on the road trip because one of the other American pitchers on the team got drunk and was thrown in jail. Who knows? In my frustration, I rearranged the owner's office before I left.

After that experience, I am back with the A's, from one crazy team to another. We picked up a new player. He is a former first-round pick of the Texas Rangers, and he has been around a few years. It is weird, but his father hired me when I worked at the Ford assembly plant. He was the headman in the human resources department.

The player is an outfielder. He can run okay, throws okay, but he can't hit. One thing he does have, though, is great drug connections. We become friends although he doesn't play much baseball for the A's.

So it is February now. The young pitcher has gone to spring training, Big League Camp, and he has a real shot to make the big league team. He throws well, but he starts the season at triple "A" bummer.

The A's have a day game today. It is in Tijuana. I don't pitch, but I pinch-hit. We win, and it is another long drive home, but at least the skipper has gas money.

We are playing in Santa Maria this weekend. It was different now than before. Still, this was a great place to play baseball. We don't have a great ball club right now. We have played here before and did pretty well, once. This was a tough place to play.

We lose the opener on Friday night. I'm pitching the Saturday game. It starts okay, but in the second inning with one out, the batter hits a roller to second, and the ball goes right through the second baseman's legs for an error.

The next batter up throws his bat at the first pitch. It was a hit-and-run. Well, the runner didn't run, and now this USC college kid has to come out to the mound to get his bat with me berating him the whole time. So "Play ball!" the umpire cries out. I am on the rubber in the set position when the runner takes off for second base. I step back, turn inside, and feed my second baseman the ball. He then tags the runner, and he is out. Not so fast, the home plate umpire has called a balk. He called the balk because I didn't throw the ball to first base first. I stepped straight back, breaking contact with the pitching rubber, and at that point, I became an infielder.

Look at the fucking rule book, jackass! Any Little League umpire knows that this was not a balk. The call stands, and I am furious.

Now I pitch my best when I'm in a controlled rage, and I'm there right now. The skip lifts me. This makes me even madder. It was a long ride home, and we didn't win a game.

Well, things pass, and we are playing an exhibition game at Long Beach State College. They have won their conference and want to play a practice game before the national tournament starts. It is to be a two o'clock "Huego," and I am on the bump.

I go six, give up one hit, a home run on a 0–2 pitch. The catcher for Long Beach State took a ninety-plus fastball out of the catcher's glove and deposited it over the right-field fence in the fourth inning. Damn good piece of hitting.

Now I open the seventh with a single. The pitcher, the dumbass that he was, tries to pick me off. The first baseman then steps on my hand, and I have a hole in it. No biggie. I can finish. But no, not today, the skip has another plan, and he pulls me. We win anyway.

Now it is time for the NBC tournament, and we don't have that good a team, and the team chemistry is terrible. Somehow, we make it to the championship game. I am good to go, but the skipper has other plans, a junior college pitcher. He gives up fifteen runs in five innings, and we lose.

Meanwhile, my pitcher is in the big leagues now after a June call-up, and he is making the best of it, and he is making the big bucks now, and it is so well-deserved.

Now we learn the real lesson of professional baseball. Getting to the big leagues isn't so hard. It is staying there that is difficult. I mean, you constantly have to reinvent yourself. It is difficult. What I mean is that most players have raw talent, but the finesse, well, that takes time.

It is now September, and winter ball has started. We have a pretty good winter squad. A team called the California Red Sox called today, and they want a game. I have never heard of them. They have a field for the game, and it is off the 5 Freeway. I've seen the field before, many times, but I have never played there.

Well, this is a nice field, but it is tiny, a real bandbox if you know what I mean. It is 390 feet to dead center and 300 feet down the lines.

When the opposing team shows up, it is easy to see why they picked this field. These guys are huge, each, and there are at least fifteen of them. And to boot, they have all played pro ball. Hell, one guy hit thirty-five home runs for the Cleveland Indians last year.

So the game began, and the other dugout is laughing it up—oh, and there is a faint odor in the air.

"Son, is that marijuana?" the skip asks me.

"Maybe," I say.

He, the skipper, then starts some eighteen-year-old left-hander who hasn't ever pitched and who does not want to be out there. His dad is making him pitch, and his dad is a contractor, and the skipper is doing some business with him, so the kid gets to pitch. Bullshit! One the of things that I dislike about the skipper.

The kid walks, the bases loaded, and the thirty-five homer guy is up. The skipper makes a trip to the mound. The kid says he has a sore arm—more bullshit! So the skipper puts me in the game, and I am pissed, and I told you already, I love to pitch in a controlled rage. I fan the next three hitters. My fastball and slider both have the hop tonight; in other words, I'm on.

We have a Black guy playing first base tonight, and it is his first time playing with the A's. So about the fifth inning, the Black guy who is playing with us for the first time starts bad-mouthing my pitching. What the fuck? This is this guy's first game with us and his last. The next inning, I get a comebacker and the throw to first, and the ball has a little giddy-up on it. That shuts him up. I go eight innings, strike out thirteen, including the thirty-five homer guy three times. I hat-tricked him.

Now it was the bottom of the ninth, and we are leading, 3–0. In his wisdom, the skipper brings in some guy from Cal State–Fullerton, and as I have said, we are leading, 3–0. He walks the bases loaded and throws the ball out of the yard. We lose, 4–3.

After the game, the thirty-five homer guy walks up to me and says to me, "I don't remember your name, but I have seen that slider before."

It is a long bus ride back to Santa Ana.

My pitcher is back home now, and we have the normal routine—going up early, five-mile run, calisthenics, then breakfast. Next, we go to the beach for a few hours. He plays beach volleyball. I have mixed feelings about this activity. My main concern is the stress on his arm. And there has also been quite an influx of people into our social circle, and not all of it is good.

One guy is a Canadian. He is in the oil and gas business. He sells shares in drilling projects. He is from Edmonton, and he was, according to him, a backup quarterback for the Edmonton Eskimos in the Canadian Football League. I have never heard of him, and I lived in Canada for four years.

We are throwing a football around when my pitcher reminds me not to turn this guy's fingers back.

The beach is pretty mellow, but there is always one. My pitcher's girlfriend is at the beach with us today. She's eighteen, and she also his stepsister—questionable, I know.

He has been with her for a few years. She is a looker and a cheerleader at her high school.

So anyway, some yahoo is on the beach with his camera, and he wants to take her picture. Apparently, I am in the way of his shot. After exchanging compliments, he starts to approach us. He is a pretty good-sized fellow. He walks up to me and starts to grab me by the throat. Bad idea. I hit him with a six-inch straight right hand. He is out cold. We pack up and leave. The days turn to weeks, and it is Christmas and then New Year's.

The year is now 1984, and it is an "Orwellian" year. George Orwell once wrote a novel about 1984 and big brother. His prognosis, well, it is oh so close. The nanny state is growing.

I have been doing a little business with the outfielder, whose father worked at Ford. He is a good kid. But he is just so sloppy and careless, like stopping to make a phone call at a phone booth and leaving his identification and half an ounce of cocaine in the phone booth.

Well, it wouldn't be long before he got busted with ten pounds of cocaine. That got him a ten-year sentence in the state penitentiary. I've been in prison. I know this kid pretty darned well, and I don't think he can handle ten years. And apparently, I was right because he married the warden's daughter, and that was apparently the get-out-of-jail card he needed.

One of the players on the A's is from Alaska. He graduated from college and was substitute teaching. The only problem is, you get paid when the term is done or some nonsense like that. Anyhow, he is living in the "cave." What is the cave?

The cave is an upstairs dorm in the back of the shop. Anywhere from two to eight ballplayers are living there rent-free, and my Alaskan buddy is one of them. The shop is huge with the business offices up front and the mechanics bay in the rear. I mean, we could actually make money if the skipper cared, but his wife, Mama, is an heiress, so that is all that matters.

She has her own business and an office just down the street, where she provides mailing lists to her clients. Then there is the daughter. The drug addict nightmare from hell. She had to do a pee test, and she knew she was dirty. She was running around the shop, trying to trade sexual favors with the ballplayers for a bag of urine. Real class act.

Then there was Quincey the Dog—the bipolar, half pit bull, half boxer, yes-sir half boxer and half pit bull, and as mean as a rattlesnake.

One day, we had a delivery driver come to the shop to make a delivery. He was a Black man. Well, Quincey attacked him, unprovoked, and the crazy dog had the guy on the ground. He had the guy's foot in his mouth. It is a good thing that guy was wearing steel-toed boots because Quincey ripped one toe right out of the shoe before we got him under control.

Then there was the time he, Quincy, went after the skipper. Well, the skipper got out his .357 Magnum and was going to execute the dog, but the drug addict daughter was shielding the dog from her father's rage.

The final straw came when this crazy animal attacked me. I hit him with a left hook and spun him around in a complete 360-degree circle. Well, he got up, and he shook his head as if to clear out the cobwebs, and then he charged me again. This time, I caught him with an uppercut that caused him to flip head over paws and knocked him completely senseless. He knew he had had enough.

The skipper gave him away the next day. So that's the way that the ball bounced for Quincey.

Chapter Fifteen

Northern Lights

The outfielder, my new buddy and business partner, had a source for bales of marijuana. They were about twenty-five pounds or so, and the quality was good. He also has cocaine and a lot of it. I didn't want to be involved in that, but I knew someone who did, and I introduced them. The cocaine didn't interest me. There was too much violence associated with it.

For example, I had been selling some cocaine lately for a couple of Peruvian surfers.

The problem with the cocaine trade? It was expensive, and the buyer didn't always know what he was getting. You can "cut" it. By that, the supplier mixes nearly pure cocaine with other substances like baby laxatives.

There were different types of "caines": lidocaine, benzocaine, and novocaine. *Don't forget Coca-Cola*. After all, it was, as the advertisements proclaimed, the "real thing."

How did the railroads get built? *Coca-Cola*, that was how. Only a few decades ago when cocaine was legal it was in everything. This including the favorite American beverage *Coca-Cola*, which had a cocaine content of about 20 percent liquid cocaine. In fact, a derivative of the coca leaf continued to be used in the Coke production process.

I had taken a half ounce on the front. That means I didn't pay for the coke. They gave it to me to sell, and I sold it to some bikers from

Garden Grove. They had tried to make it into freebase for smoking. Freebasing or smoking cocaine was the newest fad. A really exhilarating high but also quite addictive. So the user inhales the fumes or smokes the residue left from boiling it with sodium bicarbonate.

Freebasing had become the newest way to get high on cocaine although snorting lines off a mirror or glass surface through a straw or a rolled-up dollar bill was still the most popular way to get cocaine high.

Soon the newest fad for cocaine users became a tiny spoon worn around the neck on a gold chain. The coke spoon signified a person's acceptance of the use of cocaine.

Next, these chemical-processed drug users would be doing the same with crystal methedrine. The world had changed once again and not for the better.

Many lives were ruined. As it turned out, it was not cocaine, but one of the countless other types of caines on the underground market. Needless to say, when the bikers threw the whole half of an ounce into the mix, they were quite disappointed to get just one gram back. It should have yielded almost what they put in. They were pissed, to say the least. I gave the bikers their money back. It was bunk coke.

Now I have to go and give the bad news to the Peruvians, and this is what I hate about drug dealing. So I go over to their apartment, and to my surprise, when I get to the apartment, there was a thirtysomething guy at the apartment too. I walked in, and this neatly dressed, well-groomed man was wearing a cardigan sweater with a big bulge under it. Gun! I immediately pinned him against the wall. I am not letting him pull that gun out. So we struggle a little, but I eventually overpower him. I reach inside his sweater and grab the gun. The pistol is a Colt military .45. *What the fuck I think to myself?* I clear the weapon and disassemble it, then spread it around the living room.

"Let's talk," I say, and they agree.

After a few tense minutes, we get the mess straightened out. It turns out the older guy is with the Peruvian government and he has a diplomatic passport. He is the smuggler. How hard can it be to smuggle with a diplomatic passport?

Now I'm not burned out on baseball, but I'm in the doghouse with the skip. It is not that I am in the doghouse. I just don't like the way he treats some players, and the cave, that's a different story altogether.

The guy from Alaska has managed to get kicked off the team. I let him stay with me and support him until he gets paid, and he goes home, but we stayed in touch.

You know, it was that time of the year once again, and the pitcher is off to spring training, and I have no place to play.

I could play for the A's if I was willing to put up with the skip's bullshit. So I call my guy in Alaska and tell him, "I'm coming up, and I am bringing a bale with me. Can you find me a place to stay?"

Yes was his answer. I am back in the smuggling business.

It was cold, colder than I have ever been. I had the chills for two days, but I was in Anchorage. I had sent the pot by airfreight ahead of my flight. There would be nothing to worry about. I would pick it up as soon as I could.

I met with my baseball friend, and he introduced me to a friend of his.

This guy had lived in Anchorage for his whole life. He was a native Alaskan, and his family was there when Anchorage was founded.

He was a senior at the University of Alaska and played on the hockey team. He had a house with a basement, and I rented the basement for a quarter pound of pot per month. That was a deal, so I rented a car. And I drove to the airport and picked up my luggage, I mean marijuana.

As it turned out, I was introduced to another guy who lived way out on the Kenai Peninsula. He was also a baseball player and had played college ball at Fordham University in New York. In addition, he could move some pot as well.

I now had two movers in different parts of Alaska and no conflict, so far. But that would change. I moved the product in about five or six days and flew back to Orange County to reload. This was going to be a sweet year. I was making almost a thousand dollars on a kilo.

I had made a couple of runs, and they all went smooth. I had not had any real problems except for one—and it was a big one. The guy whose house I was renting was not the problem. It was his girlfriend. She has a problem—cocaine.

On my fourth trip up to Alaska, I came up almost six thousand dollars short. I moved the next month. I still did business with him, but his girlfriend was out.

I heard they had a baby boy who died a few months later of sudden infant death syndrome. I thought the evidence pointed in another direction, but without an investigation by authorities exactly where, that would go remained to be seen.

I moved to a little rental house. I kept to myself pretty much, except for a foray out to Chilkoot Charlie's once or twice a week. Hands down, it was probably the best bar on the West Coast. I had spent many a night in that place drinking my blues away. The place was a two-story bar with bands upstairs and down. It was always packed.

The year was cruising along, and the pitcher was due to arrive back home in Southern California. That meant my working vacation in the long summer days of Alaska would be wrapping up. I made one more trip this year. I got a couple of bales, and I break them down, weighing out quarter-pound bags and pack them in footlockers.

Then to the airport. I catch a flight to Anchorage after dropping the goods at the airfreight terminal. Then I hop on an airliner, but we only make it to Seattle. Engine trouble.

This is the first time I have ever experienced difficulty with an airliner. We will have to stay in Seattle overnight. Bummer. I guess airplanes do crash once in a while.

I have been flirting with this little honey on the flight. As it would happen, she was sitting right next to me. They, the airlines, can only get so many hotel rooms, and to my surprise, she asks me, "Do you want to share a room?" They probably have two beds. So we share a room, and it had two beds. I didn't get any sleep, but I did get the phone number where she is staying in Anchorage. But it was a phony. *I feel so used but in a good way.*

So the baseball playoffs are in full swing. I am sitting in a bar in Downtown Anchorage having a beer. The Kansas City Royals and the Detroit Tigers are about to tip-off. The regular-season major league umpires are out on strike. Last year, it was the players who struck baseball. Unions? What are they good for?

Major league baseball was using replacement umpires who will be calling the games. Last winter, we, the A's, got introduced to this umpire who had umpired in the American League for fifteen years. We met him one night in Escondido. We were playing a doubleheader at the high school there. They had lights, so it was a night game. The Escondido team is in first place by a half game over the A's. We have a guy who pitched triple "A" for the Royals who is starting the first game, and despite giving up two home runs to the same guy, we win.

The second game begins, and the skipper starts this little lefthander over me. That was a dumb move. But as luck would have it, he gets in a collision at first base in the first inning and his ribs are bruised. He is out, and I am in.

Now because this is a doubleheader, the games are only seven innings long. I come in with two outs in the first and a man on first base. I immediately punch out the batter on three pitches. I'm on. I strike out fifteen and throw a shutout. I hat tricked the guy who hit the two long balls in the first game.

So we head to the nearest watering hole to celebrate our victories, and the skipper invites the umpire.

"Man," he says to me, "you could have won the World Series tonight. You have got some damn good stuff. How come you aren't pitching in the big leagues?"

"That's the sixty-four-thousand-dollar question," I say back to him.

So he starts hanging around the shop a couple of days a week and playing pinochle.

I guess he had a little bit of a racist attitude, but more importantly, he used a "balloon" chest protector, and major league baseball was switching to the under-the-shirt "armor" protective gear for its umpires. Either way, he was out of professional baseball, and he was running an umpiring school in San Diego.

So we are playing pinochle regularly, and he is partnered with the catcher from the Tigers. No big deal.

Fast-forward to the 1984 major league baseball playoffs between the Kansas City Royals and the Detroit Tigers, and the umpires are on strike, and they are using replacement umpires as previously stated. Guess who's behind the dish? That's right, the man from San Diego. And who's playing third base for the Tigers? That's right, his pinochle partner from the shop in Santa Ana.

So the game begins, and the pitcher for the Royals, a big right-hander who won twenty games this year during the regular season, is on the mound.

The former catcher and now third baseman is at the plate.

"Strike one! Strike two!" the umpire bellows as a pair of ninety-five-mile-per-hour fastballs sail right down the middle of home plate.

This is going to be a quick at bat. A third screaming fastball is launched by the Royals hurler, and it is right down the middle, the middle of the plate.

"Ball one!" the umpire cries out.

Now I'm not sure, but I think that the umpire said something to the batter after that pitch.

He probably said, "You better swing that fucking bat!"

And he did.

He dribbled a ninety-nine hopper through the left side of the infield for a base hit, and the rest is history. He got a bunch of hits, including the home run, that propelled the Detroit Tigers to victory over the San Diego Padres in the World Series of 1984.

Racism was as prevalent in baseball as it was anywhere in society, and it can overwhelm you. It goes both ways. Blacks hated Whites and Hispanics and Latin Americans too. In short, everyone hates everyone. It can be fierce, but on the field, you have to play together.

Rumor has it that one time, a big Black slugger came to the plate in a game this particular umpire was umping. The first thing the umpire says was, "It smells like shit around here." That's the kind of thing that we really don't need. So after fifteen years, they, major league baseball, said goodbye to him. I am not particularly a racist; rather, I am an equal-opportunity hater. I hate all races equally, and by the same token, I respect all races equally. So I handle it by just not talking with people I don't like.

So this is my last trip to the north country, Alaska, and once again, it is cold. I'm not going to miss the cold, I will tell you that.

So I get my product distributed, and I am just waiting for the payoff. I go to Chillkoots and I'm standing outside the bar, and right across the street is the Alaskan Bush Club, a fully nude bar. I don't do strip clubs or do prostitutes.

One of the girls had just gotten off work from the strip club, and she walks across the street, and she strikes up a conversation with me. Well, one of the life lessons that I have learned is about women.

If a woman talks to you, she is interested. But if she touches you, she wants you. That's called chemistry, magnetism. The next thing you know, we get a motel room. All night long, and the next day, I am a noodle.

There are a lot of women in Anchorage more than you would think. And they are all prime specimens too. No slouches in Alaska. I mean, the sex trade is pretty heavy here, and bordellos are legal. A decent-looking woman can make a hundred grand in about ten months, a good nest egg.

I guess it was in about June, or maybe it was in July, the guy whom I'm renting from has a slow-pitch softball team. They have entered a tournament down south in Soldotna.

That's a fishing town in Southern Alaska, where the crab and cod boats go out to make their catches, commercial fishing. It was good money but is also dangerous as all get out.

So I go with them to the tournament.

I meet this guy in a bar, and we are talking, and he asks me, "Ever done any panning?"

"Gold panning? No," I say.

The next day, he takes me gold panning in a stream just outside town. He, not I, finds about a half of an ounce nugget of gold—of all the luck.

So back in town, we win the softball tournament and are about to head back to Anchorage when I run into him. The kid from Seattle, whom I set free a few years ago—what an oddity—has been working on the fishing boats and keeping his nose clean. That was great news.

So it is November now. I'm home and conducting workouts with my pitcher although a few changes have come about. He has bought a condominium and has moved in, and his sister is living with him. The girlfriend is gone.

Now that I'm not smuggling, I am back at the office with the Orange County A's. It is the usual weekend doubleheaders and games during the week. We have the catcher with the Detroit Tigers playing with us still. I know him. We went to the same high school. It is amazing how players wind up playing on the A's.

"So, son, where have you been?" asks the skip.

"I have been just traveling around," I say.

He doesn't know it, and I'm not telling him, but I made almost eighty thousand dollars from my activities in Alaska. Of course, I spent half of that on whiskey and women, and the rest, well, guess I just blew it. Oh, and Alaska is as expensive as hell.

I mean, don't get me wrong, Alaska? Well, it is beautiful. I saw moose, the aurora borealis, salmon swimming upstream. It was spectacular. I met this one guy who had served two tours in Vietnam. He was a hunting guide. He was taking a group out to Kodiak Island to hunt bears. "Did I want to come along?" Well, at first thought, what an adventure, and then I had second thoughts. Those bears are not bothering me. Just let them be, so no bear hunt for me.

It is now late September, and I have told everyone that this is it for me. I am retiring. There is one person, though, that I really like and sort of trust, the kid from the Kenai Peninsula. I ask him if he wants to continue the business. He says that he does. I tell him I will airfreight bales to him at a slightly discounted price. When we have done a few shipments, he can come down to Southern California and buy the product and ship it to himself, and so it is agreed.

I send him the first bale. He gets it no problem. I never hear from him again. No good deed goes unpunished, and nothing is going to be okay.

Chapter Sixteen

Ghost Bus

The year is 1985, January 2, and we're on the baseball field, where we belong. This is going to be a banner year. I can feel it with the kid now set to be in the major leagues. I guess he really isn't a kid anymore. He is ready to go to Florida for spring training, so I take him to the airport, and he is off to spring training. He is invited to the Big League Camp, and even better, he has a guaranteed spot on the big league roster.

What's really cool is that I got the kid his first endorsement contract last winter. I mean, he has a glove and shoe contract, but this is an outside endorsement, and it was with Wham-O, the Hula-Hoop- and Frisbee-making company.

Last year, while he was pitching for the Tides, at triple "A," Tidewater, the young hurler, was out on the beach. He was throwing a Frisbee on the beach when an AP photographer saw him throw the Frisbee with his foot and snapped "the shot."

The photo went national, and we got a promotional contract. The company Wham-O made up these miniature Frisbees with his signature emblazoned on them in the Mets colors of course. Everyone was happy.

Then came the trade to the Cardinals, so they switched to red for the Cardinal colors. But alas, the baseball would come to an end after the Cardinal trade. But it was a heck of a run while it lasted.

The skipper, meanwhile, is running the A's, and he has bought a professional baseball team. The Idaho Falls A's. No, seriously. This is a team that plays in the Pioneer League, which is a rookie league.

"By god, son, you are going to be the pitching coach!"

"Um, no, I'm not. This is a league full of eighteen- to twenty-year-olds, and babysitting is what it amounts to. No thanks. No, I will stay here and run the shop, the A's, and look after Mama. So it is settled I'm staying put."

The pioneer league was a bus league, no airplanes, no trains. It is a bus league, so Mama buys the skipper a used Greyhound bus, and it is off to Idaho Falls he goes. With him are half of the A's who are too old to play in the rookie league, so do you see where this is going?

Next, the skip buys a house with a big basement, another cave, and this is where the players will live.

The next problem pops up when the city wants the skip to post a "performance" bond for the season in case there are any damages, charges, or, heaven forbid, unpaid bills.

"No problem," the skip said. "I will post my gold mine in Colombia."

"I am sorry, but that will not suffice," said the mayor.

The battle lingers on.

The skipper has promised the field manager's job to two different people, which is crazy because we all know who is going to manage the team, the skipper.

The situation comes to a head one night. One of the men that the skipper has promised the manager's job too has found out that he may not get the job, and he was pissed, really pissed.

So he comes to the house, and he and the skipper have a shouting match, which is okay because the players are there. So he leaves, and the players all retreat to the basement to get some sleep.

Well, the fired manager goes to his car, gets an aluminum baseball bat and returns to the house, and knocks on the door. When the skipper opens the door, he is hit with the bat. He managed to get his arm up to deflect the blow, but in the aftermath, he has a broken arm, a compound fracture no less.

To the hospital emergency room they go. Now the skipper is one tough son of a bitch. No anesthesia for this man—no, sir.

"Scotch," he says. "Bring me some scotch," and so they did.

While the skip sips on his scotch, the doctor sets his arm complete with a few screws.

Now the A's are doing just fine. We are playing at the local college—that, by the way, were never before allowed us to use the field.

So I have just one problem. I have a catcher who can't catch. And he is a whiner. He is one of the skip's boys. I would tell him to pound sand if it was my call. We were playing a Sunday game, and it is in about the fourth inning, and I have this boob behind the plate. There is a runner at second, and the batter singles to left field. The runner is trying to score. The outfielder fields the ball and unleashes a mighty throw to the plate. Now the catcher is out in front of the plate, and he is in a pretty good position, but he has the mask on. Good thing too because he never gets a glove on the throw, and it hits him right in the face. That's it, you're out of the game before you get killed.

It is Monday. I get to the shop at about seven thirty. Mama shows up just minutes later. That's unusual because she usually goes straight to her shop at around nine. She tells me that the skipper has a broken arm. She wants me to get on a flight to Idaho Falls, get the bus and the skipper, and bring them home.

"No players are to be on the bus. Do you understand?"

"Yes, ma'am," I reply.

Well, I didn't know the whole story yet, but I do know the skip is not clumsy.

So I touch down in Idaho Falls, and the skip meets me at the airport. We get some dinner and a drink, and I hear the story firsthand. First thing when we get back to the house, I confront the players. They all know me and my reputation, and they are scared to death of me. I tell them two things: one, the team is folding, and two, you have to make your own way back home or wherever you are going, but you are not on the bus, Mama's orders.

So I spend the next day getting the bus ready for the journey to Santa Ana. Fuel is the most important thing because we have no fuel permit, which means we are not stopping at any weight stations. We will just run them.

Now the weight stations are also the "port of entry" for each state, and by law, if you have a commercial vehicle, you are supposed to stop at each one and show your papers. Papers? We don't need any stinking papers!

Cops like to hang around baseball teams. I don't know why. Most of them can't play, and this situation is no different. So this Idaho State Trooper, who has been hanging around the team, stops by the house, supposedly to say "adios," a goodbye meeting. It is the last night in Idaho Falls for the skip, so he comes by under the pretext of saying goodbye. He is a big guy, probably six feet two, and he weighs about 220 pounds. We get into a spirited discussion.

Some of the players have been talking to the ex-manager, and they have told him that I was coming and that I was a Vietnam badass and I was coming to kill the bat swinger.

Well, he goes to the police with this information. So this cop seems to know a little about me, a little more than he should.

I tell him, "I am there to get the skip and the bus, and we are leaving tomorrow morning."

"With that said, anyone, and that includes you, who would try to harm this old man will pay a heavy price."

And now with that having been said, "I'm going to ask you to leave," and so he did.

Well, it turns out he had a SWAT team surrounding the house and they had evacuated the neighborhood. He thought that not only was he going to entrap me, but he was also going to get Mama too. The charge was going to be conspiracy to commit murder for hire. What a giant red-nosed bozo the clown he was!

The next morning comes, as they always do, and the Greyhound was heading south on Interstate 15. Next stop, Santa Ana.

About ten o'clock at night, we hit a detour. The skip is drinking milk. He is doing this—drinking milk with no scotch because "calcium" is what you need to heal broken bones, he tells me. And me? Well, I have a case of Heinekens I am working on.

I take the detour, and it is a rough one. A two-lane road with no lighting. We pass through a small town, and I mean small, if you blink, you will have missed it. There is a guy hitchhiking."

"What was that?" the skipper asked.

"A hitchhiker," I replied.

"Was he White?" the skip asked.

"Yes," I answered.

"Well, damn it, son. Pick him up."

"Okay, will do."

So I stopped the bus, and then I backed it up, and I opened the door.

"Where are you going?" I asked.

"I am going to Encinitas for the flower festival," the long-haired hippie-type replied.

"Hop on board," I told him. "We are going to Santa Ana."

It is right about now that you can hear the theme song from the *Twilight Zone*—you know, the Rod Serling show.

Anyway, this guy climbs on board the bus, and his eyes get really big when he sees that there are no other passengers on the bus. Is this a ghost bus? he must have thought to himself, and the skip, well, the skipper is handing him a beer.

He takes the cold Heineken, and he goes to the back of the bus, and he sits down, and we don't hear a peep out of him the whole way to Santa Ana.

We are back at the shop, and it is business as usual, and our business is baseball. We have a game set for this weekend in Ontario. I love the stadium in Ontario. It is one of those old early nineteenth-century wooden facilities. It is a great day for baseball; in fact, "let's play two."

In Southern California, there are maybe twenty of these vintage, classic, old ballparks. They are constructed of wood and are just so grand, and I love playing at them.

Most of them were built in the 1930s by major league owners for spring training. The Pacific Coast League also used them for their spring activities. They have a large seating capacity, that's for sure, but it is the construction that really stands out. I mean, they are all wooden facilities.

"So I have one thing for you to do," the skipper tells me. "Drive out to Riverside and pick up a bus for me."

It turns out that it is an old school bus. No sweat, sounds simple enough, except when I get to Riverside, the bus has no windows and, worse, no windshield.

"Excuse me, but is it even legal to drive?" I ask the yard attendant."

He shrugs his shoulders, tosses me the keys, and says, "Good luck."

Well, it is hotter than hell, and there is a pretty steady hot wind blowing right into my windshield-less face. That was some drive, I will tell you that, but I made it.

Now there are some perks to being the veteran on the team. The skipper? He never met a "stranger." I mean, they were all his "cousins," which is where the phrase "Cut it out, cuz" came from. So everybody is family. We always had some White trash living in a motor home or a trailer on the property.

One of the perks was Donna. A sweet twenty-year-old, beer-drinking, rosy-cheeked girl from the Midwest, Iowa to be exact. Man, she had a set of tits on her that would make any man take notice. Strawberry-blond hair, she was a real peach.

Now I had a weekly hotel room that I kept for my business needs, and frankly, I couldn't sleep in the shop. So I had her over one night for a swim and dinner. She did not do oral sex, so we just screwed all night. They moved on shortly thereafter.

Skip has a paint booth on the lot out back. He rents it out when we are not using it. He rented out it last night for four hours. The guy was painting a VW bug. Well, he didn't get the car out of the booth on time, so Corky rolled it out front. It had to be pushed because it had no transmission or engine. No big deal, we thought. But the guy that owns the car is there to pick it up, and he has another guy with him, and they think otherwise.

Skipper and I pull up about eight o'clock in the morning. This guy starts right up on the skipper. He, the skipper, has his arm in a cast from his last argument, so he is no threat.

So this guy is saying that when we moved the car, we smudged the paint job.

"Fine," says the skip. "You can bring the car back later and spot it in."

Well, that's not good enough, and the guy starts to grab the skipper. Whoops! Big mistake because I am involved now, and I am not talking. I drop the guy who's assaulting the skipper, and the other guy comes up behind me and puts me in a full nelson. Meanwhile, the other guy gets up. So I flip the full nelson guy over my head and land him on his back, hard. Then I hit the second guy again, and he goes down again. So this guy I hit for the second time tells his buddy to go and get a hammer. I tell the skip to get the .357.

By now, there are ten ballplayers standing around, watching—not helping, just watching. They, the foiled customers, take their VW and skedaddle, and we go to the yard. Nothing like an early morning workout to get the blood flowing. I throw a two-hitter. We win. But the talk in the dugout is all about how I saved the skip from the two thugs.

We still have the Greyhound bus, and it just so happens that one of the baseball promoters in the area is promoting a big new tournament. It is to be called the "US Open Baseball Tournament."

There will be four American teams and four international teams competing. We got a berth because the skipper is letting the tournament's promotor use the Greyhound bus to shuttle the teams back and forth from their lodgings to the field.

The tournament is going to be held in Palm Springs at the Angels' spring training facility. The Cuban national team is going to play, and it is the first time in twenty years the team from Cuba has ventured into the United States for a ballgame.

"Welcome, amigos." I may get to pitch against the Cuban national team. That would certainly raise my value if I could beat them. I'm in great shape and throwing the ball really well, and I have never lost a game at this facility in a dozen opportunities.

Hot? It must have been a 110 today. Well, we got the bus here and turned it over to the people that are running the tournament. We go to the hotel and check in. We are playing Japan tomorrow in the tournament's opening game. Dinner, beers, and bed, that what's on my agenda.

The San Diego Stars have also been invited to participate in the tournament and had accepted. I have a good personal relationship and rivalry with them.

About seven in the morning, the skipper was at my door. They want to see us in the hotel manager's office, he says.

Apparently, a security guard has alleged he was roughed up late last night. Could it have been the "Werewolves of London again?" No, it was allegedly me and the center fielder from the "San Diego Stars."

We exchange pleasantries with the manager. Then before the conversation goes one word further, the skip pipes up with, "Well, is he okay? Is he in the hospital?"

"Well, yes and no," the hotel manager replies.

"The guard is okay, and no, he wasn't hospitalized. He was treated and released."

"Well," says the skipper, "that leaves my guy out. If my guy had hit him, he would still be hospitalized," and with that, we got up and adjourned the meeting.

It finally got straightened out later that day. It turns out that the security guard, "Rent-a-cop," made up the story to make himself look like a hero. Instead, he just looked like a dumbass.

We get to the yard for the game against Japan, but the skipper is not with us. He has returned to Orange County to deal with his drug-addict daughter, but before he left, he named me as the "manager for a day."

The game started following some pregame opening ceremonies and a little pomp. I don't have that great of a team, to be honest. One or two ex–minor leaguers and a bunch of college kids. I start with one of the pros. I've been working with him a lot. He has come a long way, and he is about ready to resign.

OUTLAW LEAGUE

Now the Orientals (Japanese) are not a power-hitting team, and this complex has a pretty good-sized yard. It is 320 down the lines and 420 to dead center. Not a hard place to pitch in at all.

So the Japanese team is all about getting it right, the game, the game of baseball. They beat you with sound fundamentals. Mostly hit-and-run put the ball in play. Little ball to the max. And the defense, they play impeccable defense.

We are trailing, 2–0, at the end of three innings.

I call a meeting, and I say to the catcher and the pitcher, "Throw the four-seamer up in the strike zone to these guys and get them to hit the ball in the air. This is a damn big yard."

We tie it up in the eighth inning and win it in the tenth frame. Next up, Australia.

But first, the San Diego Stars are playing the Cuban team tonight, and I'm not missing this one. The stands are full even though it is a hundred degrees out. That's the problem with having a pro ball team in Palm Springs. It is just too damn hot.

Seeing the Cubans play made me realize how difficult it is to pitch against full-grown men swinging aluminum bats. The ball comes off the bat with about a 15 percent increase in ball velocity. That is a lot. Plus, you can't break them. Fastballs, on the other hand, become homers instead of shattered bats.

Anyway, the stands are full, and from the looks of the crowd, they are mostly Cuban. This is a big deal having the Cuban team coming here to participate in this tournament.

Now we all like to feel safe. The security that surrounds the Cuban team is seemingly tighter than that surrounding the president of the United States. But the Uzi carrying security, it isn't to protect the players, but it is to keep the players from defecting.

The crowd is really into the game. They are really excited. They are betting on every pitch, every inning. Will it be a strike, a ball, a fastball? You'd be surprised what they bet on.

It is a typical Cuban phenomenon.

During infield, I am in the stands, and I can hear the seams on the baseball whistling on the throws home by the right fielder. That's some kind of arm! The game is pretty entertaining. The Stars were actually leading at one point. I really hope I get a shot at the Cuban team.

But first, there is the task at hand. The Australian national team is pretty good, and they are managed by some ex-big leaguer.

The skipper is still not back yet, and it is almost game time. I get the team ready to play—you know, hit infield, outfield. My pitcher today? Well, I have not seen him throw, but I did talk with him before the game.

He told me he was only going to pitch five innings.

I said back to him, "Good luck making five."

College pitchers, sheesh. I wouldn't start the douchebag, but it is the skipper's orders.

The kid starts and goes five strong innings, a pleasant surprise, as he ate up some innings. We were ahead, 3–0, when he came out.

So I bring in a left-hander. He throws good low nineties. I have been working with him for a while on his command and a split-finger pitch. He would eventually sign a professional baseball contract and pitch a couple of years in the big leagues for the California Angels. There were only two things the lefty couldn't do—pitch the first inning of a game or the ninth inning; other than that, he was a "World beater."

So I bring him in in the sixth, and he pitches three shutout innings, the sixth, seventh, and eighth.

It is the ninth inning now, and I have a little ex-Giant farmhand loose and ready to go. He isn't a real hard thrower, but he has a great curveball, and we have the heart of the order coming up, and they all bat right-handed hitters.

I'm just about to tell the lefty that he is done when the skipper is in the dugout. Where in the hell did he come from?

I tell him, "What's up?"

And he asks me if I'm crazy pulling the lefty. Well, from a man who has made some pretty stupid pitching moves, it almost a compliment.

"Okay," I say.

He stays in. He walks the bases loaded and throws the ball out of the yard. We lose, 4–3. The skipper heads back to Orange County.

The next day was a day game with the team from San Bernardino. There was some bad blood between the teams, so it should be an interesting game. I start an ex-Giant's farmhand, and he walks everybody in sight. But he isn't throwing the ball wildly or all over the place. Could it be the umpire? Are we getting "homered"?

In about the fourth inning, I have a little chat with him, the home plate umpire, and the calls straighten out a little bit. I know when I'm getting homered, and this is definitely a plain blatant example of that issue. We are definitely getting homered.

Well, even with this blatantly bad umpiring, we are winning the game somehow. The ninth inning comes along, and we still have a lead. It is the bottom of the ninth, and the bases are loaded with two outs for the opposing team.

The batter lifts a fly ball to left field. It isn't that deep, and it is playable. My left fielder drifts with the ball, but he doesn't get back where he can get position on the ball; in other words, he let the ball play him. He reaches up and snares the ball, and the ball goes right through the webbing of his glove. We lose the game. That is two bottom of ninth-inning defeats in a row. We had fourteen hits. They had twelve walks.

South Korea is up next tomorrow night at seven o'clock. I should get the start. It isn't Cuba, but it will have to do. We are at the yard, and the skipper is there.

"Glad you could make it. Am I starting?"

"No," he says. "You are doing a terrific job of coaching."

So I take off my uniform and leave it folded in the dugout. They lose the game and me, for a while anyway.

For a while turns out to be the next day when my phone rings. It is the skipper.

"Please come and see me," he says.

So I do.

It turns out that he is completely perplexed by his daughter's drug addiction, and he wants me to kill someone for him, his daughter's boyfriend, as a matter of fact.

"Cut it out, cuz," I say to him. That's a serious favor.

He explains to me what he has been going through for the last week, and this guy has his daughter strung out on heroin.

"I will look into it," I say.

So I do. I go up to his house and check it out. It turns out that I don't have to kill the guy. I just have him robbed and terrorized. It works. He leaves the girl alone, and we got a half pound of cocaine for our efforts.

So I move to Las Vegas. My guy is pitching in the big leagues, and I am at a loss personally. I find the local "adult" baseball team and play with them for a bit. The manager is a real boob. I learn that the local triple "A" team needs a batting practice pitcher. It isn't much, but I'm throwing every day and working out, and that's the rest of the summer for me. The fall is coming, and my pitcher will be home soon back to Orange County.

I love Orange County. Newport Beach is the bomb. The beaches, the weather, the social life. Now I am back in Orange County, and I'm with the Orange County A's. Everything is mellow for now.

We are playing in the NBC winter league, and it is almost entirely a pro league with the tournament being held the first two weeks in December.

We make the finals. I went ten wins and no losses, and all were complete games, and oh, we're going to Palm Springs in the winter when Palm Springs is nice.

The winter finals are the best, two out of three. I persuaded my Mets pitcher to come along. Between him and me, we should sweep. We have been throwing daily, and it won't hurt him to throw one game before we shut down our throwing for two weeks for Christmas. The catcher for the Tigers is with us, and we have a pretty strong team.

The weather is beautiful in the Southern California desert, and we are ready to get it on.

Our opponents are the Cucamonga Mets. They are managed by the current Cardinals big league manager, and he has several major league players on his roster. Our starter, the Mets pitcher, goes six, and we win the opener. I go eight the next day, and we win the championship. And now a couple of weeks off.

Chapter Seventeen

The Challenger

The wheels of time keep on turning. They will stop for nothing, and time is the enemy. The year is 1986, and it is January 2, and we're on the ball field. This year, it is different. We have more major leaguers. I mean, there were some names, and there was some talent out here on the field.

Still, no catcher, though, so I will be the primary bullpen catcher.

We have this one guy. He is the "closer" for the Angels. When he warms up, he stands fifty feet or so away from you and just let it rip. No one will play catch with him. All the veterans look to see if he is throwing batting practice first, and if he is, they all head to their positions for fungoes and let the rookies get their swings off him.

It is late in January, and we had just arrived at the yard when the news broke. The Challenger, which was supposed to lift off for a manned space mission, exploded, killing all the astronauts and a civilian school teacher who was on board. A terrible day for our country and the space program, and it is my birthday.

Here is a new wrinkle. We are playing a game. The Cincinnati Reds scout has brought in a team, and he has some talent. A Mets outfielder, the Cardinals' closer, they have talent all right, but so do we, except we have no catcher. "I'll catch," I pipe up, and I do. Nine innings, and I got a couple of hits to boot. It is pretty fun to play in a game with that much talent. We lose.

One of the players out here is a shortstop who had rotator cuff surgery. Then while rehabbing the shoulder, he dislocated it, lifting weights. Gritty little guy. I do some extra work with him, even throwing for him on Saturdays. He has signed with the Angels. We also have the Angels' third baseman working out with us.

Normally, there are not many coaches out here for these workouts, but the Boston Red Sox pitching coach is out this season. He is interested in me after seeing me on the field for a couple of weeks. But alas, my age is the problem.

"You can throw it," he says.

Well, it is time for the players to report to spring training. There are a couple of stragglers—guys who are going to Minor League Camp. One of these players was a ten-year veteran. He was released by the Cleveland Indians because, well, basically, he was the worst pitcher on the worst team in major league baseball.

I remember one day he walked up to me and said, "I see you working with the younger pitchers. And well, if you see anything in my delivery, don't be afraid to say something."

Well, how did you stay in the show for ten years with that stuff? is what I was thinking.

I opted for diplomacy, and I said, "Okay, we will have a bullpen session."

This guy had gotten into some bad habits, pitching-wise, and some bad mechanics followed. Fortunately, I have the knowledge and drills to fix his mechanics.

The first thing we started with was his set up. I got him to shift his feet a little bit to make it easier to get his front leg into the pitch. The real problem was getting him to stay back, keeping his weight back.

So I tell him, "Get your weight on your heels and keep your shoulders back."

Now for some, stop drills. In stop drills, you stop at every point in your wind up. This creates knowledge of where you should be and corrects your balance. You will never see one of my pitchers off-balance. Now bend your back and finish the pitch head low and on the glove.

We work a few weeks, and I ask him if he wants to pitch in a game.

"Yes," he says.

The A's are playing the La Fonda Stars. I call the skipper up and my guy is starting. He pitches five innings, and it goes really well. He is off to camp with the Oakland club.

So right at the end of our voluntary workouts, the two Angels players tell me to be in Palm Springs to throw batting practice for the big club. I go to Palm Springs, and I get the job. After thirteen or fourteen years of trying to get to the big leagues, I have made it. I'm in the big leagues.

True, I am only the batting practice pitcher, but things happen, and I will be ready if they need a fifth starter. One chance, that's all I need. The thrill that you get when you put on a big-league uniform is unexplainable. I mean, it is absolutely euphoric.

Big-league locker rooms will bring you back to earth in a hurry, and this clubhouse was all that.

There is so much jealousy and paranoia. It is unreal, and the more ego you have and the more money you have, it just heightens the tension.

And then there were just plain old-fashioned bullies. My locker was right between smiling George and the rookie center fielder. The twelve-year veteran outfielder is trying to make the club.

The manager is trying to make him a "small ball" player. You know, hit-and-run, "small ball." I don't think that will work in this case. I tell him, "Just do what got you here." He hits a pair of homers, and he makes the team. I never did see him smile.

The Ghetto, One South, that's what this reminds me of. All, or most of the Black players, have their lockers in this row. No problem, us low-rent guys can deal.

The big left-hander was that guy. You know the type, the team bully. He is always trying to intimidate someone, and he runs roughshod over this one reliever. I don't know why the guy takes it, but he does.

Now it is me that he sets his sights on. One day, while I'm working, throwing batting practice, he is in the clubhouse up to no good.

He gets a roll of white athletic tape and attaches a strip of it on the front of my locker next to my name. Then he scrolls on the tape the words "Is a faggot and dickhead."

So I come in from practice, and it is there staring me right in the face. There is no hiding it. I take a shower, and I leave the facility. I probably have some sort of workplace lawsuit available, but I have a better idea.

The next day, they, the defamatory comments, are still there.

"You're not going to take that down?" asks the shortstop.

"No, no, I'm not," I say.

My plan is to get some reporter in here so I can show him how juvenile and bored and lazy these big-league pitchers are. I know who put the defaming graffiti on my locker. It is no secret. I can tell by the language. He doesn't bother me again.

We had this Black reliever, and I'm playing catch in the outfield with him.

"What are you doing here anyway?" he asked. "Are you an actor prepping for a role?"

"No," I said.

The next day, we were tossing again, and he says to me, "You are from the commissioner's office, aren't you?"

"No," I said again.

The third day, he throws me a forkball.

I told him, "It didn't move."

He then throws me his ninety-two-mile-per-hour "heater," and I throw the baseball back to him at ninety-five.

"You're trying to take my job," he says.

"Bingo!" I said.

It was too bad. He overdosed later and died from cocaine. That was a real shame.

The next morning, I'm on the field early as usual. I'm walking down the right field line, and I reach the bullpen area. I spy a young rookie left-hand pitcher sitting on the bench.

"What's up?" I ask.

He replies that one of the veteran right-handed pitchers is coming out to show him how to throw the curveball. I thought to myself,

No forty-year-old pitcher is going to show a twenty-one-year-old pitcher how to throw a pitch. That would cost him his job.

These were secrets of the trade, and baseball is so competitive that those secrets are protected. The manager was cool, the "Little General" they called him. And he, after the first week of practices, would ask, "Who is that guy that has been throwing batting practice? He throws pretty good." He thought I was some free agent, trying to audition. He was right. Can I get one lousy start? Please! You won't be sorry.

Then one morning, that almost happened—a start in a major league game. It is the closest I have come to pitching in a major league game, and it was oh so close.

It was a Monday, and the Cleveland Indians were in. We are playing two nine-inning games, a "B" game in the morning, then the "A" game in the afternoon. This means that there will not be batting practice today, a rare day off for me.

Now "B" games are for triple "A" players and your big-league backups. One of our left-handers, not the bully, is scheduled to start. The starting pitcher, today's starting pitcher, has a bad back and can't go. Could this be my shot?

The manager and the coaches talk about it and decide to go with some younger triple "A" pitcher. Damn it, that could have been the break I have been looking for fifteen years, and it was oh so close. It was pretty emotional for me, to say the least. But you can't show your emotions.

The owner of the Angels, the "Singing Cowboy" as he is called, is at the yard every morning, where he watches the morning workouts and then the afternoon game. He watches intently from a well-behind home plate.

Now the owner is old, at least in his early eighties. I hear that he has a half pint every morning for breakfast, and he just about owns the entire city of Palm Springs. This team is built to win the World Series. The cowboy has opened the saddlebags for this brood of immature spoiled brats. It is truly amazing.

Who is the biggest star of the big stars? He is the right fielder. He just was lured by the "Cowboys" purse strings, and they got him away from the Yankees, where he has won a couple of World Series championships in the past. Does he have one left in the tank? The loudest guy in the clubhouse, he is also the hardest worker.

The Angels have this eighty-year-old coach with the team. He is kind of a novelty. He once roomed with the "Sultan of Swat," the "Bambino," the one and only Babe Ruth. I used to protect his back while he was hitting soft fungoes to the "straw who stirs the drink" when I was not throwing batting practice. Not once did he get hit.

As it often does, spring training is over, and we are breaking camp. What to do with me? Anything at all is what I say. They have made a decision, and they are going to keep me. Then just a short four hours later, and my major league career is over. I get released. That was the saddest day of my life.

I pack up. What else could I do? And I head to Orange County. I'm cruising in my Porsche when a highway patrolman pulls me over and writes me a speeding ticket to go with my pink slip from the Angels.

Back in Orange County, I am sitting in a diner, eating a steak dinner, and pondering my fate. That's when the television blares out a commercial for the weekend series between the Angels and the Dodgers—the Freeway Series. It is an Angels' commercial, and it is from spring training, and who's throwing batting practice? Yep, it is me.

You know, it kind of became a game inside a game for me to make it to the major leagues. Some challenge it was, but I eventually almost accomplished the feat. Okay, I had some big-league time, but not nearly what I should have had. I mean, there were times when I was broke and homeless and I slept in my car. But I never gave up as long as I thought my stuff was good enough.

Well, I resumed working out with the older veteran pitcher as he had been released by the Oakland A's. I call the Angels and ask the pitching coach to let him throw batting practice. They agree, and he signs a triple "A" contract, and eventually, he makes the big club. So there is nothing for me here now in Orange County.

I move back to Las Vegas and join the triple "A" Las Vegas Stars as a batting practice pitcher. The season is going along pretty smoothly when the Angels triple "A" team comes in. The veteran right-hander is with them. We have lunch, and he tells me if he has a good start in Las Vegas, he is going to get called up to the big club. So what do I do? I give him the scouting report on the Stars hitters, and he throws a two-hitter over seven innings. Pretty accurate scouting report, I'd say.

So I'm sitting in a bar, watching Monday night football when a news announcement comes on: the New York Mets have acquired the first baseman from the St. Louis Cardinals for two pitchers. A reliever who had forty saves a year ago, and you guessed it, my pitcher. The kid has been traded to the Cardinals.

Well, the St. Louis newspapers waste no time in lambasting the manager of the Cardinals, calling the trade the, "worst trade" in Cardinal history. And that is saying something because the Cardinal baseball history is a long one.

So upon their arrival in St. Louis, the manager calls the two newly acquired hurlers into his office.

"Let's get right to it," he says, and then he pulls out two FBI photos from his desk. The photos showed the former first baseman exchanging money for cocaine, and he tells the newly acquired chuckers that the former first baseman will be out of baseball by the end of the season with a "lifetime" ban. What could go wrong?

He, the manager, sends my guy to triple "A," and the reliever, well, he was a bust. The disgraced first baseman who bought the cocaine, well, he led the Mets to the World Series championship. There was one thing that could go wrong, and it did.

The season is over for the Stars. What to do now? I go back to Orange County and work with my pitcher, and I throw some games for the A's. One note, I led the Pacific Coast League in hitting. To be more exact, the first baseman led the league in hitting. I just threw for him. To be precise, he didn't even know my name. He just called me, "You, motherfucker!" I had broken all his bats by the end of the season.

Chapter Eighteen

On the Air

So the kid is a Cardinal now. He will report to the Cardinals spring training facility. He pitched at triple "A" almost the whole season last year because the manager couldn't deal with the flak from the trade.

The year is 1987, and we are on the ball field. It is early in January. I hope this is a better January than the last one what with the Challenger disaster and all. The training goes well, and he is off to spring training.

I'm off to Vegas. I go out to the Stars to see if I can catch on.

They have a new manager this year, so who knows? I go out and throw a few times, and the manager says to me, "Can catch bullpens?"

"Yes," I say.

So he wants me in uniform for the games as a bullpen coach. I would still throw batting practice and hit fungoes. A full-time coaching position? How much does it pay?

Well, the next day, I go to the yard, and he tells me, "We don't need you out here."

Well, we get into a conversation, and he says to me, "Well, I played ten years in the show. Where have you played?"

"Yeah," I say back to him, "the only reason you played in the big leagues is because all the real men were in Vietnam fighting."

So he has a fungo bat in his hand, and he throws it at me, and he misses, and the bat hits the batting cage.

"You never could hit anything with a bat," I chime in. "I'm gone." And the Stars? They go on to win the whole Pacific Coast League.

So I met a guy last summer. He is an electrician, and his father owns an electric company. He wires commercial properties. I go to work for them for eight dollars an hour, starting time 4:00 a.m.

I have also met another guy. He is a city bus driver and a father who wants his son to be a ballplayer. Now the high school kids in Vegas have a rough road when school is done. You must go out of state if you wish to continue to play baseball.

There is only one college baseball program, the University of Nevada, Las Vegas, and no two-year schools at this time. So the bus driver and I rent a van, a fifteen-passenger van, and haul a busload of ballplayers down to Los Angeles for a college tryout day. I have at least twelve or fifteen college coaches at the workout, and it goes really well, and we do it again the next year.

So the electrician played for the Red Sox at triple "A," and that was as high as he made it in the States. Then he played one year with the Yakult Swallows of the Japanese league.

A baseball school, that is what this town needs, I tell him. His parents have a vacant lot, and it is about a half of an acre of land, just sitting empty. We can use it, they say.

We build cages for batting and build six pitching mounds and go into business, offering hitting and pitching instruction. We do a brisk business, and now it is time for our first baseball camp. This is a winter camp. I get a couple of pros to come in to help with the instruction, rent two baseball fields, and we have morning and afternoon sessions.

We draw more than two hundred kids to come out at fifty dollars a head. But trouble is brewing. The parents, especially the mother of my new partner, is nagging about everything that was nothing. I have investors who see my vision and who will back it. But alas, the school is shut down. She said it was due to liability. I say the only liability was that I wasn't a Mormon.

The kid has managed to hurt himself in spring training. A pulled hamstring while "racing" another player is the issue. Boys will be boys, but this is just plain stupid. It will cost him six weeks and another month before he gets back to the big leagues. Last year, he started the season with the Mets before being traded, and the Mets won the World Series.

Now he is with the Cardinals, and they are going to the World Series this year, and he's hurt. Finally, in late June, he makes it back to the big club but doesn't pitch that well. It was later in the month when he got the call-up. The Cards were on a West Coast swing, and he was to be the starting pitcher at Dodger Stadium. He goes six and gives up a three-run homer, and the Cards go down in defeat. The team leaves him off the playoff roster. Too bad because they are playing the Dodgers in the playoffs. We go to the playoff games the Cards win the series but eventually lose in the World Series to the Minnesota Twins.

I was back living in Vegas. I talk with the kid, and he is okay with his winter workouts. I have pitching lessons, so I am busy six days a week. I also go to Orange County and pitch for the A's once in a while.

I served an infantry combat tour in Vietnam. I was a point man for the Fourth Infantry Division recon platoon. For eleven months, I have seen more combat than most. For those of you that don't know what a point man is, I will tell you. He is the first person to walk on a patrol. Simply put, he is the leader, and your fortune rests with him.

I am at home watching television when a movie comes on the air. The name of the movie was *Platoon*. Well, I watched it, and I didn't sleep for two damn days. I thought that shit was over—that shit meaning Vietnam. I guess not.

No winter workouts at the college and only a few games with the A's. The year is 1988, and it is January, and I'm bored as hell.

I am selling golf equipment. I have never played a round of golf in my life. But I have a knack for sales, the gift of gab, and I easily outsell the other salesmen on the floor.

The store manager, who is just okay, wants me off the floor and in the back room on the phones. The company is apparently doing a big phone business. I balk at the switch as I am making good commissions on the floor. It is the phone room, or I am out. I guess it is the latter.

I have been pitching for some team here in town, but it isn't like pitching for the Angels or even the A's for that matter. But I make do.

There is a tournament in town for teams with players aged thirty-five and over. A team from San Diego, the San Diego Gems, are playing in the tournament. Now there are quite a few ex-San Diego Stars on the team. They call me to pitch for them. The little center fielder from the A's is with them. I am sick with the flu or a cold or just the plain old crud.

We win the first game and then set out to do some drinking. The little center fielder has about three hundred dollars just burning in his pocket. So he gets into a blackjack game. I say to him, "No, I think you should play at that table over there," so we pick up stakes and move.

Well, as luck would have it, he wins thirteen thousand dollars. A pretty good night. I tell him to wire half of the winnings home. So we play out the tournament, and we win it too boot.

Fall is here now, but winter is closing in. I'm just doing my pitching lessons and driving to Orange County to pitch a game for the Orange County A's. The skipper isn't doing so well, health-wise. He is getting up there in the years.

I have picked up a radio show in the mornings in Las Vegas. The name of the show is *Sports Play*. It is a morning sport handicapping show. Now I'm a radio host—sweet.

The show is part of a sports magazine that runs for one hour, five days a week. It is produced by one of my clients from the baseball school. He asked me one morning if I had listened to the parent show, and if I did, what did I think about it.

"Yes, I have listened, and I think you need a sports handicapping segment." After all, this is Las Vegas the sports betting capital of the world.

"Hmm," he says. "That's a pretty darn good idea," he adds. "Could you put a show together for me?" he then asks.

"I think so," I say. "Give me a fifteen-minute slot starting on Monday at eight fifteen in the morning. I will broadcast for twelve minutes with three minutes for advertising."

Got to be making something. It is a deal, and I have some work to do.

Now the Stardust Casino is about as big as you can get in the world of sports books and, more importantly, of sports wagering. I know the sports book director at the Stardust, and I have been a guest on the "Stardust Line," which is their nationally syndicated radio show. It aired on Saturday nights at ten o'clock in the evening.

I am thinking about going to them for sponsorship, but I have a better idea. The "Palace Station" is really climbing the ranks of sports books. I think that I will give them a try. I go to see the sports book director, and he loves my idea for a show.

Now the morning baseball lines come out to the betting public at about eight o'clock, but I am getting the daily baseball lines at six thirty in the morning, a full hour and a half before they become public and one hour before my show airs.

I write the show going over all the days' action, and then I give out a five-team parlay, a three-team parlay, and the clincher, my "dog of the day."

Now in baseball, you bet on what they call the "money line." In other words, if you bet on a favorite, you would lay, or wager, $130 to win $100 or a total return of $230.

Now if you bet on the underdog, you would wager $100 to win $130 or a $230 return. So as you can see, the dog wager is the way to go. Sometimes the "dogs" are as much as a 3 or 4–1 play. Pretty enriching if they hit, and they do.

Sports betting? It is a big-money market. These sports books are the brokers. Baseball is a good bet because you have multiple dogs to bet on each day.

As the season rolled on, the radio station would get calls, wanting to know what I said about this game or that one, sometimes as many as fifty calls in a morning.

Someone was listening.

The Cardinals shortstop has a new book out, and the producer of the show wants an interview with the player.

"I can arrange that," I say, and I do.

The Cards are in San Francisco for a three-game series with the Giants. I have several players that I know on the Cards. So I call the clubhouse, and I get a left-hander on the horn. He was someone that I had worked with in the past.

"Does the shortstop want some exposure for his book?"

"Of course, he does."

"Will he do an interview on our program?"

"Of course, he would."

"So how are you?" I ask.

"My shoulder is killing me," he says, "and I'm starting today."

Well, he is minus one forty-five. I will take a hundred on the Giants, please."

The Giants won. He went three.

It is a beautiful fall day, and my telephone rings. I answer it. It was one of my friends who works in the casino industry. He is a pit boss at the MGM, and he manages the baccarat room, and that's a pretty high-stress job because of the amounts of money gamblers wager in there, and you, as the "boss," must okay huge credit lines.

He was a ballplayer, and he caught for the UNLV baseball team a few years back. I like him. He's good to me. I mean, he has comped me several times when I have had five or six players from the Las Vega Stars with me. I have five or six casinos that I can get anything I want, and thus my nickname the "Comp King."

So we exchange pleasantries, and by the way, he asks, "Would you mind throwing some batting practice for my son, who was a recently graduated local high school prospect?" He, the father, has a Dodger scout that is going to be there.

"Sure," I reply. "Where and when?"

"The UNLV batting cages at four o'clock this afternoon. See you there."

I show up early to get loose.

So my friend shows up with his son and this really old man. That must be the scout. He is a little old. Holy shit, that's no scout!

He has brought Al Campanis to see his son hit. That's some baseball horsepower when you can get Al to look at your kid.

So I begin throwing, and I'm trying my darnedest to make the kid look good. After about ten minutes, Al pipes up, "Can you throw the curveball?" he says.

Well, I can, but I don't think he can't hit it. So here we go, and I was right. He couldn't hit it. Afterward, as we're walking out of the yard, Al says to me, "How old are you?"

"Forty," I say.

"If I'd have seen you throw twenty years ago, you'd have been a Dodger."

Well, there were no scouts in Vietnam, except for me.

It is very rewarding working with the young pitching talent. I have had a couple of pros and lots of college players during my tenure as a pitching coach.

But when you lose one, well, it hurts. I lost one, and it is a haunting tale. He started taking lessons from me when he was about fourteen. A big tall lanky kid. He was taller than me by an inch, but he had no body weight. But that is okay. We have lots of time. Anyway, he has some personal problems—racial problems to be exact. He is a racist, plain and simple.

Well, it is a struggle, but we get through it. He graduated from high school and had a great senior year. He is just seventeen years old at the time of his graduation. There were no baseball contracts until you are eighteen, but he is more of a prospect than he is a suspect.

I want to send him to California to play at a two-year school. I know all the coaches and can get him into the best school for both academics and baseball.

His dad flies down to Orange County one weekend to see what I have arranged. Then they opt out for a Virginia military school. Now this is a really sticky point, you know. You become close, really close with your students, but you have to know where to draw the line. I can't help him if he is in Virginia, but if he is in California, no problem, I say. Well, I lost, and the boy is off to VMI, where he has two good years but no draft. The kid can pitch. Now he goes to the University of Alabama–Birmingham for his last two years.

I ran into his mother this morning in a grocery store parking lot. The news she gave me was just devastating. He had gotten addicted to heroin at the UAB, and he overdosed and died. Just sickening. If he had stayed here and gone to school in Southern California, would things have been different? And with that, we said "Aloha" to 1988.

The year was 1989, and I can tell it is going to be another snoozer. I am back with A's, sort of. I mean, I still live in Las Vegas, but I'm in Orange County quite a bit. My boat-selling buddy has a place in Costa Mesa where I stay when I'm in the county.

In spring training last year, the kid had pulled a hamstring. This year, it is his arm, and he manages to get released. He re-signs with Baltimore and goes to minor league camp, but he can't throw and is soon released. He had such a promising career, and now it is down in flames. I think it is partly mental; after all, baseball can be a tough life, especially when you are hurt, you can't play, and you are on the road. I told him to come to Vegas and stay with me, but he opted for Newport Beach.

We have another friend who had played fifteen seasons, mostly in the minor leagues, but he does have some major-league time. He is a catcher, and he has an affinity for blow. That's a problem.

So he has been invited to spring training in Florida. He has been hot and heavy with this one girl on the beach, and now it is time for reflecting on what I said previously about marriage and baseball. We all know her. She is a nice girl, an heiress, and she owns a house right on the beach. They get married. Remember what I said about professional sports and marriage, oil and water, they do not mix.

So he took her to spring training with him in Florida, and he was cut on the last day. They drive home to Newport, and it looks like it is over for him.

But the phone rings a couple of days after they arrive home. It is the New York Yankees. They have an opening at the triple "A" level. Is he interested? Yes, hell yes, he says. He tells his new bride, and she responds by immediately filing for a divorce. It is a lonely life being a ballplayer.

It was June, and I get a call from a guy in Ontario, California, and he has a baseball team. We had played him before when I was with the A's. I don't know about him as a player or manager, but he had some talent on his team. I know that much. Do you want to manage the Expos in the summer tournament?

"Why not?" I say.

So I took a couple of weekends and managed the team in the tournament, but we didn't do that well.

One occurrence that caught my attention and not only my attention but the whole world's attention, the OJ Simpson debacle on television. Yes, it was the low-speed chase on national television, where the police were trying to question Simpson about the murders of his wife and her friend Ron Goldman. What a fiasco.

Well, the skipper didn't take kindly to me managing the competition. The Fourth of July is here, and I spend it in Newport dunes at a beer, barbecue, and cocaine bash. The next morning, I hop a jet and fly back to Vegas.

The year is rolling along, and that's one thing about time, it just keeps on marching along, and I'm not getting any younger.

Now the main story in politics this year has been the Iran-Contra affair. Apparently, some members, high-ranking members, of the National Defense Committee have made a deal to trade arms from the United States to Iran in exchange for the freedom of some hostages being held by the Iranians. It is a sordid affair and very embarrassing for the president at the time who is Ronald Reagan. Despite the whole messy deal, George Bush, the current vice president, will become the next president of the United States.

In the world of baseball, Nolan Ryan surpassed five thousand strikeouts this year, and he became the first player to achieve this milestone. Shortly after that feat, Pete Rose, the all-time hits leader in major league baseball, agreed to a lifetime ban from major league baseball, and this also excluded him from entering the Hall of Fame. The charge was that he bet on baseball games, his own team's games at that, while he was the manager of the Cincinnati Reds, the team he spent his whole career with. And he lost the bets.

As a fan of baseball and someone who has been around the game a lot, I'm not torn by this decision, but I find it a little hypocritical.

First, let me state for the record that I am not a Pete Rose fan, never have been, the reason, well, the main reason is that he never got a hit off me. And it is a fact that betting on baseball games is a violation of baseball's golden rule: "Thou shalt not bet on baseball games." But he broke that rule when he was managing but not as a player, and there is a difference. His stuff? Game-used equipment, the bat and ball that made up the record, and his jersey are all in the National Baseball Hall of Fame. So where is Pete?

It has been quite an interesting year in baseball. Bart Giamatti has died while in office. Yes, the sitting commissioner of baseball had a massive heart attack, and it took him out. The new baseball commissioner is Fay Vincent. It is he that will head major league baseball.

The other events that made up 1989 were the number of arrests for treason, spying, and government misconduct. It seems like the whole world is turning into a corrupt wasteland—corruption spawned by Richard Nixon.

And so it is that this year has passed too. The last two years have been pretty quiet for me. I need to shake things up a bit.

Chapter Nineteen

Red Alert

What this town needed was a good solid summer college baseball team that could play in the National Baseball Congress tournament in Wichita, Kansas.

Las Vegas so deserves to be represented in this national tournament. I persuaded the local paper to run an article on the sports page about my plans to start a summer college-level baseball program—the Las Vegas Reds. After my request, the *Las Vegas Review-Journal* ran a full-page article for me titled "Red Alert."

I held tryouts right when all the college kids were coming home for the summer. Man did I hit the jackpot when about fifty strapping young ballplayers showed up for the Memorial Day tryout. This was a testament to the popularity of baseball in Las Vegas, one that would continue to blossom as the city became a long-standing home for triple "A" baseball.

I explained to the players, "We are a first-year team and that this is instructional ball. So don't take it too seriously, have little fun, and improve your game." I advised them, "Do your work and develop your game. Constant improvement is what we are looking for. The one thing I won't put up with, besides jewelry on the field, is disrespecting anybody that's out here, players, coaches, or volunteers. Do your work and keep your mouth shut unless it is baseball you are talking about."

I knew all the college coaches in Orange County and a few in Arizona. I quickly arranged a fifty-game schedule that included weekends at home and Wednesdays in Orange County for a nine-inning game.

We also played a Tuesday "B" game. My friend, the bus driver and former candidate for mayor, had taken over an American Legion team. He promptly got kicked out of the league because he simply couldn't get along with anybody. So I have some "A" players and mostly some "B" players, and I can use these players for my "B" game.

The first game that we played, he had this old white-haired guy coaching with him. I had never seen him before, but he knew what he was doing.

It turned out he was an old minor-league player and manager. He had played thirteen years of minor league baseball and then switched to managing and coaching. He finished up with the Hollywood Stars. He then naturally went into acting, and he did a lot of commercials.

Bing Russell, the father of Kurt, had purchased the Portland Mavericks of the old Pacific Coast League. He then hired his friend and a former minor leaguer to be the manager. He was quite a character. He was voted the most popular manager in Portland's baseball history.

My team was okay, but there was one problem. I have a coach who can't coach at this level, at least the way I wanted to see this team coached. The final straw came when I had a real good NBC baseball team in for a weekend series.

In the second game of the series in the seventh inning, they had a left-handed pitcher who had just been released from double "A" on the bump. He was darn good. We had gotten a leadoff single off him, but we were down two runs.

I put my coach's son in the game to pinch run. I gave him explicit instructions to take a two-step lead.

"Your run doesn't mean a thing. Don't get picked off," I told him in the dugout.

Then what happened next was inexcusable. On the first pitch, he gets thrown out trying to steal second base.

The next inning with one out and a man on third base, this same coach sent the runner home in an attempted steal of home plate. There were two strikes on a dead-pull hitter. It was a disaster, and I was about to have a mutiny. I told the guy he couldn't be on the field, but he could do other things to help the club.

"No," he said. "You are fired!"

I found that pretty amusing because I had started this team, owned it, and had installed him as president.

This set off a one-week fiasco about who was running the team. To make things even better, the Henderson newspaper published the whole damned soap opera the following week on its front page. There was no doubt who was running this club. That would be me!

My next move was to get the old guy, the old minor league manager, to coach third for me. When he saw what I had going, he jumped right on board. This was the start of a fifteen-year friendship.

I realized there was going to be a little bit of babysitter and big brother in me to these younger players.

"Live life at your own risk," I told them. "Girls are a big problem, but that is in my purview."

Why did I say this? My talented lefty had been talking to me about pitching and then suddenly had switched the conversation to nightclubs and women.

"You are not old enough to be in a nightclub, are you?" I asked.

"Yes," he said. "Last night, this really cute girl was talking to me, and the next thing you know, I went home alone. I thought I had her in the bag."

I reminded him of the facts of boy-girl life.

"If they talk to you, they are interested. But if they touch you, then they want you. It is chemistry 101, human magnetism."

As it turned out, I was right.

We made it through the summer pretty easily, and we won more games than we lost. The San Diego Stars were going to Wichita. They wanted one of my pitchers, the talented left-hander.

The San Diego team's owner had purchased an entry into the US Open Tournament, which was being played in Ontario, California, this year.

Because of this trade with the Stars brewing, the situation became problematic to play in both tournaments for the Stars. To resolve it, I traded the left-hander for an entry into the US Open.

I needed money and some players because most of my guys had already returned to their college campuses. Regardless, I managed to find enough decent players to compete.

It was the morning. We were leaving for Ontario. I had rented a fifteen-passenger van. Some of the players were driving in their own vehicles.

My phone rang at six in the morning. It was the owner of a casino on the Las Vegas strip. His son was my center fielder. The kid had a stroke of bad luck. He was an outstanding athlete at Las Vegas' premier Catholic school, Bishop Gorman, which has a reputation for being nationally ranked in sports.

He was drafted by the Baltimore Orioles, but he turned them down for a football scholarship at the University of Arizona, only to be stricken with mononucleosis. After he recovered, he had essentially lost his scholarship and turned to baseball to restart his athletic career.

He was playing on my summer team to revive his chances at a professional sports career or at least to get a scholarship to a college. A scholarship to Fresno State college is what he got. Then he played in the College World Series, and he signed with the Baltimore Orioles. Not too shabby.

The casino owner says to me, "Meet me at the hotel valet parking in fifteen minutes."

"I will be there," I say.

Well, I pull up, and he is standing out front.

"Good morning," I say.

He then hands me an envelope with fifteen one-hundred-dollar bills inside of it.

"I do not want anybody to go hungry," he said. "Have a good trip."

We head out to Ontario. The first game for us is a night game against the Mexican National team. I have this ex-first rounder scheduled to start. He had Tommy John surgery and is still trying to figure it out. He was a real hard thrower. Now he has to make an adjustment and become a pitcher.

Simply put, I don't think he can locate the ball.

He calls me about three in the afternoon. "I can't make it," he says. "I'm sorry."

Well, shit, I knew he would let me down. So I do the only thing I can. I start the game on the mound. Now I have a history with the Mexican baseball league. It was, in fact, an open tournament, so there were no restrictions on age for players. In other words, I could pitch at age forty.

I have never lost to a Mexican team, and today is no different. Despite not having pitched in a game in months, I throw eight innings, and we shut them out.

The next day, we get a no-hitter from our pitcher, and we have won our first two games.

I am starting my lefty today, and he is my best. Well, he was up drinking and screwing all night, and he shows up a limp noodle, and he simply got the poop beat out of him. It is by far the worst game this team has played all summer.

Next up is the team from Fairbanks, Alaska. I have a right-handed starter, I think. He is the punter for USC, and he had to be in Los Angeles for a stress test, but he will try to make the game.

He does, and he throws a dandy, eight innings of no-hit baseball. Now I have the major-league catcher from the Tigers in the game, and he hits a three-run homer. We are looking good.

In the ninth, my center fielder starts a brawl, and when it is over, he is ejected, and we lose the damn game.

Florida is our next opponent, and I have no pitching, so on three days' rest, I give it a go. Five innings is all I get. A Texas leaguer, which drew chalk down the right-field line, did me in, and I took a rare loss. So the tournament is over, and we pack up and head back to Las Vegas.

Anyone for winter ball? A new adult league has emerged. I don't know if it is new or not, but suddenly, there are a lot of teams playing baseball in Las Vegas this winter. We enter the league. The old guy is going to manage, and I am just going to pitch or maybe play a little first base.

Well, we, the old guy and I, know a lot of baseball teams, and we get a lot of games in Southern California, as well as league play in Nevada.

Now I have become good friends with the old guy, and as I have stated previously, he is quite a character himself. So one day, he says to me, "We are going to Los Angeles for a movie audition. Don't worry, you already have the job."

"Okay," I say. "What job?"

"The pitching coach," he replies.

Apparently, Paramount Movie Pictures is making a baseball movie about some Mormon kid who throws a hundred miles an hour, but the lad is torn between being an elder in the church or a baseball player. The old guy was going to be the home plate umpire, he told me.

"Does the big Cardinal righty want to come too?"

"I'll ask," I say, and I do, and he does. So we, the three of us, go to Hollywood for the audition, and sure enough, I got the job.

So it is five days a week, twelve hours a day of shooting scenes at Dodger Stadium. I wouldn't have cared if it was twenty hours a day, seven days a week. It was, after all, Dodger Stadium for Christ's sakes!

This was pretty interesting work to me, and I could see myself being in this profession. How do I get a break? This is a real movie, twenty million dollars' worth. *A Talent for the Game* is the name of the movie.

It is starring James Olmos, who plays the scout, and Lorraine Bracco, who plays the girlfriend. Oh, and forty ex-major league ballplayers. They had to hire ex-players because the actors couldn't play baseball.

There are just so many things that can go wrong on a shoot. It is amazing. Here are some examples.

One day, Lorraine's girlfriend is trying to be all macho to impress Lorraine. She is playing catch with one of the pitchers in the cast. He is a sinker baller, and if you don't catch the ball just right, you get the ball on your thumb, and it hurts. So the next day, she shows up wearing a bright new shiny thumb cast.

You need fans in the stands, right? So they, the producers, are having problems getting fans in the stands for the big shoot. They decide on a mass giveaway promotion to get some fans in the stands. They give away refrigerators and a car, and they advertise it on the radio. It was quite a big deal, and they got forty thousand attendees.

The only problem was thirty-five thousand of the audience are Crips, and the other twenty thousand or so are Bloods and Rolling Fifty's. These are the most notorious and violent gangs in Los Angeles. And our security? We have poor security. Well, it didn't take long for a riot to break out in the stands, or was it a big gang fight? I don't know, but somehow, we lived through it.

So one day, I'm standing in the dugout, and the director comes up to me and asked me, "What would the players be dong during the national anthem?"

I tell him.

"You have a great face," he tells me.

"Well, I am available. Make me a star" is my response.

So we are filming a scene in the clubhouse, and it was not going well. They can't get the manager's language right for the pregame meeting.

The problem is that the manager is an actor and he can't comprehend what would be going on in the clubhouse before a game, and furthermore, he doesn't grasp the relationship that he has or should have with his players.

After about five shoots, the director comes to me and asks me to write the script for the scene. It takes me about a half hour to write the scene. We come back to shoot the scene, and it goes perfectly. It was so perfect they cut it from the movie.

The next day, we are on the field. The director and the stars were sitting in director's chairs along the third baseline. I'm shagging throws for a coach who is hitting fungoes from the third base side of the batting cage.

I turn to the three amigos, and I advise them, "These guys are pros, but even professionals make mistakes. So pay attention!"

Well, sure enough, the shortstop uncorks a rocket, but it is an errant rocket. The throw is headed right for Olmos's face, and he is looking away. He, Olmos, now looks back on to the field as the ball is hurtling toward his face. It is was about a foot away, and then it happens. A loud *pop*! And I snatch the screaming missile right out of his face. If that throw would have hit him, it could have been disastrous. Just another good deed and a great grab.

Now the food was outstanding. These movie people really know how to put on a spread. The set has a caterer, and he has a great variety of gourmet foods. The ballplayers have all gained ten to fifteen pounds what with prime rib, steaks, lobster, and desserts galore. I stay away.

So we are shooting the game scene. It is two o'clock in the morning. The marine layer has set in, and the field is soaking wet, and it is a mess. The players, well, they are tired with full bellies and just want to go home. We wrap the shoot, and we all made it out alive.

The fall of 1990 arrived, and a new professional baseball league is being formed. The inaugural Senior Professional Baseball league was being formed, and it is going to be a winter league played solely in Florida.

A tourist attraction and baseball card signing event are what the league really is designed to be. The league has six teams all playing at spring training sites. The hitting coach for the Las Vegas Stars is rumored to be the manager for the "Tampa Bay Sun Sox."

Now the minimum age for players is thirty-five, and I'm now forty-two. Maybe I will go see the guy. So I do, and I wind up throwing batting practice for the Stars for the rest of the 1990 season.

The manager for the Stars at this time is an okay guy. He hails from Santa Maria, home of the Indians. His brother umpires games there. He was probably the boob who called me for a balk back in '86 or whenever it was.

The manager is going to play in the senior league as is the pitching coach for the Stars. That's funny because he can't even throw a strike during batting practice.

One day, the manager steps into the batting cages for a few swings. I was on the mound. Eighty-five down the middle, "Strike one!" bellows the little left-handed reliever who is umpiring from behind the batting cage. Then a changeup floats in.

"Strike two!" the player umpire calls out.

Then a knee-buckling slider comes blazing in and, "Strike three!" calls out the little lefty from behind the batting cages.

The pitchers are just getting ready to hit, and they are all gathered around the batting cage. I showed the manager up in front of the players. Uh-oh!

The manager? He is as mad as hell. He throws the bat and walks over to the third base dugout all the while screaming a long list of profanities, mostly directed at me. He is as pissed as a man can be. He sits down on a chair at the top of the dugout steps and bellows out at me.

"You know, I don't have to let you come out here and throw!" he shouted.

I think I am in the doghouse, and it only took me two days.

I finished throwing batting practice. It took about fifteen or twenty minutes, and I walked over to where the manager is sitting.

"I'm sorry," I say. "I don't know what happened. It was the devil. The devil made me do it."

The next day, we are on the field for batting practice. The manager is throwing, and I am shagging in center field. Our big home-run, hitting first baseman, is in the cage. The manager delivers the pitch, and the batter launches a towering fly ball to dead center field. I turn and take off, and I make the catch over my head without ever looking back.

"That was the best catch I have seen all year," the manager tells me later.

Guess I'm out of the doghouse.

Now I have traveled to Tampa Bay to be a Sun Sox hurler. When I get to Florida, I find the team's office and check in. We are staying at the Holiday Inn. I'm one of the first players to arrive, so I get a room to myself. That's cool.

The next day, I'm out at the field, and there are a few other guys out also. It is hot, in the nineties, and the humidity is 90 percent too, pretty miserable. One guy pops his elbow and has to have Tommy John surgery. He was a left-handed pitcher, and it is only the first day.

When I get back to the hotel, to my surprise, the Detroit Tigers catcher, whom I have played with for years on the Orange County A's, is in the lobby of the hotel.

"Welcome aboard," I say.

He has a rental car, so we have wheels. What to do at night? That is the question. The days are filled with practice. So being the sleuth that I am, I do some investigating, and I found a bar that sponsors the team.

I call them and asked, "What's up? Are there any women in that bar?"

They answer that question, "The bar is right across from a big shopping mall," and about nine o'clock, the place starts jumping.

We head over to the fine drinking establishment, and sure enough, the place is jumping. We play pool and tell the bartender that we are with the Sun Sox. The catcher is wearing his World Series ring.

"Sun Sox players drink for free," the bartender said.

So we start downing Greyhounds.

I met this girl, and we coaxed her into our pool game. It turns out that she works for the Sun Sox baseball club. We wind up getting a twelve-pack of beer to go, and we left for her place. She has a roommate, and she is as hot as they come. Things are going pretty well, for now.

We stumble into the hotel lobby just as everyone is getting up for breakfast. We eat and then go to the field. Well, I have an easy day. I'm in the outfield, shagging, and one of the veteran pitchers is hanging out with me. This guy might be a Hall of Fame member. I don't know.

Anyway, I tell him about the bar and Sun Sox players drink for free. Well, I don't think any more of it.

I just know I am getting a good night's sleep, and I do.

Early the next morning, it is breakfast and then the yard. I am throwing today. I do my work, and then I am shagging in the outfield with the same pitcher from yesterday. I look at him, and he isn't quite right.

"What's up?" I ask.

He and another pitcher, a veteran major leaguer, were together in the outfield. He starts out with, "Some guy told me where we could drink for free."

"So we went there, and man, he was right. Man, I'm fucked up."

"Now I thought you had to be a pretty straight, laced guy to pitch twenty years in the big leagues. Guess I was wrong."

I guess it is all about being a whore and learning to pitch with a hangover.

Pitching mechanics have greatly changed over the years and through the decades of baseball. The old-timers like the Walter Johnsons and Burleigh Grimes and Sal the Barber ruled. Then it was on to the fifties and Warren Spahn and Lew Burdette and even into the sixties up to the Bob Gibson Sandy Koufax era. They all had great big windups and could throw numerous innings. Not at all like today's game where pitchers make a fortune and are looking to be in the showers after five innings. This is mostly due to the players union, I suspect. Today's pitchers are more compact in their deliveries. They use less energy to throw fewer innings is how I would sum it up.

I remember the old knuckleballer telling me one time how he was pitching for Texas. The game was in Minnesota, and it was freezing cold outside. In the seventh, he wanted out of the game. He was starting to get frostbite. It was so cold. Well, they have some twenty-five-year-old in the bullpen, and he says he can't get loose.

Once when I was a kid, my dad took me to a ball game at Dodger Stadium. I was about eleven years old. It was the Dodgers versus the Milwaukee Braves. I confronted Burdette and Spahn from the stands as they were on the field for smoking cigarettes. I am sure they took heed; after all, I was eleven years old.

The hitting coach from Las Vegas is not the manager of the Sun Sox, but he is going to be a coach. The new manager is an ex-Orioles pitcher, and he cuts me immediately.

This comes the day after the catcher, my buddy, told me that I was playing the other pitchers "under the table." What was I going to do now?

I make my way to Lakeland, the training facility of another team set to play in the league. I introduce myself and ask if they need any pitching help. What I got was the most honest answer I have ever gotten from a baseball player in my life.

"Yes," the manager says, "but we don't have any money."

There's a problem. I can't play for free. I spend a couple of days with this club, but alas, it is true. I can't play for free.

Chapter Twenty

Night Train

I headed for Las Vegas, and I was pretty disappointed. The catcher wound up marrying the girl from the bar. That was a big mistake as he did four years in prison for nearly beating her to death. Wow, I didn't see that one coming.

Back in Las Vegas, I was pitching for the Orioles scout team. My good friend, the old catcher, had become a full-fledged scout and had assembled a team of prospects.

I finished the year on that note. One thing though that is sad and funny; at the same time, my father has been sick lately. The doctors didn't know what was ailing him because he was suffering from mesothelioma, a debilitating lung disease caused by exposure to asbestos.

They prescribed steroids for him, prednisone.

"You should take one before you pitch," he suggested.

I'm not really into drugs of the steroid and performance-enhancing type, but I did use anti-inflammatories once in a while. I was not thrilled about the idea of steroids even though it seemed like a high percentage of professional athletes during this time of the "steroid" era were engaged in "chemically enhanced" workouts. It was a twist on the old saying, "Better living through drugs became better athletes through steroids." After a little coaxing, I took some of my dad's tablets with me.

Holy shit, what a difference this stuff makes!

I was throwing in the midnineties at age forty-two. My father? He passed away the following June from cancer.

As we moved into 1991, the last year was a sobering one, to say the least. My father's passing was the most significant event of the year. We had some rocky times, but in the past five years or so, we had been pretty close. It was quite painful to lose him.

I was still pitching for the Orioles as the season turned to Indian summer in Las Vegas. The old guy had become my new best friend and drinking buddy. We were playing in the league here in town, and we had the best team because we had all the pitching.

The pro season was about to start. The kid is with the Royals now. He was destined to begin the season in Memphis, which is the Kansas City organization's double "A" team.

"Good luck," I told him.

He called me about two weeks into the season and asked if I could drive his car to Memphis. I had never been there, so I was off like a shot to Tennessee.

I spent about a week in this cool country music capital with Graceland and the mouthwatering Memphis barbecue. But the best thing about this city was the Peabody Hotel. The walking of the ducks happened there every day at about five in the afternoon. They had a red carpet rolled out for the mallards to waddle in from the pond. It was quite a spectacle.

When I returned to Nevada, I checked in with the Las Vegas Stars.

"Do you need help with the pregame?" I asked the manager, who was the same guy from last year whom I had buried at the plate.

"Yes," he said.

So I had a job for the summer. Better yet, I could use the bullpen for my private pitching lessons for high school prospects.

That was pretty impressive when these budding pitchers could have full use of the best facility in the state for instructional pitching. Plus, it was accommodating for the kids because of its central location. I was set for the summer.

The catcher for the Tigers, or the ex-catcher for the Tigers, has a team in Southern California. I venture to Southern California to play with them. Flashing back, it was the summer of '89. The "Quakes" is what the team was named.

In one game, we didn't have nine players to play the game. We were in Downtown Anaheim. There were plenty of drunks around. So the catcher gets this old Black wino to play right field. We bought him a couple of bottles of "Night Train," and he was good to go. Now besides the Gallo brothers, Night Train has killed more people than cancer over the years. Cheapest wine you can buy, and it packs a punch.

We are going to Santa Maria to play the Indians. I hate to be redundant, but Santa Maria is such a beautiful place. And this team of theirs, well, it is fifty years old, and the team's program looks to be the size of a telephone book. This is what I had envisioned for my team, the "Reds." But alas, it wasn't to be.

You need support. It isn't a one-man operation to run a ball team although some may think they can do it. And money, you need plenty of that.

So the fall and winter are coming, and I'm not getting any younger. The kid is out of baseball now. His arm problems proved to just be too severe for him to continue on throwing.

Now it is December, and he is up here in Vegas for the playoffs, the NFL playoffs. I get them a complimentary room at the Sahara. While we are there, I met this lady from Arizona. She represents a sports artist from the East Coast. She wanted to display his art and sell some of it if possible. The art is top-quality stuff, and I may need a real job soon, so I jump right in. She is having trouble getting permission to set up her display. No problem, I say, as I know the owner. And like magic, she is set up. Well, I get her a room too. I mean, she can't sleep in her van. Well, I sort of shack up with her as she ain't too bad-looking either. She is a nice Catholic girl. I mean, I like Catholic girls. They are usually as horny as hell, and this one was right out of that mold. So I help her with her show, and I made a little money, and we get along pretty well.

Before leaving for Arizona, she tells me that she is doing a show at the Cow Palace in San Francisco. It is the national sports show and big sports show at that.

"Would you be interested in working the show with me?"
"Most definitely," I say. "I'll see you then."
"Oh no," she says. "I'm coming back for the Super Bowl."
"Super," I say. "See you then."

I really don't know what to do with myself now. I'm now forty-four years of age, and my big-league hopes are severely dashed. Whether I could pitch in the big leagues is irrelevant. Nobody is going to give me a chance at this age. So I am thinking this art deal might be my next best shot. I think this guy's stuff is really the bomb. I sold a few pieces around town for top dollar, and the pitching and hitting lessons? They aren't cutting it. There is another guy in town doing a similar business, but he has his own facility—you know, dirt. He is a millionaire. Anyway, food for thought.

The Washington Redskins are playing the Buffalo Bills in the Super Bowl—it is Super Bowl XXVI to be exact—and sure enough, my new partner is back. I get her set up at the Sahara Hotel, and we work the whole week and the game on Sunday, and in reality, it is a pretty successful week, and the year is 1992.

She asks me again if I can come to Arizona on the thirteenth of February and we will load the van for the trip to San Francisco and the National Sports show. It is being held at the Cow Palace and do I want to make the trip and work the show. She has a friend who lives in San Francisco and is out of town, so we have a place to stay. "Perfect," I say. "Yes, I will be there." So I drive to Arizona to the home of major league baseball's spring training, which is exactly what I should be here for.

So once in Arizona, the girl introduces me to this sports memorabilia dealer from California. He is a little Jewish character. We begin a conversation, and he tells me that he represents Frank Robinson, the Hall of Fame outfielder and current manager of the Baltimore Orioles. He says that he arranges all of Frank's personal appearances; in return, Frank sets him up with players to do signings. You know, bats, balls, anything connected with baseball. We become friends until his death at the hands of a real modern-day Jezebel. It is in the year 2003, and he had developed diabetes, really severe diabetes.

Well, he was trolling the internet, looking for information about his newfound disease when he found her.

She was trolling on the internet too, nude, looking for a sucker, and one thing led to another, and he moved to Arizona.

This woman had been a fifteen-year critical care nurse. She knew the ropes. So one weekend, they come to Las Vegas to do some signings at the Stardust Hotel, and he went into a diabetic shock, and she did nothing to help him. I mean, a Coke, a sandwich, anything. But no, nothing is what she did for him. Then two days later, she takes him to the emergency room. She doesn't call an ambulance. She drives him to the emergency room. He was already dead.

Well, the story she told the investigators had a little different ring to it. She said that she took him to a dialysis center first, and they told her to drive him to the hospital. I say bullshit. Any medical professional in the world, except for her, would have known to call an ambulance right away. I say bullshit. And that's exactly what three dialysis centers told me.

Back to the here and now. I have my baseball bag in my car—never leave home without it. The little sports memorabilia dealer tells me that he was at the Brewers practice yesterday, and the manager was asking people in the stands if they could hit fungoes or throw-batting practice. Hmmm, that's right up my alley.

So I go over to the Brewers training facility the next morning bright and early. And sure enough, he was right. They need help.

"I can help," I say. "Let's talk about money."

"Let's see what you can do first," they say. "Be here tomorrow at eight o'clock in the morning."

So I go to their practice the next day. I know the pitching coach. He is from Orange County. I beat him in college baseball, and I beat him when he pitched for the La Fonda Stars team. I don't like him. He is a trash talker, one of those "draft dodger" types, from back in the day.

Anyway, practice begins, and we are out in a backfield doing infield drills. I am playing second base. Why? I'm here to pitch, and from the looks of this staff, I could make this team easily. This is a typical Milwaukee team. The team is rich in on-the-field talent and hitters galore, but the pitching? Well, that's another story.

So practice is going. The grass is still damp with morning dew when the coach hits me a grounder, and this is a double-play situation. I field the ball and feed it to the shortstop. It is a perfect feed, and it hits him right in the chest. Literally, the throw, flip, whatever you want to call it, hit him right in the chest. The Dominican kid who is playing shortstop doesn't get leather on my throw. Everybody is chuckling. It is bad etiquette to laugh at professionals, but this was so funny that you couldn't help a little chuckle.

After the infield practice, it is time for the pitchers to throw. I am playing catch with their ace. This guy can't even locate the ball. I mean, we are just playing catch. Sixty feet at the most, and I am picking one-hopper and fielding balls off my shoelaces then one over my head. Me? Every throw I make is right at his chest.

Finally, it came time to throw batting practice. The Brewers had an "A" game this afternoon, and I was going to throw batting practice for the starters. This was a championship-caliber team, except for the pitching. The team reminded me a little of the 1986 Angels ball club.

Batting practice began. I was throwing four-seamers right down the middle. These guys can hit, and I'm bringing it pretty good, so good, in fact, there are only a couple of balls in the batting cage.

The center fielder steps in the batting cage, a surefire future Hall of Fame player. He pounded one over the center field wall.

I turned to the coach who was standing behind the mound and remarked, "That was a good one."

"That was nothing," the coach said. "The next guy can really launch them," he quipped.

Hmm, we will see about that.

When I was with the Angels, I just threw polite batting practice and didn't really show my stuff. The big burly hitter stepped into the batting cage. He had brought three bats out to batting practice with him. We did the bunt drills, then it was time to start hitting.

This stocky guy was looking for a fastball over the heart of the plate, which he was crowding to protect the outside corner. I threw him a fastball on the outside corner, and he whiffed at it.

My next pitch was a fastball, about ninety-two miles per hour waist high and tight. He took a quick swing, and the ball broke his bat right above the label.

He kind of smirked in disbelief. Then he grabbed bat number two and took a practice swing.

I hurled another four-seamer right down the middle. He took a mighty swing and made contact about six inches above his wrists. *Crack went the bat!*

That thirty-four-inch Louisville Slugger looked like a broomstick that somebody had just splintered over their knee.

He chuckled, shaking his head as he stepped out of the box and grabbed the third bat he had brought to the cage.

Are you ready, meathead? I thought to myself. He stepped back in the cage and dug in. I threw another fastball and he took the pitch without swinging.

Then he stared at me as if to say, "Bring it on."

And so I did. This was a screamer inside again, and it shattered that thin handled bat just below the label.

With that, batting practice ended. I had broken all three of his bats in five pitches.

As we were walking off the field, the future Hall of Fame shortstop called out to me.

"Hey, hummer. That was the best batting practice we have had all year. Thanks," he said.

I went back to the clubhouse to talk with the powers to be about money and a contract.

What they offered me instead was pretty darned paltry.

"I can't live on that," I said. "I mean, what am I supposed to do rent a room?"

With my luck, I would get mass murderer Jeffery Dahmer for a roommate.

I could hear it already. "What are we having for dinner tonight?"

He answers, "Liver. Yours?"

"Um, thanks, but no thanks."

No, I was going to San Francisco for another commitment.

"Here's my phone number. Give me a call if you come up with some decent money."

My phone never rang.

So what is the National Baseball Hall of Fame (HOF)? Well, in 1936, a young man, an heir to the Singer sewing machine company, decided that times were hard.

It was the Great Depression, and prohibition was taking place. It was in Cooperstown, New York, that the HOF was conceived. It is a real honor to be included in the HOF, and two of the guys on this Brewers team are slated to be inducted into the "Hall" soon after their playing days are done—the center fielder and the shortstop.

It is funny how baseball and beer go together so well.

Cooperstown was the hops capital of the United States, at least on the East Coast. So when prohibition came along, the growers couldn't sell their cash crops. The town was headed for the tombs, bankruptcy—they couldn't make a living.

So in 1936 along comes this heir to the Singer sewing machine company. And he created the "National Baseball Hall of Fame." It opens its doors for business in 1939, and a dandy idea it was.

Now all three major sports (baseball, football, and basketball) have a "Hall of Fame." But baseball is the oldest and the best. It was also in 1936 that the first Asian Professional Baseball league was formed in Japan. So there is a little history lesson.

We are off to the Cow Palace in San Francisco and the National Sports Show, a three-day event. Naturally, I start things off by getting a speeding ticket on the Interstate on the way up to San Francisco.

We arrived in San Francisco and the house where we are to stay. It was a pretty nice house, and we did pretty well at the show. "The straw that stirs the drink," the former Angel outfielder, is at the show also, making a guest appearance. He hangs out at our booth for a while.

So we wrap up the show and head back to Arizona. We have one stop to make on the way, and that is in Rancho Cucamonga. We are supposed to do a charity event for a San Francisco Giants outfielder. The girl wants to blow it off and just go straight through to Arizona. I get a motel room and tell her to get some sleep. I shower and shave and head out to the charity event. It is really nice. There are a lot of former big leaguers and some current players at the gala. I set up the art pieces in a nice display, and by the end of the evening, I have sold all my pieces. A good night indeed.

The outfielder would go on in a hellacious turmoil to break the single-season and the all-time home run records. The issue? Steroids! It would become the biggest steroid scandal yet. Hell, they were all doing it.

I went back to the motel after the gala. I got some much-needed sleep, and we rolled to Arizona the next day. Now once back in Arizona, I find out that she has a show on Sunday next. She doesn't want to do it. So I stay and do the show and make good money once again. This is a great product, and it basically sells itself. I have come to the conclusion that my partner is lazy. On top of that, she is mixed up with some weird cult. There are all kinds of crazies in the world. I think most of them, the female ones anyway, live in Sedona. I think she is just another version of that. I am probably like, no, make that definitely cutting bait. And so I do. Back to Las Vegas.

The baseball season is starting up, and the Stars have a new manager. He is a younger guy, younger than me anyway. He is definitely a man on his way up the ladder of success. He is ticketed to be next to the manager of the San Diego Padres. The hitting coach is still the same guy who has been here for the past two years. I go to see the old hitting coach. He introduces me to the young skipper. I mean, this guy is just a few years younger than me.

He okays me to throw batting practice, so I'm set for this year, and my old buddy the Orioles scout has his scout team, and I throw for him occasionally. Then, of course, there are my pitching lessons. It is a full plate. I'm not getting rich, but I am having fun and enjoying life. Sometimes that's all you can really ask for.

Chapter Twenty-One

Hot Dog Up and In

Now it is early in the 1992 season. I have a right-handed pitcher that I have been working with who throws pretty well. He's just finished school at USC, where he played football for four years and baseball for three.

There is a gaggle of baseball scouts who have been coming out early to watch our batting practice. I ask them if any of their organizations need any pitching help at "A" ball.

"Are you looking for a job?" one of the scouts pops off sarcastically.

"No, but I have a younger pitcher who is."

The Yankees scout pipes up right away with a yes.

"I will have him out here at three tomorrow afternoon," I say.

Well, the Padres' assistant general manager is in town to inspect the troops, and he gets wind of the kids' tryout with the Yankees.

"Mind if I attend?" he says to me in a kind coy voice.

"The more, the merrier," I say.

The show is on, and I catch the kid's bullpen, and he smokes it.

"We will take him," the Yankees scout says.

"But I need to make a phone call first. I will be right back."

Back in 1992, mobile phones were just coming on the market, and they were expensive. So he had to go to a pay phone, and the swoop occurred.

Not to be outdone, the Padres' assistant general manager, who needs no permission to sign a player and has the checkbook with him in his pocket to boot, pulls it out. A twenty-five hundred dollar bonus to the player and five hundred dollars for me, a "finder's fee." This is a pretty good day.

The Padres have hired a new scout. He is a distinguished World War II veteran. I will spend the next two years watching baseball games with him. He has managed quite a few different major league teams, and he was a surprisingly friendly guy.

After World War II, men were welcomed back from the war as heroes, men of honor, a far cry from the name-calling, spit-on-you protesters that I faced. And get a job in baseball? No, not on your life. I think three or four Vietnam veterans played in the big leagues. It was just plain disgraceful when you consider the number of men conscripted for war during the period.

I haven't talked about my time in the service very much. That's because it was so horrific. And then when we came home to the United States, it was like we were monsters. Killers and rapists, they called us. And nobody wanted to be associated with us. Problems? Oh, we had problems all right. Society was our problem.

The Padres have a center fielder who got signed because he could run fast. Unfortunately, that's just one of the tools you need to play major league baseball, and in fact, it is the least of the five major tools. Hit for average, hit for power, catch the ball, throw the ball (arm strength), and finally foot speed. One out of five was what this kid had. *So how does he get on base?*

This guy is a Black kid from the Deep South, and he is just plain dumb. So the manager tells him to come out early and to work on bunting.

"Who is going to throw for me?" he asks.

"Maybe the Bullet [my new nickname] will throw for you."

He asks me and I say, "Yes."

Now I am a pretty good hitting and bunting instructor, and in about two weeks, I have a pretty good foundation laid down for him, and he got some bunt hits in games.

So the team holds a kangaroo court, and he decides to put me up for a fine for teaching him to bunt. He got traded to the Seattle Mariners shortly thereafter, and they sent him to single "A" ball. That winter, he got busted for selling cocaine. It was probably lactose.

My legend has grown pretty substantially over the years. What legend? The "Comp King," that's what legend. Many nights, I am taking three or four players out for dinner on comps after the game at one of the better casinos on the strip. It is a pretty sweet life I've built for myself, if only there was some money involved. Oh well. So the season draws to a close, and I am pitching winter ball for the old Orioles scout.

I like to drink and enjoy the nightlife as much as the next guy. The Sahara is my favorite haunt. So I'm in the lounge one night just relaxing and doing my lounge lizard thing. "Cookie Jar" is playing, and he is a pretty good entertainer.

I meet two young ladies from Washington State. I do not pay for food or drinks. As long as I am in the casino, the owner's orders. So I put the two girls on my tab.

"Can you say ménage à trois?"

I can, and that's what I am thinking.

I'm dancing with one of the girls, and when we return to our table, there are two Black guys sitting there, trying to make it with the other girl.

Well, almost immediately, a brawl breaks out. I am holding my own when I feel someone at my back. It is the casino manager. He is an old Air Force veteran, and we are friends. I get along with him. He has a concealed weapons permit, and he is carrying a loaded .40-caliber semiautomatic handgun. That's good because a lot of gang members frequent this lounge. Well, the brawl clears, and we all go home. I missed out on the girls from Washington.

Celebrity batting practice, that's what we have today, and today's celebrity is none other than Jerry Seinfeld.

"Who is that?" I ask.

The owner of the team says, "He is an up-and-coming comedian."

"Never heard of him," I reply.

"Will you throw for him? They are shooting a commercial for an HBO special. If you throw for him," the owner says, "you can skip pitching regular batting practice."

Hell! I'd rather throw for the players, but I can see that's not happening.

So I go through my warm-up routine and got loose. Then I am sitting in the dugout, waiting to start the commercial shoot, an older gentleman sits down next to me. He asks me, "Are you going to throw for my son?"

"Yes," I say. "Is Jerry your son?"

"Yes," he says.

"He was a hell of a high school baseball player, and he is going to take you deep."

"Really?" I say.

"Got any money, say, fifty dollars?"

Well, the bet's on, and I love a good challenge. The session started, and the batter can't even touch the ball. This ain't high school.

"What are you doing?" everyone screams at me.

"I made a bet with the old guy sitting over there in the dugout," I respond.

"Whatever the bet was, you won it. Now let him hit the ball."

I never did get my fifty dollars and no tickets for Jerry's show either.

"No hits for you," says the baseball Nazi.

About a week later, the Dodgers farm team, the Albuquerque Dukes, are in town. They are leading the league while we are mired in the basement buried in last place. Mondesi, Piazza, Martinez, this may be the best Dukes team they have ever had. So it is the day before Pedro is due to pitch, and he is the "King" of the league. The local paper, the *Review-Journal*, has written a story, a full-length feature story, on how great of a minor-league career he has had. Really?

The next day, I tell the manager that I am throwing for the starters today. I don't usually assert myself in that way, but that story on an opposing player, well, that just kind of stuck in my craw. I have played a lot of baseball, and one thing I don't like is losing, and this team was nothing but losers.

So the manager concedes, and hell, it is about a hundred and ten in the shade when batting practice starts. The heat was nothing compared to what I was throwing that bright sunny summer day. No one can get the ball out of the cage against me.

"Bullet, what in the hell are you doing?" asks the third baseman.

I responded by saying, "What do you think you are gonna see tonight? Let's get ready."

Pedro went three and a third, and we totally knocked the shit right out of the ball, his shortest minor-league appearance ever.

Later that evening, I was in the stands, running the radar gun and charting pitches. I am sitting right behind home plate with the Padres scout and former major league manager. There are two Dodger executives sitting there in the stands with us. The one guy, who is a senior vice president, says to me, "I have never seen anyone throw that hard in batting practice."

I am not sure what he meant by that. It worked. It was the highlight of the season.

The year by now had turned to be 1993, and once again, it's Super Bowl time. I'm down with a cold. My phone rings, and it is the little sports memorabilia dealer. He lives in Santa Monica.

"What's up?"

"Nothing," I say.

"Well, I need to come to Las Vegas for a few days as they are doing something fumigating or whatever to my apartment. So I have to be out for a while."

"Okay," I say. "I will get you a complimentary room at the Stardust. Is that okay?"

"Yes," he says. "See you tomorrow."

So he rolls into town, and he gets settled in. I go over to meet him. I have a beer, and he meandered over to a baccarat table. He won fourteen thousand dollars. He upgrades to a suite the next day. Then as usual in the gambling world, he goes right back down to the casino and loses it all back, right? Wrong! He wins another eight thousand dollars.

It is really late at night by now, and we go across the street to the Riviera to check their odds on an upcoming fight. The favorite is undefeated, maybe forty fights or so, but the challenger is pretty good too, and so this is going to be a marquee matchup.

There is a woman ahead of us in the sports book. She's betting a grand, a thousand dollars, on the challenger.

"Are you crazy?" I ask her.

The champion could roll out of bed at six in the morning with a blind hangover and knock this guy out.

She retorts without skipping a beat, "My friends have been with your champion, and he hasn't trained one day for this fight unless you call fucking and drinking all night a training routine?"

Well, we passed on a fifteen to one shot, and the challenger won by unanimous decision. Whoops, we missed one.

So the next day, the little Jew is on the phone, and he's doing what he does, dealing. We get everything we need to build football plaques—nice plaques with three Buffalo Bills and three Dallas Cowboy stars.

Meanwhile, we set up an assembly plant in the two-room suite. I get a couple of ballplayers to come over and we pay them to assemble the plaques. Meantime I am around town getting sites to sell the plaques and we settle for three locations.

We are going to make fifty dollars on each unit, and we have a hundred plus units. We sell just fifteen plaques. Disappointment abounds. My little buddy goes back home. I, in the meanwhile, sell the rest of the plaques to sports bars for the upcoming football season for twelve dollars each. They use them for halftime giveaways. Fortunately, Dallas and Buffalo were on the Monday night football schedule, quite often following their respective Super Bowl appearances in the previous season.

Baseball is back in season. I can manage one more season, I think. But there is one little problem—the manager does not want me back for the '93 season. I am mildly surprised.

The team is up for sale, and the player development contract with the Padres is also set to expire.

They, the Stars, provide the field, but they are contracted to major league franchises for labor. In other words, the Stars have no say in who plays here.

My phone rings. It is the current owner of the team.

"I have told the Padres that you are going to be a paid coach on this year's team. Are you okay with that?"

"Yes! Hell yes!" I answer.

We have some talent this year. Lots of older players with major-league experience. We open in Phoenix and lose, 2–3. Both losses came in the ninth inning. So the team is home now. It is early before the game. The manager is in his office. A few reporters are gathered in the stands, waiting for the skipper to come out on the field so they can roast him. I am standing on the field, waiting and engaging them in a conversation. We are supposed to win this year, and we are off to a bad start.

"He isn't coming out," I tell them. "He is on the phone with the major league club. Can I help you?"

They fired questions at me as if shot out of a Gatling gun.

I compose myself and say to them, "This club has more talent and, more importantly, more character than any team I have seen out here, and I have been here a while."

Well, that seemed to appease them for a little bit, about three hours, I'd say. That's when we lost another game in the ninth inning, three out of four.

Baseball is a funny game. But there is nothing funny about losing. So I get the closer, and we go to the Sahara lounge and get a couple of long island iced teas.

"You know what's wrong with you?" I say to the closer. "You are a nice guy, and nice guys finish last. You have been in the league for a couple of years, and everybody knows you. You have good stuff. I mean, you have every single hitter, 0–2, yet they get on base. Throw the damn baseball up, and once in a while, don't let guys get comfortable in the batter's box. Learn to throw some chin music."

The next night, we are leading in the ninth, and the manager summons the closer into the game. The count is 0–2 on the first hitter he faces. The closer backflips the hitter with a ninety-four-mile-per-hour fastball. Next pitch strike three. He goes on to record eighteen saves in eighteen opportunities and is promoted to the big club. Long islands work every time.

The pitching coach for the Stars is an ex-big leaguer. I like him, but he isn't a very good pitching coach, and he is pissed that he is not in the big leagues. I think he was the one who went to the manager and pooh-poohed me at the start of the season. I am no competition to him. I pose no threat. We are getting along a lot better.

So it is all-star time—a time when there is a lot of movement in baseball. By movement, I mean, trades, promotions, and demotions.

This year, we are having an "alumni" game. Whatever that means. I mean, I've heard of "old-timers day" but an alumni game?

In '86, we had the real deal old-timers game. Earl Weaver managed the American Leaguers and Dick Willams, who would later become a Padres scout, managed the National League entry. Jim Bouton was there in the outfield with me, the original tell-all "baseball" book writer.

Oh well, I guess I'll play a couple of innings. It is the fifth, and I am playing first base. My turn in the batting order is up. I launch a fly ball down the right-field line. It is going to fall. I round first and head for a second. I make a great pop-up slide, but I am out.

Later on, while sitting in the stands, a Texas Ranger scout says to me, "Was that you sliding into second base?"

"Yep, it was me."

"Well, that was a pretty fine slide," he says.

"No!"

"That was a pretty fine throw," I say.

Scouts always miss the point.

We are in the first place by five games at the all-star break, but that doesn't matter because we play halves in the Pacific Coast League. That means that we are all even, each team that is, to start the second half. Still, that's pretty good for a team that started out one and three. The second half is going to be harder, though, because we have had so many player call-ups.

I have a fan club. It is just a small one. I usually hit fly balls for the outfielders during the last part of infield and outfield. I must say my fungo skills are pretty good. After hitting for the outfielders, I practice hitting foul balls for the catcher. So I face toward the outfield and hit fly balls back over my head into the stands behind me. I have about ten or so kids with their gloves, and it is quite a sight to behold and a big hit with the kids.

Then one day, the owner of the baseball team comes to me. He asks me about a broken window in the parking lot.

"No, I don't know anything about that," I tell him.

Could it be that one of my fungoes found its way up and out of the stadium and into someone's windshield? Only the shadow knows for sure.

It is just another day in paradise, and I'm walking down the left-field line to the clubhouse and, *whack*!

I am the recipient of a half-eaten hot dog right on the side of my noggin. The mustard and ketchup are dripping slowly down my face. Now, fortunately for me, I'm a towel guy. I always have one with me for sweat. So now it has a new use: hot dog cleanup.

I turn, and there is a ten- to twelve-year-old girl standing there in the stands. She is standing by the rail in the first row.

"Did you throw that hot dog at me?" I calmly ask her.

"Yes, I did," she boldly answers.

"Why?" I ask.

"You are a bum," she says. "You pitched lousy last night."

I say to her, "You are mistaken. That wasn't me. I am a coach," adding, "You are right, though. That was a pretty bad pitching effort last night."

I have a brand-new baseball in my back pocket, and I then walk over and give it to her.

"And don't throw it at anyone," I scold.

I'm not the pitching coach, and you can get in trouble by sticking your nose where it shouldn't be. It is nearing the end of the season. We have some shaky pitching with both our starters and in the bullpen.

One guy, a lefty reliever, comes out to run with me. I mean, it is hot, really, it is Vegas hot, and no one wants to run with me.

"What's up?" I ask.

"Well," he began, "the pitching coach says my mechanics are bad, and they are in need of a complete 'rebuild,' and the manager says he can't use me in games anymore."

"My first question to you is, Do they know that you are consulting me?"

"Yes. I asked them, and they said it was fine."

"Okay. It is like this. You don't have a plus fastball, but your breaking ball is okay. Your problem is pitch selection, and by that, I mean your location. You throw everything away from the hitter, and guys take you all over the yard. What's the simplest fix?" I say to him.

"I don't know," he says.

"Pitch predominantly inside. Cut the field down. Learn to throw foul balls, then go away to get hitters out."

He says, "That's pretty simple. Cut the field down. Make them beat you in the small part of the yard."

So the manager puts him in a game. We are getting beat 15–4 in the fifth inning. Well, he throws two perfect innings. The manager puts him in again and gets the same results. He throws twenty scoreless innings to close the season. That's why the pitching coach has issues with me or had issues. I guess they are over now.

I'm standing in the outfield shagging balls during batting practice. The people that run the audio are playing music.

"Land of a Thousand Dances" is blaring, and I'm dancing all the dances. A couple of outfielders are out in center field with me when the batter lifts a fly ball our way. I move over a few steps and settle under the ball when, out of nowhere, a baseball glove flies in front of my face. Well, the glove obscures my vision and the ball hits me right in the head and then bounces over the fence. Pretty hard-head, I'd say.

I'm not pissed, but the outfielder who threw the glove is nearly in tears; after all, that was a pretty bush league thing to do.

Well, the season draws to an end, and this is will probably be my last. We don't win the second half. We finished in second place—still, a pretty respectable showing. So the playoffs begin. We are playing Colorado Springs, the Cleveland Indians triple "A" affiliate.

We win the first two games at home then on to Colorado Springs for a two-game set. We lose the first game, but it is the best of five in the playoffs. Now this is the first time the Las Vegas squad has made the playoffs since1987, so it is big deal, and the owners are quite pleased.

It was pregame, and the manager is pitching batting practice, and the starting pitcher is in the cage. The first pitch hits him right in the side of his head. Why not two? And that is exactly what happened. The second pitch hits him right square in the side of the head. This is not boding well. The game starts, and we get absolutely buried back to Vegas for game five.

It is a beautiful fall day in early September. I throw batting practice for the Stars; after which, I take a seat in the third base dugout and watch the Sky Sox take their batting practice.

What a show! They hit every ball out of the yard. I have never seen that before. I mean, a whole shopping cart full of baseballs, and now it was empty. They had to stop their practice early because they had hit all the balls out of the yard. I go down the tunnel to the manager's office.

"How did they swing it?" he asks.

I tell him.

Then the game starts, and they continue right where they left off in batting practice. The final score is 21–1. And that's a wrap on the season and pretty much on my baseball career. The manager is getting promoted to the big leagues, and the coaches? Well, they are all fired.

I will say this. I have been the batting practice pitcher fungo hitter and even caught a few bullpens for five of the last eight seasons.

I led the league in hitting all most every year I was out with the Stars. In the '86 season, it was the first baseman. And then in '91, it was an outfielder. He couldn't play the last two days of the season because of some tendinitis behind his left knee. He needs the at bats to qualify for the leagues batting title. What's he gonna do?

I go up to the guy and ask him if he wants to play tonight. He is a young Black guy. Well, I'm an old vet by now, and I know a few tricks.

So I tell him, "Let me rub some DMSO on your leg."

"Okay," he says.

"Are you clean?" I ask.

"Yes," he says.

"Okay, this is going to sting," I say. "And pretty soon, you're going to smell like garlic. The dugout will be hating you."

So I rub the solution, DMSO, on his leg.

"That stings," he says, and immediately, he tastes garlic in his mouth. He went four for five that night. The next day, he comes in, and he can barely walk.

"Hey, Bullet, I want to play tonight," he says. And so he did, and he went two for three.

Now let me tell you about DMSO (dimethyl sulfoxide). It is a solvent, and it is great for athletes and also works pretty well on horses. It is a weird substance. It will clean the grease or ink off anything and is used to clean commercial printers also.

When applied to humans, it goes right into the bloodstream and dissolves clots that occur from bruising.

It was illegal in the United States until the 1990s. I started using it on my shoulder before I would pitch in Mexico, where it was legal.

Then in 1992, our catcher was flirting with hitting four hundred. So batting practice is an important part of the game; in fact, all pregame is important in my opinion, and I am a pretty good pregame coach, but no one sees that.

So the rest of the year is spent doing lessons and pondering life without baseball and what that is going to be like.

Chapter Twenty-Two

Keep Your Own Counsel

The year 1994 became a milestone for major league baseball because the season started with a players' strike. The owners, meanwhile, threatened to use "scab" players who were willing to risk crossing the picket lines.

I could still pitch pretty well at age forty-two with my fastball clocking ninety miles per hour. And I was healthy. As a bonus, the pitching coach for the Angels was now the team's manager. So I had a connection.

I had been pitching for a team during the summer in a citywide Las Vegas league. Some guy in town had started a National Baseball Congress team. Does that sound familiar?

The pitcher from the University of Southern California, whom I had groomed for the Padres, had been released, so we became the starting pitchers—the ringers.

The games were pretty uneventful. Other than one bad start I had on a windy day in Petaluma, the kid gave a stellar performance, eight and two-thirds of no-hit baseball. I, on the other hand, threw an absolute stinker of a game.

The Petaluma team was better than decent, and the players knew this field like the back of their batting gloves. The grass diamond with well-kept base paths graced this older wooden ballpark befitting the game as it was played in the early 1900s when baseball was still baseball. From home plate to dead center field was at least 400 feet, and it was 320 feet down the lines.

The former USC Trojan and ex-Padres farmhand threw eight and two-thirds innings of no-hit baseball, only to lose the game when the right fielder dropped a fly ball. That was a heartbreaker.

I took the mound for the next game. I had an absolutely terrible group of fielders playing behind me.

"Play ball!" the home plate umpire shouted as he pointed his index finger at me.

The game was being broadcast on the local AM radio station, and the Petaluma team had some fans in the stands.

There was one fan in particular who got my goat. He was yelling at me on every single pitch. This went on for seven innings relentlessly.

By the top of the eighth, I had had enough. I left the dugout and sauntered into the stands. I maneuvered through the seats where this heckler was sitting. He was looking away from me, so I just walked up and sat down in the seat next to him.

Then when he turned around, there I was, sitting right next to him. I'm a pretty good-sized fellow, and I've got a little sweat soaking through my jersey. His eyes opened widely, and his brows were raised as he was surprised as hell to see me.

"Hi," I said. "How are you?"

"Fine," he replied.

But it was obvious however that he was not so fine. I could see it in his gray eyes.

"You have a pretty good voice," I said calmly. "In fact, it feels like you are right on my shoulder screaming in my ear the whole time I am trying to pitch. Do you think I could pitch this last inning without the fanfare? Could you, would you, be quiet for just one inning? I would greatly appreciate it."

"Okay," he said.

I finished the inning, and we packed up our gear to get ready for the trip back to Las Vegas when the guy came down to our dugout. He invited the whole team over to his place for a barbecue. We declined, but it was a nice gesture on his part. Baseball fans are the best.

When January of 1994 rolled around, my sports memorabilia dealer isn't feeling well. He needs a caretaker, and that's me, at least for a while. He has been diagnosed with severe diabetes, and I'm in Santa Monica taking care of him.

I heard that the Seattle Mariners are having an open tryout for "Strike" players. They are offering a flat fee of a hundred grand if you can make the team. I showed up at the tryout, and it is just what I expected, a big fat joke.

The tryout was being run by some high school scout, and it is just a big mess. After four hours, I finally get a chance to throw. It takes me about five minutes to pitch two scoreless innings with no base runners. The only scoreless innings thrown that day. The scout told me that I don't throw hard enough. I told him to get in the batter's box and we will see how hard I can throw. What a dip shit.

I go back to Santa Monica and call the Angels. I am told by the manager that the Angels would sign me in a second, but the strike is ending tomorrow, and there will be no replacement players playing baseball this season.

In December 1993, my phone rings, and it was the skipper.

"How are you doing?" he asks.

"What's up?" I say.

"The A's are playing in a tournament. Could you come down and throw a game for me? And by the way, do you have any players that you bring with you? Oh! And one more thing, I have cancer, and it is terminal."

Well, that's just dandy.

"I will be there," I say. "And I will bring a couple of players with me."

"Great," he says.

So the tournament was on, and we played pretty well, and we make the tournament finals. One note that merits mention, there was a woman playing with one of the teams. She had played for the Silver Bullets, a professional baseball team that was sponsored by the Coors Brewing Company. She came up against me, and it was a good morning, good afternoon, and good evening three fastballs, and she was back on the bench.

So the championship game begins, and I am on the mound. I pitch all nine innings with fifteen strikeouts.

I brought two players down for the tournament with me. One is a triple "A" infielder with the Phillies, and the other is a big-league outfielder with the Brewers. They both can play the game to death, but the outfielder is a firecracker, a Cuban kid.

Well, in the fifth inning, he strikes out and shows the umpire up by marking the batter's box with his bat. This gesture is to show the umpire where the pitch was in relationship to the home plate. The umpire took exception and ejected the outfielder from the game.

Now I take exception as the umpire is full of himself. So the next inning, the catcher calls for me to throw a fastball inside to the batter. He sets up on the inside part of the plate. The umpire sets up right in the middle of the plate, leaving his right arm exposed.

I throw pretty damned hard still, and I put a fastball right square on his wrist, and I broke the guy's wrist. Delay of game? This was to be my last real game. I am going to miss baseball.

In March, I go to Orange County to see the skipper. He is in rough shape. The cancer is spreading to his brain and has gotten in his bones. He asks me if I can stay with him and be a caregiver. Well, now I have two patients, the sports memorabilia dealer and the skipper, one in Santa Monica and one in Orange County.

The sports memorabilia dealer has found some girl in Arizona, and he is moving there. So that leaves me free to take care of the skipper. He passes away about six months later. I remember it clearly. I had the Dodgers game on the radio. It was just set to start when the skipper took one last gasp, and he was gone. He died right in front of me.

I've had some interesting times in baseball, but the time with the skipper and the Orange County A's was by far the best.

The Outlaw League is a harsh place to hone your craft. Filled with bullies and half wits. It can be trying at times.

Once, we had a game at Buena Park High School. The umpire was this big fat guy. I mean, he must have weighed three hundred pounds or more. Anyway, I am pitching, and this guy can't call balls and strikes. So in about the third inning, the skipper gets into a shouting match with the idiot. Finally, I get between them. Then the sprinklers come on, and the game is a washout.

The skipper says to me, "That guy was pretty big, weren't you a little nervous?"

"No," I say. "I was standing on his foot. Have you ever tried to throw a punch with someone standing on your foot?"

It has been thirteen years of pretty much year around baseball. I've had my ups and downs with the skipper. He was an eccentric fellow and the best liar I ever met. He could look you right in the eye and tell you a whopper and you would inevitably believe it. For that, I give him kudos.

Anyway, that is at least 100 games a year times thirteen, and I have probably won 275 of those games and another 100 or so games for the Orioles. I have been very lucky to have been associated with two of the greatest managers ever to manage in amateur baseball.

The old Oriole scout was an actor and all-around, great guy. We had a lot of good times too, but I will tell you the truth, he used to schedule the worst games.

Like on this one Saturday, he had a game in Los Angeles. It is at Locke High School. No big deal, me and the kid from USC will pitch it. Now this is the high school that produced Ozzie Smith, the great Cardinal shortstop. So the field should be decent. Hah!

The infield was covered in broken glass, the pitching rubber and home plate are just loose, and to make things better, we are the only White people around for about ten square miles. At least it was a day game.

Another time, he has a game with a "Korean" team. A bunch of young Korean lads has a team, and they can't play a lick. I show up, but I'm not playing, at least I wasn't anticipating playing, but he has only eight players. All right, I will play first base. So the manager, the old Baltimore Orioles scout, has this guy throwing for him. A big college kid who will eventually pitch in the big leagues, and he can throw pretty hard. I'd say at least in the low nineties.

He has one small problem. He can't locate the ball, and he walks the first six batters. We score twenty runs in the bottom of the first. An easy win.

I would be friends with the Oriole scout until he died a few years later. What a man.

There are no spots in the Hall of Fame for the outlaws who played or managed in the Outlaw League—umpires for that matter too. If there was one, a Hall of Fame, these two former managers would get in on the first ballot. Me? I would probably sneak in too.

Major league baseball is an interesting way to make a living. I think I would have done very well. Like they say, "It's easy to get to the big leagues. It is staying there that is hard." You have to reinvent yourself, kind of like what I did with the veteran pitcher.

I think I deserved to have had a shot, and I would have been a twenty-year guy. But with a snitch for a high school coach and then the Vietnam War, which I then parlayed into a forty-four-month prison stretch, well, let's just say it was a long shot for me to ever to make the major leagues.

I won't lie. It was the money I was after. That's why even a year or better yet five years was important to me. Maybe if I was Black, I would have gotten signed, kinda like when Billy Martin signed Ron LeFlore, the Black outfielder whom Martin discovered in a Detroit prison. Nobody scouted prisons when I was there, Vietnam either for that matter.

Vietnam veterans, especially combat veterans, are perceived to be damaged goods with tarnished reputations. Hell, it was only Vietnam! We don't have the plague. For Christ's sake, we are not all baby killers and rapists.

Hell, if a man can serve in Vietnam, he deserves a chance, a wide opportunity at professional sports. I mean, we are not zombies.

Or maybe the powers that run the major leagues thought that if we were dumb enough to get drafted and sent to Vietnam, we were probably too stupid to play on any baseball team. The stigma of Vietnam did so much harm to returning veterans it is not even funny. Who is the main culprit in this character assassination? The media. They quite simply ran us into the ground!

Baseball has changed so much over the years. They keep getting new commissioners, and with that, the commissioners keep trying to reinvent the game. Why don't they just police the leagues for drugs and fouls and collect their fee and leave it at that?

But no, we have to have men on base to start extra innings, designated hitters, and pitch clocks to speed the game up. You don't need the clock. If you want baseball to run right, get rid of the television commercial time-outs for one thing. It is not about the game anymore. It is about the money and how much of it can the owners put into their pockets.

What do the fans want? Now there is a good question, I think, and it is just my opinion that the fans want to see a good, clean, well-played baseball game, about two or three hours in length at most, not these four-hour fiascos featuring what seems like million-pitching changes. And the designated hitter rule? That can go as well. Just give me the old-fashioned game of baseball with the rules I used to play by.

And the players' salaries, well, they are totally out of hand. I am sorry, but no one is worth fifty million dollars for one season. And the long-term contracts? I would simply say no to them!

You could also level the baseball playing field. How? Stop signing fourteen-year-olds from the Dominican Republic and other regions where they have no labor laws. You are undercutting your own people by signing children. They would be better off going to school and getting an education. But no, they are paid adult wages and therefore have value to the gangs that ultimately run these third-world countries.

These boys, these children, are ballplayers, but ultimately, they become drug mules for their sponsors.

In the United States, you have to be eighteen years old to sign a professional contract, and that's about the right age. The "Players Union" is also a problem.

So that is the story of the Outlaw League as I lived it, and I did. Lots of baseball games on bad fields in sometimes unforgiving conditions. There was basically never a dull moment, at least in my life.

In a tragic but not unexpected turn of events, I was killed yesterday in a plane crash. How many kilos did he have with him? my buddies quipped. Another said he never did like to fly. Maybe the skipper has a spot for him was the final quip at my funeral.

Well, if you are really dead, then how can you still be writing this book? Well, that's an easy one. You see, I have been a ghost for a long time, in fact, most of my life.

September of 1969, to be exact, we were on patrol in the Central Highlands of Vietnam, and it was anything but a routine patrol. Thirteen nights and fourteen days. Raining cats and dogs the whole time. On the fourteenth day, I fell into a river that was flooded and raging. Well, I got out, but did I really?

Ever since that dreadful day, I have been like a ghost. I can advance other people in their goals. But my own life? Well, it is anything but normal. It's like no one can actually see me. It is kind of like the story *A Guy Named Joe*.

A guy named Joe was a classic World War II movie about a hotshot pilot who piles up his bomber and is killed. However, he is sent back to be a "guardian angel" to younger pilots. It is like you are in the room but no one notices you are there. So you see, writing from the grave is easy for me.

So as I look back on life and the different aspects of it, I found that playing baseball in the Outlaw League must have been a lot like playing in the old "Negro" leagues—a lot of talent but a lot of head cases too.

You would be shocked at the number of ballplayers who quit professional baseball because of their wives. The worst thing you can do, in my humble opinion, is, be a professional athlete and get married at a young age, especially if you are a pro athlete.

Life is so demanding in the minor leagues, and the odds of ever getting to the big leagues are not good.

But that's one thing I never had to worry about, nagging women. I stayed single. It is weird, though, that I have no children. I mean, what's up with that?

Well, I'm sterile. My sperm is dead. How can that be? Agent Orange, that's the culprit. When I was in Vietnam in 1969, I was

OUTLAW LEAGUE

operating in the area where the Army was spraying the dangerous defoliant. I got sprayed with massive amounts of this carcinogen-laced spray on a daily basis. The government denied any responsibility.

Then there are the Southern "belles" who scour the minor league ballparks all over the South. They are looking for a way out of some small Southern town, and the ballplayer, he is just the ticket. He is looking for the same ticket out of town.

The pay isn't that great in the Outlaw League; in fact, it is non-existent in most cases. I'd say 99 percent. I mean, some owners will pay you fifty dollars, but that is about it, and me, it probably cost me to play. I won't deny that fact.

And the chances you will wind up in the Hall of Fame? Pretty good. If you have the entrance fee, but that is about the only way you will get into the Hall of Fame.

The Outlaw League, I will tell you, is real—as real as you and me. These are men striving for real to make it to the big leagues, even if it is just for a cup a joe with the big boys.

People all know the names of big leaguers. Even the most obscure major leaguer has notoriety. It is called publicity. In the Negro league, the players didn't have much publicity or very much of it anyway. And in the Outlaw League, they had even lesser media coverage.

What are these leagues all about anyway? That's easy. They are about the three gifts of baseball—fame, fortune, and notoriety—although some players become notorious.

There are many baseball players who can't handle the whole aspect of being who they are. So they deal drugs or get involved with fraud. Character issues are what it boils down to. And they just don't have it, the character aspect.

Systemic discrimination cost me a baseball career. I never looked at it that way before. But looking back now, I am not so sure. I am pretty sure that occurred, and the fucking Vietnam War was the catalyst. Let's talk about it. It is all over now but the crying, and there won't be any of that. Simply, there is no crying in baseball. I have stated that before, and I am not crying now, just telling a story based on that fact. Let's be clear on that point.

Baseball players are born. Not everyone has the ability or, more importantly, the desire it takes to play the game.

It doesn't matter who their father or grandfather or uncle was. Do you know someone in the game? That's the question. That's where the jobs are, and how you can get one? Nepotism is alive and well in baseball. Systemic discrimination was practiced against Vietnam veterans, returning veterans, combat veterans who deserved to be first in line for the good-paying jobs, like paying professional baseball. But quite factually, they were not.

Mix this in with the signing of fifteen-year-olds from South America, the American player, the young American player, and the aging veteran has no chance!

I know if I had been given the chance, I could have been a productive, effective player. Is it that someone didn't like me enough to give me that chance? No, that's not it. I had the stigma of a Vietnam War combat veteran. I stank of it.

I dominated the Outlaw League for thirteen years starting in 1979, and believe it or not, the talent, the competition in the Outlaw League was pretty good.

I can thank the military-industrial complex for making me unlikable. After all, that's who is running the world today. The weapons makers, the warmongers, striving to sell that next bullet or rifle or whatever piece of military hardware he can.

People were leery of returning Vietnam veterans. We were extremely hard people to like, I guess. Hell, liking us was nothing—trying to understand us was impossible. I harbor no grudges, though, as I played all the baseball that I could. I was quite successful as a player and had a damned good time doing it.

The military-industrial complex, you say? What is that? you wonder. Well, it started way back in history in the days of old. Men began fighting, and other men gave them the tools to fight with weapons.

Well, pretty soon, they had standing armies ready to conquer the world at the slightest provocation. Yes, sir, holding armies with fully armed soldiers, and they have the biggest and newest weapons on the market. Nowadays, they have rockets, machine guns, tanks, ships, and airplanes. The military-industrial complex has come a long way in just a short time.

How does this affect your and my life? you ask. In many ways, but the most significant way it affects you? You pay for it. Every single piece of military equipment. You buy all these magnificent weapons of destruction, but better than that, you serve, and sometimes you serve by being forced. I mean, you can't have a war without soldiers, and what is the best way to get those soldiers? Draft them. Conscript them. You get top-quality prospects at slave wages, and they have significantly diminished rights, and that's perfect for the military. If there's a draft running, you had better be running too. Baseball, football, and basketball all have drafts also. Which would you rather be in?

From the food you eat to the clothes you wear, it is all provided by the MIC. They are basically in your everyday life. How can you invade a country that really doesn't want you there under the provision you're aiding them? After all, you can't claim self-defense, can you? Is the world at peace right now? *No*! Could a peacetime economy even work? We may never know.

We, the United States, are involved in several actions, conflicts. That is what wars are called now—"conflicts." And we are involved in multiple actions that are being waged around the world.

What if we lived in a peacetime economy? Would that be better? What are the chances of that? The military-industrial complex got a hold of me, and my life was changed forever and for the worse. So my advice to you, the reader, is quite simple. If you feel the cause is worth it, and most are not, then, by all means, join up and fight. If the cause is not so strong, just say "hell no" and don't go. It is really that simple.

Life goes on after death—at least in my case, it does. So let's take a little trip in the rearview mirror, a look back.

When my father passed away—actually, it was a short time before he passed—he sat down with my stepmother and me to discuss his passing. He wanted to make sure his small estate would be passed along as he wished. So an agreement was made between the three of us on that subject.

My stepmother was to get full control of the estate until she passed. Then it would be split up 60 percent to me, and the other 40 percent would be split up between the three other siblings. Sounds grand. doesn't it? My stepmother passed away about two years later, and I was right.

There were larceny and hatred—hatred for me in her heart. She left me $500 out of about $250,000. Well, I raised hell, and the three surviving siblings split the money equally. And that was fair.

I was never sure about the degree of hatred and larceny in that woman's heart for me. But that final gesture on her way out summed up the entire history of our relationship.

Racism! What do we do about it? Is it right? Is it fair? Racism has been around in history forever and is destined to be around until the end of days. You just can't help it. But it should resort to a competition of which race can be the best. Think about it for a moment. All races striving to be their best. It would be amazing! I think every person has a little racism in them. Why do you ask? The reason is that every person has pride, or should have, in who they are and what they are. Without that fact, they have nothing. They are nothing. It is just a natural fact of life and a good one in my opinion.

I am White. I am proud of what I am. I am proud of who I am, and believe me, I have had some challenges with that one over the years. Don't hate people for the color of their skin. Competition between races is good. Assimilate into society. Be a part of the mix. Blend right in and go unnoticed. There is an idea.

The marijuana business has been on a roller-coaster ride for some years now. It was legal in the 1930s, then it wasn't. Now it is legal again and sold in shops freely. Well, not freely. It is heavily taxed. The government (state) has just about taxed the herb so heavily that you can't afford it. That's not right.

And what happens when the federal government wakes up and decides they want a piece of the pie too? Will there be back taxes owed? There is a federal tax stamp on marijuana. The tax was already placed on the product some fifty years ago. The levy was one of fifty dollars an ounce. Although I believe that tax was repealed in 1969.

What about other drugs? They were all legal at one time or another in history too. Hell, cocaine was in just about everything back in the day. It was hailed as the cure-all for whatever ailed you. It was the dumbass Nixon who was the real drug war crusader. The war on drugs is a big fat loser, just like Vietnam was. Fraught with lies and misinformation, it still plods on today with no clear end in sight. End it. End the war on drugs.

Set it up so that all drugs can be purchased legally. Tax it but do so reasonably, not as a punishment. The world would be a much better place. And maybe, just maybe, there wouldn't be as much drug use.

I am a person who has spent his life looking out of the front windshield, a forward thinker if you wish. I am not much on rear-view mirrors. You can't spend your life looking backward. But it was kind of interesting to take a little trip down memory lane. I cleared up a few things that I really did not understand until now. I think that all folks should do that at one time or another. You know, kind of get in touch with yourself. It's true, "You don't need a weatherman to know which way the wind is blowing," crooned Bob Dylan. And he was right!

Baseball is the final note in the trilogy. What is wrong with baseball today? Nothing! you say. Baseball is just fine!

Then why is the commissioner trying to fix the game every other day with some new rule or regulation?

Because baseball is not okay, that's why. What do the fans want? It is simple. They want a good, fast-played, well-pitched game that lasts about two hours. That's what the fans want. And it would be simple to give that to them. But will the owners ever see the light?

It is like my old friend, the actor and Baltimore Orioles scout, said to me one time, "Baseball has survived me and more idiots than any sport in history." I can't argue with that logic.

In life, you can do two things: follow leaders or keep your own counsel. Listen to all parties, but ultimately, you must keep your own counsel.

The End

Epilogue

This story is a bit unusual, and I am aware of that. I hope you enjoyed it, not only because it is told through the eyes of a veteran, and a combat veteran at that, a man hardened by war and what followed through prison and systemic discrimination.

It has been touted as a story about baseball, but more so, it is a story of life, love, and the pursuit of happiness through the game of baseball, as told through the eyes of the one person who lived it.

And although the protagonist doesn't distinguish himself by achieving his goal of becoming a major-league pitcher, he fulfills his destiny in other ways, including through baseball.

What is it that makes an ordinary young American man from a middle-class family take the chances that our protagonist took? Risking life, limb, and freedom he partakes in war, then the marijuana trafficking business. Was it for the cause? What about money?

Well, it was a little of both, but more importantly, you felt like you were doing something worthwhile. You know, fighting for the little guy who just wants freedom from an oppressive regime like that of Dick Nixon's. Everything the man said was just an outrageous lie. What has happened to the "American way" of life anyway?

I will tell you what happened to it! Politicians who depend on the military-industrial complex for their lively hood. That is what happened to it. Lifetime politicians. It is a worldwide phenomenon—this thing called the military-industrial complex. And it is the real problem.

I was never very religious as the story has told you. So I don't believe in God or Jesus. By the same token, no devil worship either. No, I just went by the "You're okay, I'm okay" philosophy. Trust and verify sounds good to me. I am not a Republican or Democrat.

Just give me the best man or woman for the job. Term limits are a must for the future of this country—this country, the United States of America.

Quite simply, America has gotten old really old. She is stale, and she stinks. We don't need rioting and looting. Just a quiet simple change at the top, and by change, I mean a change of attitude. Race? I don't play the race game either. Life isn't that complicated unless you make it so. I certainly did a fine job of that, complicating my life. But don't you know that I had a little help?

My advice to you: Live your life on the straight and narrow and do not complicate it. Know what you want, then go and get it! There is nothing wrong with being successful. Everyone should do it.

Every single one of us is born with a talent—a special talent that is unique to every person. Discover that talent and go with it as far as it will take you. Baseball players are born.

Their talent is that they can play the game of baseball. It is just baseball, and that's all that it is and all that it ever will be. Just enjoy it and don't get into a big fever about yourself. After all, you're not saving lives. We need to take a serious look at our social structure and then look at ourselves as a society, and that's for sure.

The most important thing you can do to ensure your health, wealth, and security is to "learn at an early age, to keep your own counsel, the secret to living a happy life."

About the Author

Robert L. Foust, a Southern California baseball pitching prospect, went from throwing fast balls to lobbing hand grenades. "I had three draft interests in 1966: the White Sox, the Red Sox and the Army. And the Army won." In South Vietnam's central highlands in 1969, he served with a long-range reconnaissance team, Echo Company, 2nd Battalion, 35th Infantry Regiment. After the war he probably has the most compelling story of combat veterans in pursuit of a professional baseball career, appearing in spring training with the California Angels in 1986 after spending four years in a federal penitentiary for smuggling marijuana to Canada.

CPSIA information can be obtained
at www.ICGtesting.com
Printed in the USA
LVHW040818090621
689684LV00005B/267